It takes a specialized task force to bring down the most notorious criminals, FBI agents with the guts to go for the glory, and the smarts to know what rules to break—for justice and for love . . .

Avery Coppola is a woman on the run—not from the law, but from the lawless. Her ex-husband, mafia boss Dante Coppola, never forgets or forgives, especially since Avery stole incriminating files from him. For now, she's found sanctuary in the North Country of New Hampshire, working as a waitress to support herself and her ten-year-old sister. But not only are Dante's men on her trail, so is the FBI . . .

Special Agent Vincent Modena is at the end of his rope. After a year-long attempt to infiltrate the Coppola organization, his only chance to ensnare the crime lord now lies with the ex-wife. After locating her, Vincent makes contact, unafraid to use his good looks to capture Avery's attention. But she turns the tables on him with an intoxicating combination of innocent beauty . . . and the mind-blowing skills of a stone-cold killer.

On the run from Dante's hit men, Avery takes Vincent on a wild ride of danger and deceit, hiding a secret that could destroy Vincent's trust in her—and in himself . . .

Visit us at www.kensingtonbooks.com

Books by Kris Rafferty

Caught By You

Published by Kensington Publishing Corporation

Caught By You

Kris Rafferty

LYRICAL PRESS
Kensington Publishing Corp.
www.kensingtonbooks.com

First Electronic Edition: March 2018
eISBN-13: 978-1-5161-0813-8
eISBN-10: 1-5161-0813-2

First Print Edition: March 2018
ISBN-13: 1978-1-5161-0816-9
ISBN-10: -5161-0816-7

Printed in the United States of America

To Michael. You know what you did.

Chapter 1

"Deming? Are you insane?" Special Agent Vincent Modena was in the back of the FBI's surveillance van, kneeling knee to knee with Special Agent Cynthia Deming, the task force's profiler. It wasn't Deming who was the problem; it was the five-pound flounder she held by the gills. It was staring at him, and smelled hideous.

"Your cover is a week-long fishing trip. You're too clean." Deming narrowed her blue eyes, and then slapped the fish against Vincent's chest.

"Stop!" He grabbed her wrist, processing the moment. Rich, blond, gorgeous Cynthia Deming, in a black Dolce & Gabbana suit and heels, was on her knees swinging a fish. Nope. He was living it and still didn't believe his eyes. Meanwhile, the flounder hung limp in the air between them. "I'm supposed to keep Avery Coppola *in* the diner, Deming. Hit me with that again, and the smell will chase her *out*." She broke his grip, seemingly teetering between agreeing and having another go at him with the fish.

Special Agent Jack Benton, FBI task force team leader, jumped from the van's passenger seat into the back. "What the hell?" He grimaced, glaring at the profiler and Vincent, as if Vincent had anything to do with the fish. He didn't.

"Exactly," Vincent said. "What the hell, Deming?"

"What's with the fish?" Benton's black hair hung in his face, obscuring the intensity in his blue-eyed gaze. His year-long deep embed with Dante Coppola's syndicate crashed and burned yesterday, requiring the task force to extract him. His split lip hinted at the bruises and abrasions hidden beneath his conservative black suit and tie, but it was the banked rage that made his team nervous. Benton hadn't taken time off to shake his role of gunrunner, and some deep embeds needed more recovery time than others, but he'd escaped with a lead, so Benton wasn't going anywhere. The lead was, Coppola hired contract killers to find and kill his ex-wife and her little sister. Rumor had it, when she'd divorced him three years ago, the ex-wife left with incriminating files. Now, Coppola knew where the ex-wife was, and so did Benton. It appeared as if the task force lucked out and got here first.

"The fish is necessary for authenticity," Deming said. "Modena's too…" She waved a hand at him. "Handsome."

"Hey, Benton." Vincent held Deming gaze and then winked. "Deming thinks I'm handsome."

She shook her head, barely paying attention to Vincent. "Maybe *clean* is a better word. After a week of backcountry camping, he wouldn't be this clean." She used the back of her wrist to nudge a blond lock off her cheek. "No one sleeps outside for a week, lives off fresh catch of the day, and doesn't suffer from puffy face and bad hair. Avery's clever and distrustful. She's had to be to escape detection for three years with a sister in tow. With contract killers on her scent, she'll smell a rat if Modena doesn't commit to his backstory."

"She'll smell something." Special Agent Harris Gilroy was the task force's official driver. Blond hair cropped to his head, brown eyes, mid-thirties, he looked like an Irish bare-knuckle fighter, crooked nose and all.

"His backpack is enough of a prop," Benton said. "Get rid of the fish, Deming."

"Fine." She tossed it into a Styrofoam cooler, and then stripped off her latex gloves, throwing them inside, too. She seemed on edge. Yesterday's violent extraction of Benton had notably rattled her, rattled them all, as did the dead bodies the team left behind. And when Deming was rattled, she distracted herself with details—like Vincent's backstory and a fish—so Vincent tried not to take the fish assault personally.

"Our warrant is to surveil Avery Coppola's apartment," Benton said. "Unfortunately, I couldn't convince the judge that rumored files containing alleged evidence is grounds for a search warrant, so we watch and wait for Coppola's men to make their move. If the files are in her apartment, she either surrenders them, or we need probable cause to take them. If Coppola's men find her, maybe make a move on her at the apartment, we've got them and our probable cause, so cross your fingers. Modena, you keep an eye on her at the diner while we set up the cameras outside of her apartment. I want any potential attack on video. Let a judge and jury see who these monsters are, and if we're forced to bust into her apartment to save her, and happen to find evidence, they'll be forced to make our findings admissible in court. Time is short, folks. We have no idea when Coppola's men will show, but this isn't rocket science. If she has files, which my contact assured me she does, it's probably hidden in her apartment. Coppola's men have to know that."

"Yeah, about that, Benton," Deming said. "I think I should go in the diner instead of Modena. Look at him. He looks dangerous. She'll think he's a contract killer, maybe run, and ruin the whole operation. We can think of a different backstory for me."

"Deming, you'd be walking into a backwoods diner wearing Dolce & Gabbana," Vincent said. "Do you really think you'll get anywhere near her without making her suspicious? And Benton knows I have advantages you don't have." He allowed a slow smile to crack his lips. "Leave the ex-wife to me."

She shook her head, still not convinced. "But—"

"I know. I know. I'm handsome, clean, *and* dangerous." Vincent winked, trying not to enjoy Deming's annoyance too much. Being on the sidelines was twisting her in knots. She wanted in on the action, and he didn't blame her, but he'd waited too long to meet Avery Coppola to just give this moment away. "I think you're crushing on me."

"Blow me, Modena." She turned toward Benton, waiting for his decision.

"We stick with the plan," Benton said. "Modena, go."

Gilroy reached into a console between the two front seats and produced a bottle of Febreze. He aimed it into the back of the van and sprayed with no concern for whom he doused. Between the fish smell, and being gassed by Gilroy, Vincent found it a relief to spill out into the parking lot, backpack slung over his shoulder.

As the task force sped off in the van, heading down the street toward Avery Coppola's apartment, Vincent walked toward the diner, passing a multitude of beat up SUVs and trucks, listening to his hiking boots crunch gravel underfoot. The chirping of birds, the breezes rustling through maple and oak leaves, it was a nice change from the city. August in the North Country of New Hampshire, mountainous. Vincent was enjoying himself, and the diner's aromas wafting through the air. His stomach growled as he approached the door, but his thoughts were all on the woman inside.

Avery Coppola. *Damn.* Her name had been popping up in the Coppola case for a year now, but Vincent had only actively studied her for the last few months. He was a little ashamed to be this excited about meeting her... Dante Coppola's one vulnerability. Avery was the crime lord's ex-wife, so probably poison, without conscience. Totally his type. Vincent's ex-wife taught him a thing or two about women like that. On his second tour in

Afghanistan, she'd sent him a Dear John letter paper clipped to divorce papers. It had a way of changing a man's paradigm real quick. It certainly forced Vincent to see things more clearly. Women were mercurial at best, self-serving at worst. It was weird to know he had something in common with a murderous crime lord. Both he and Coppola married women who'd betrayed them.

He'd memorized Avery's pictures. She had the look of an innocent, red-headed imp, and seemed younger than her years. She certainly didn't look like someone who could inspired an ex-husband to hire contract killers to off her. Not a sterling personal recommendation, and yet, the contradiction tickled Vincent's curiosity. What would she be like? Or rather, how best to bend her to his will?

Benton wanted to try and flip her, see if they could convince her to give up the goods on her ex, rather than make the Feds slog for the evidence, but they didn't have enough intel to know how best to approach her. Deming, the task force's profiler, suggested they feel her out with some casual conversation. Benton had tapped Vincent, and he'd report back to the team after they'd finished installing security cameras around her apartment.

Just meeting her would probably answer most of the questions his team had. Then, if all went as planned, they'd find the leverage they needed to flip her, and she'd help break open the task force's RICO case against her ex-husband. If *that* went south, she'd either face jail time or risk a bullet between the eyes. Dante Coppola wasn't pulling his hit on her anytime soon, and now that he knew where she was, she had a target on her back. The FBI would offer her protection, if she was willing to deal, but they couldn't make her accept their help. No, that would take persuasion. And that was where Vincent came in.

He smiled as he opened the diner's door. A bell chimed overhead, announcing his arrival. It was old-fashioned and kitschy, and he liked it. As he stepped inside, he finally admitted to himself that he'd been anticipating this meeting with Avery Coppola since he'd first seen her photo nearly a year ago. He was excited, and when his gaze zeroed in on her behind the diner's counter, his chest tightened because he knew… This was going to be fun. Lots and lots of fun.

Chapter 2

Avery's feet were already hurting and it was only late morning, four hours into her eight-hour shift. She was bored and restless when the bell over the diner's door chimed. Like Pavlov's dog, she had a reaction every time it rang, but instead of salivating, her stomach tightened with dread. Another customer requiring a smile and chirpy greeting.

Then she saw *him* and her day suddenly wasn't so boring.

Scruffy, lots of stubble, he was deliciously sexy; strong jaw, aviator sunglasses, dark brown disheveled hair, his red flannel shirt was open, revealing a tight black T-shirt stretched over a flat, muscular stomach. Her eyes zeroed in on his silver belt buckle, and then she spent a moment or two imagining what his black jeans were hiding. Yum. Yum. Yummy.

Avery bit her lip, fiddling with the rings on her fingers. It was a nervous habit, but this guy made her nervous in a good way. He pushed his sunglasses on top of his head, unveiling eyes so green and vibrant she had to will her jaw not to drop. He approached, propped his backpack against the counter, and scanned the room. Avery quickly looked away, her pride fighting with her instinct to gawk.

Nat Harris, a retired barber who ate at the diner every day, was sitting at the counter, chuckling under his breath, because he'd caught her wanting something she couldn't have. Embarrassed, Avery found it hard to meet Nat's gaze. He was a man who knew a thing or two about not getting what you want. He'd struggled with wanderlust his whole life, but between raising siblings and keeping his business afloat, he'd been stuck in North Conway, New Hampshire for thirty years. Retired now, he lived to travel, and was taking a cruise next month. The brochure was on the counter between them.

Nat nudged his coffee cup toward Avery. "Can I have a refill, honey?"

"Sure thing." Despite Nat's preferences, she refilled it with decaf instead of high octane. He had a bad ticker, so she ignored his grimace and instead focused on the brochure, its bright colors and exciting pictures. A clutch of wistfulness had her grimacing. Not for the first time, she was reminded she was where Nat had been, raising a sibling, out of options, feeling life passing by. Avery wanted to travel. She wanted to be anywhere but here, but choices had consequences, and she had the life she deserved.

Jaw-droppingly handsome man sat his fine self at the counter, slipped his sunglasses into his shirt pocket, and made Avery's heart pound just a little bit faster. She told herself to play it cool, to enjoy the moment without inviting too much comment, and when she felt his eyes on her, despite her better judgment, she looked back at him.

Only he wasn't looking at her eyes. Ostensibly reaching for a menu, he leaned, *peering* over the counter and openly admired her legs. His gaze moved slowly up her body until it connected with hers, and then he smiled. Yikes. Handsome man was coming on strong.

It made her regret not blow drying her auburn hair straight this morning, but instead allowing it to air dry into waves that fought the restraint of her ponytail. And her practical "nurse" shoes? She regretted not wearing a heel, something that said sex kitten, rather than bed pan. She regretted not changing her beige and cream-colored uniform this morning, when she'd realized it still reeked of syrup despite being washed. This man had Avery regretting a lot, down to not putting on makeup, not even a smudge of lipstick.

Releasing a sigh that had become habitual, Avery forced a smile, because she knew it wasn't her lack of blow-dryer, laundry expertise, heels, or lipstick that ailed her, it was her lack of options. She'd made decisions that had unavoidable repercussions, and now she had to live with them. This handsome man wasn't for her. He was for other women. Women who hadn't…well, hadn't sold their souls.

"Coffee?" She set a cup and saucer before *handsome man* and then offered the choice of the two coffeepots. Her nerves were getting the better of her, making her hands tremble, and not just a little. The bitter brew inside the pots quivered. "Decaf or regular?" He briefly ran his hand over his mouth as if hiding a smile. He discombobulated her, and from all appearances, he'd noticed.

"Caffeine, please. I've been camping for the last week and I'm desperate for a decent cup. And a full night's sleep. I came to the great outdoors tense and irritable, and now I'm leaving tense and irritable. I thought nature was supposed to soothe the savage beast."

Pouring his coffee, Avery aimed for a polite *though disinterested* attitude. His ego seemed plenty stroked, and her pride was stinging from failing to hide her attraction. Her one move was to make it clear that her being attracted to him didn't buy him anything.

"Is that what you are? A savage beast?" She'd unintentionally allowed the last two words to fall from her lips like she'd enjoyed saying them. Damn. She sucked at standoffish.

He chuckled, ignoring her question. With a glance at her name tag, he seemed to settle in for a long talk, studying her as if later he'd be quizzed on the details. "Patty? Nice name. Mine's Vincent."

Patty Whitman was Avery's alias. "Pleased to meet you, Vincent." She replaced the coffeepots, and then turned back to him, wrinkling her nose. "It smells like your fishing trip was successful." He did reek, and it made her wonder if focusing on that flaw might dampen her raging hormones. It didn't take long to acknowledge little would. Maybe if he were unkind? Yeah, that would do it.

He wrinkled his nose, too. "Sorry. I had a disagreement with a fish and the fish won." He scanned his menu and seemed overwhelmed by the options.

"You're lucky you didn't meet up with bears." They would have eaten him alive. She sighed again, wondering how Vincent tasted. His lips were perfect and quick to smile. They probably tasted divine.

"No bears." He rolled up his flannel sleeves, eyes still perusing the menu.

No customer was attempting to catch her eye, so Avery leaned her hip on the counter and lingered. She recognized his tattoo immediately. A cobra entwined around a human skull over a cross of rifles, and the moto *one shot, one kill* written under it. He caught her looking, and instead of eagerly discussing the tat, like every other ink fan, his smile lost its authenticity, and he rubbed his hand over his forearm, as if it bothered him.

"Sniper," she said. The word popped from her mouth, and she regretted it immediately when his smile faded. A veteran who didn't want to talk about his experiences killing people? Totally understandable. There were plenty things in her life she didn't talk about, especially to a stranger while slinging coffee in a diner. "I saw that art in a tattoo magazine once." It was a lie. She'd seen it on too many arms, on too many men who'd taken their skills to the marketplace, but she didn't say that because she didn't want questions, such as, why a waitress in North Conway, New Hampshire, knew about sniper tattoos.

Vincent tapped the menu. "What do you recommend?"

"The burgers are good."

"Cheeseburger plate then," he said, "with onion rings instead of fries. And Coke." He leaned forward, his brows lifted, and suddenly he was all charm. "Did anyone ever tell you what amazing green eyes you have? I have green eyes, too."

"Yes." She smiled. "I can see."

He peered closer, studying hers, as if it were a perfectly normal thing to do. "There are gold flecks in yours, and—"

His pause lengthened and seemed strange. "And?" she said.

He no longer focused on her eyes, but rather on her gaze. His smile widened, grew flirty. "They're stunning. Rare. They go along with your hair. Less than two percent of the world's population has red hair."

"Hmm." She tried to repress a smile and failed miserably. "I think I've heard that before."

He faux frowned. "Then I need to up my game. When is your shift over?"

Whoa, Nelly. That escalated quickly. And *oh* how she wished she could be *just a girl*, being picked up by *just a guy*, who wanted to be with her at the end of her shift. But she wasn't. Time to set boundaries.

"Why do you ask? Looking to take me home to mother?" Her returning smile was playful, but the shake of her head made it clear whatever he had in mind was not happening.

"Now why'd you have to go bringing my mother into this?" He feigned hurt, but she could see she'd amused him. The guy liked a challenge, apparently, and Avery was having a hard time pretending she wasn't enjoying herself.

A glance over her shoulder told her no orders were up, so she leaned on her elbows, taking what pleasure she could from the interaction. "Mother's tend to keep people honest," she said.

His smile couldn't have been naughtier. "I like honesty."

"Yeah?" She licked her lips, repressing a smile. "So, where do you see this going?" His chuckle was scandalous, and had a few customers taking note. The guy certainly didn't mind her calling him on his shit. In fact, she suspected he liked it, and *damn*...so did she. "You. Me," she said. "We hook up during my lunch break, I bring you to my apartment, we spend a glorious hour of nasty, mind-blowing sex—"

"Liking where your head is at." He was smart enough to know she was teasing, but confident enough not to be offended. It was a giddy-inspiring combination.

"—on the bed, the couch, in the shower, drinking water off each other's skin." She lifted her brows, smiling, not in the least surprised to discover she would love to live out that little fantasy. "We'll make naughty memories to last a lifetime, all in the span of an hour's lunch break." He leaned on the counter, moving his face closer to hers, lips cracked with a smile.

"An hour isn't enough," he said, "but if you insist."

She laughed hard enough to throw her head back. "You're incorrigible." Then she stepped back and clipped his order slip onto the order carousel.

"If I insist, huh?" Hot and bothered, Avery knew if she continued their flirting, there was no way she'd retain even a sliver of what pride she had left. "I have a feeling women insist a lot with you."

"If I was a good boy, you wouldn't want me." He winked.

Ugh. Truer words were never spoke. How else to explain her ex-husband? Still. This guy didn't know her, and Avery didn't like that she'd become so transparent that even a stranger could read her.

After a polite but dismissive nod, she grabbed the coffeepots and walked away, moving from table to table, refilling cups. The whole time, she had to force herself not to look at him, because she knew he was looking at her. She could see his reflection in the mirrored wall behind the counter. *Vincent.* He'd suddenly become the embodiment of all things she'd given up three years ago. Her penance. Her punishment. And not for the first time, she resented the restrictions of her fate. Resented the hell out of it.

The bell above the entrance chimed, distracting her. A woman gasped and caught Avery's attention. A chair fell to the floor, but Avery's gaze remained locked on the woman's expression of horror. She couldn't force herself to follow the woman's gaze to the diner's entrance, because the chatting stopped, the utensils stilled their scraping on plates, and silence hung in the air, as if even sound feared what was to come.

Avery forced herself to move, to walk behind the counter, eyes front, seeking to make it to the kitchen before the unseen danger got her.

A shotgun cocked, and the familiar sound had her stopping in her tracts. "You!"

She didn't recognize the voice, but that didn't mean he wasn't one of her ex-husband's contract killers. It had been three years since she'd left Dante. Odds were he'd found her, and that shotgun was how she'd die.

Avery turned to face her fate. Her killer. He was around her age, early twenties, wearing flannels and jeans. Greasy, blond hair, high as a kite. The man couldn't control his twitching and suffered from facial tics. So, strung out on meth, probably. His hands shook, and his head bobbed uncontrollably as he aimed the shotgun at her. It told her that he wasn't here because of her ex-husband. Coppola contract killers weren't meth heads. They were all too sober. Yet, he still looked as if he wanted to kill her.

"You," he said again, looking at her. "Stay put." He scanned the room. "The rest of you, against the wall."

Avery stayed put and the customers moved against the wall.

The diners were freaking out, looking between the man and shotgun, and his companion, a tall, brown-haired man who hid his gaze behind lanky, unwashed hair. The companion seemed confused by the commotion.

Vincent hadn't moved. Clutching his coffee, he watched everything play out via reflections in the mirror lining the counter's wall. She supposed his Army experience gave him nerves of steel, but that didn't make her feel better. If he played hero, it was her belly that would bear the brunt of the shotgun blast. It was her guts that would splatter the wall.

The bell over the entrance door chimed again. Avery feared another unsuspecting customer had fallen into this trap. Instead, two more robbers shuffled in, guns in hand. Four total now, all in their twenties, eyes-dilated, hopped up on drugs. These two wore long, black overcoats.

Avery forced her breathing to regulate to the beat of her thumbs twirling her rings, like a worry stone. She looked at nobody and nothing, just stood near the register, rejecting the option of running to the kitchen, because it might precipitate an attack, and those deaths would be on her, so she stayed put, working her rings.

"What is going on?" The new guy was a ginger, short and stocky, laughing at the frightened customers. "I said let's get lunch, Charlie. Not rob the place." The ginger waved his pal deeper into the diner. "Jim, lock the door."

"Sure, Eric." Jim was tall, had a receding hairline, and pinched lips. He hustled to do as Eric told. Once locked, he leaned his back against the door and then unsheathed a long knife. The room gave a collective gasp. Jim ate up the reaction with a spoon.

Avery kept her gaze on Vincent, and his hands reflexively clutching his coffee mug. He seemed to be biding his time, watching the gunmen in the mirror, his expression revealing purpose, not fear. Avery had enough fear for both of them, and feared that the robbers would notice his *lack* of fear, and soon. They were already scanning the room for hints of push back, and had found none so far. Though Vincent kept his back to them, she suspected that wouldn't last long.

Eric was touching Brooke Fawley's hair. He twirled a blond lock around his sausage finger, tugging her head closer to his. Brooke sobbed, but didn't resist. Small town girl done good, she'd been accepted to UNH Durham, and everyone was excited for her. High school valedictorian, she'd earned a full ride scholarship, the only way someone from her part of town could afford the pricy school. Smart and pretty, she was too pretty to go unnoticed by the gunmen. Brooke seemed repelled by Eric's touch, but that only seemed to amuse him more. He leaned in for a kiss.

Vincent stood, poised to act.

Avery slammed her hand on the cash register's keys. It opened with a bang, displacing change onto the floor. Now all eyes were on Avery, most especially Eric's, who wandered away from Brooke, thank heaven. His interest and malice radiated from him, and with every step he took closer to her, Avery found it harder to breathe. Seeking his attention wasn't the smartest thing she'd ever done, but she was more suited to handle a guy like Eric than Brooke.

They wanted money. Avery had access to the money. Maybe she'd luck out and the gunmen would leave once they'd taken it. She grabbed a takeout bag and filled it with cash.

Jim pushed off from the door, still wielding his knife, and jumped over the counter to land next to her. He grabbed the bag of money before she could finish filling it. Then he noticed Vincent's cheeseburger plate under the heating lamp on the order up shelf. Jim poked his head through the hole separating the kitchen from the counter area.

Jim glared, getting in her face. "Where's the cook?" His breath reeked and his eyes were freaky bloodshot. Heart in her throat, Avery struggled to speak.

"I don't know. He ran, probably. There's a back door into the alley." It's what she would have done if she were Sam.

Eric walked around the counter and took the money bag from Jim. After stuffing it into his jacket, Eric waved his hand, indicating the kitchen. "See if the cook is still back there." Jim took off; then Eric grabbed the burger off the order up shelf and took a bite. "Charlie?" He spoke around his food, glancing at his cohort, the first robber to enter the diner. "Make sure you're pointing that shotgun away from me, buddy. Okay?"

Charlie squinted, blinked a few times, and re-aimed the shotgun. His pal, the quiet, brown-haired robber with greasy hair, took that moment to sit at an empty table near the door. He seemed tired, and bored.

A crash sounded from the kitchen area. Vincent leaned on the counter as if prepared to jump over, but then two shots rang out and he ducked, a mere instant before Avery did.

"I got the cook good, Eric!" From inside the kitchen, Jim shouted through the order-up hole. Hunched on the greasy floor behind the counter, Avery shuddered. Sam was shot. *Sam.*

Eric threw the rest of the burger onto the counter in disgust. "Well, hell, why'd you do that?" He waved his revolver at Avery. "Get up, girlie." Shaking, feeling weak with fear, she stood straight, only to discover Charlie was aiming his shotgun at Nat, the retired barber.

"Now we got to do them all. Right?" Charlie said. "I'm not leaving witnesses."

Vincent moved so quickly Avery only saw a blur as he put his back against the nearest wall, then her heart sank when she saw him hold his FBI wallet credentials out to Charlie...and a Glock. Damn, *handsome guy* was a Fed. She should have known he was too good to be true.

"Everyone needs to calm down." Vincent kept all the men in sight, but his gun didn't waver in its aim. It was leveled at Charlie. "Put the shotgun on the floor, Charlie. And you, Eric, right? Put that gun down. Gentle like...on the floor."

Charlie swung the shotgun toward Vincent, prompting Avery to bolt for the kitchen, just as Jim came back out, causing her to collide with him. He wrestled her into a bear hug from behind, aided by the sting of his blade at her throat.

The shotgun discharged. She flinched, and saw Vincent tuck and roll, shooting his Glock.

Charlie'd missed. Vincent hadn't.

Customers screamed, ducking, overturning tables and chairs. Charlie screamed, too, rolling on the floor—shoulder wound. Vincent must have hit an artery because Charlie was bleeding like a fountain. His brown-haired buddy, at his side, was pressing on his wound.

Vincent's Glock was aimed at Jim and Avery, and she appreciated the attention, because Jim was strong, high as a kite, and enjoying himself. The blade at her throat burned as it scraped skin.

"Put the gun down, Mr. FBI man," Eric said, "or Jim here is going to need a new shirt."

Vincent didn't blink. Eyes on Avery, he looked as if he were struggling to read her mind, though Avery couldn't have been more of an open book. She was scared, clutching Jim's wrist, trying to keep the knife's edge from biting deeper. Yet, all she saw was Vincent's hesitation.

"Shoot him," she croaked.

Jim head-butted her, but was kind enough to drop the knife an inch or two before doing it, so she saw stars instead of her maker. The stars didn't last long, because he pressed the knife back to her neck, which served to clear her head quickly.

"Blood thirsty, isn't she?" Eric laughed. He peered at her uniform's name tag. "Patty? Such a lovely name." He indicated Vincent with a tilt of his head. "Patty, Mr. FBI man knows Jim will slice you ear to ear if he shoots. Won't you, Jim?"

"Looking forward to it." Jim chuckled as a warm trickle of blood worked its way down her neck, to her collarbone, and all the while, Charlie continued to scream, writhing on the floor.

"Shut up, Charlie!" Turning his back on Vincent, who still aimed the gun at Jim, Eric walked to Charlie's side, picked up the discarded shotgun and cocked it. The brown-haired friend took one look at Eric's face and hurried to move, slipping in blood. Then Eric aimed carefully, and shot Charlie in the head.

The discharge was deafening, echoing off the diner's walls, and at that range, Charlie's head was...gone. It was messy, covering Eric and the surrounding area with blood spatter and brain. Customers' screams were deafening.

"Shut up!" Eric waved the shotgun, and everyone fell silent as if a switch had been flipped. Some people had their hands pressed to their mouths. Some averted their eyes. Most were slack-jawed, but all were silent. The diners. The robbers. Even Eric took a moment to recognize the brutality of his actions, but only Eric was smiling.

He turned to Vincent. "If I'm willing to kill my cousin, what makes you think I'm not willing to kill all of you?" He aimed the shotgun toward the customers, not deigning to look where he aimed. "Or I might let you all go free." He allowed the muzzle to point at the floor, shrugging in a playful manner. "Let's chock this up to a bad day, folks. What do you say?" He aimed the shotgun at Vincent, and between that, and him being covered with a fair amount of his cousin's remains, nobody put much credence to Eric's negotiations. "Put the gun down. No one wants more bloodshed. Right, Jim?"

Jim's body shook with silent laughter, making the knife at Avery's throat jiggle, scraping at her skin. She was no fool. She knew she'd be the first to die when things went south, and things were going south with the speed of a roller coaster on its first descent. Vincent needed to end this.

"Shoot him," she croaked.

But Vincent didn't shoot. He turned the gun so it's flat side was parallel with the floor, doing as Eric asked. Then he bent his legs, lowering the Glock, his eyes now fixed on Eric and the shotgun.

Avery's heart sank. Why didn't the Fed understand? These were killers; they wouldn't be satisfied with one or two kills. Her, the Fed, Nat, the rest of the customers, they were all going to die like Sam, and Charlie, but...

"Not today," she said.

Avery slid her fingers from Jim's wrist to his thumb pad and yanked on it with all her strength, weakening his grip on the knife as she stomped his foot. Then her back scoop-kick connected with his groin, forcing Jim to fold forward and faceplant her oncoming skull. She heard the bridge of his nose break with a snap as she upward palm heeled his elbow, loosening his choke. It allowed her to slip free, lunge forward, and with a vicious pivot toward him, wrist-lock him and strip the knife from his grip.

All in the space of two heartbeats.

Eric stared at her, stunned. Jim roared with rage and pain. Vincent opened fire.

It was confusing, and Avery lost track of who was winning, because Jim bent his elbow, breaking her hold. Avery lunged with the knife, aiming her slices at nonlethal targets, but the guy had no fear, and took all her damage without slowing his attack. He kept swinging, forcing her to parry, duck, back up and slice.

Out of the corner of her eye, she saw Eric hiding behind a table, aiming his shotgun at her and Jim, as Vincent lay down cover fire. But the Fed didn't have a line of sight. Avery did, so with all her strength, she threw the knife at Eric. He flinched, and messed up both their aims. His shot went wild, and hit the mirror behind her as Avery's knife pinned Eric's hand to his shotgun's stock.

Eric howled just as Jim punched Avery's jaw, sending her crashing backward onto the counter. Cups, plates, food were pushed to the floor, as she gained a front row seat to Vincent's fight with the greasy-haired robber. In three moves, Vincent broke the man's elbow, knee, and then jaw.

Jim grabbed her hair and dragged her across the counter, clearing the surface, and sending everything to the floor. Scalp burning with pain, she whipped her fingers at his eyes, and connected with a slimy orb, buying her time to chamber a white "nurse" shoe, and kick his groin. The fight should have ended there. *It usually ended there.* But drugged up, Jim was still in it for the win. He rushed her. Avery hook punched his temple, stopping him cold. He dropped to the floor at her feet.

Avery backed up against the wall, out of breath, her heart beating a painful mile a minute. A gunshot had her ducking, and when she peeked over the counter again, she saw Eric writhing on the ground, bleeding from the shoulder. Vincent caught her eye, his concern evident. Well, Avery was concerned, too. Jim still thrashed on the floor, clutching his watering eyes.

Vincent ran to her, peering over the counter at Jim on the floor. "Damn. You okay?"

"Do I look okay?" She couldn't catch her breath. All the robbers seemed incapacitated or unconscious.

"You scared me." He studied her face. "You sure you're okay?" She nodded quickly, but wasn't sure. "You scared me, dammit!"

"You already said that." She swallowed hard, flinched with pain, and did her best to slow her breathing.

Vincent barked out a laugh, eyes wild, smiling. "We're alive. Did *not* see that happening!"

He laughed again and cupped the back of her neck, pulling her in for a hearty kiss. His lips were warm and tasted of coffee. It was nice and confusing. When he released her, she couldn't help but want another one, and fade into the pleasure of not thinking. Then she saw Eric over Vincent's shoulder. The killer was clawing his way to the store's entrance. Vincent saw him, too.

"Dammit!" He released Avery and chased after him.

It was over. *It was over.* So why did she still feel the terror?

The customers were reviving, and their shock had found a voice. Shouts, phone calls. Avery flinched as no less than five iPhones aimed at her and flashed. Jim groaned at her feet, clearly reviving. She stomp-kicked his head without a second thought, assured herself he'd lost consciousness again, and then leaned against the wall. Her numbness was wearing off, and reaction was setting in. She wanted to faint, but there was no time.

Nate took off his belt, offering it to Vincent to help tie the robbers. Vincent glanced back at her, as if assessing her state of mind. She did her best to hide her emotions, but her panic was growing. People kept taking pictures, evidence that would end up in court. Prosecutors. Newspapers. Social media. Vincent was a Fed. All ingredients for disaster. Avery could be held for questioning, when she needed to run with her sister.

When Vincent turned back to Eric again, Avery grabbed her purse from under the counter and slipped into the kitchen...and immediately saw Sam. He'd been shot dead and now lay in a pool of blood by the phone, its receiver hanging—*swinging*—over his body. Married, three kids. It wasn't fair.

Avery hurried past, forcing herself not to think, but to escape out the door to the alley beyond. She would not cry. *She would not cry.*

Chapter 3

Vincent was still riding an adrenaline high as he muscled Eric and his brown-haired psycho-playmate to a table. The restaurant looked as if a bomb had gone off, and it gave him pause. Benton wasn't going to be happy. Vincent was supposed to chat with Avery Coppola, not tear the place up. Chairs were on their sides, tables knocked over. Everyone was sporting masks of horror. He kind of felt bad for them, remembering what it was like back in the day, when death and dying had the ability to shock him. After four years in Afghanistan and ten at the bureau, he'd come to process violence differently. Nuisance nightmares, insomnia, and a continually renewed appreciation for life. All life, whether it be innocents, or monsters like Eric and his crew.

He soon had Eric and the brown-haired guy trussed up tight with the borrowed belts, and as he stepped back to peruse his handiwork, he promptly slipped on blood. Either Charlie's or Eric's, but he found his equilibrium quick enough so as not to take a spill, but not before irritating his bum shoulder. He rolled it, and then cracked his neck, trying to work out the kinks.

He glanced at the diner's counter. "Damn." *Where was Avery Coppola?*

He'd had one job; keep her at the restaurant. If Coppola's men were trolling the neighborhood and caught up with her, there was a good chance she'd soon be dead like Charlie here. He glanced at the body, and the bloody mess on the floor and wall. Epic fail. Deming wasn't gonna let him live this down.

Then he remembered the cook, and thought maybe Avery had gone to tend to him. Dead or alive, though, odds were she'd be calling out for help, maybe even screaming, but he wasn't hearing anything like that from the kitchen, so Vincent jumped over the counter and landed next to Jim's unconscious body. After tying him up with twine he found in a nook and cranny by the register, Vincent took a moment to notice Jim's injuries. Broken nose. Clearly a fractured skull, because mother nature didn't do that to a head on purpose, and he was covered in defensive knife wounds. Vincent lost count quickly, but the slices were shallow, non-life threatening, and covered Jim from face to calves, as if the druggie's every blow or kick had been tapped off by a slice.

Shit. When the hell did this happen? Jim looked as if he'd had an epic battle with a multiarmed warrior, and Vincent didn't remember Avery having a knife fight with anyone, least of all Jim. She'd disarmed the guy, yeah, but…then again, he'd been busy taking out Eric and the other dude. Still. Something was off here.

When his knots were secure, Vincent hurried through the swinging door leading into the kitchen and pulled his iPhone from his pocket. He dialed Benton. The line connected. "You won't believe who just foiled a robbery and subdued a murderer."

"What are you talking about? We're almost done here," Benton said.

"Avery Toner Coppola, with some help from little ole me." Vincent stopped walking when he stood center kitchen, and glanced left and right. The grill area was empty. He pulled his gun, moving farther into the kitchen, looking for surprises. "Finish up at the apartment, because our girl is in the wind, and probably heading your way." He turned a corner and found the cook, did a three-sixty scan and saw he was still alone, then allowed his gun to hang at his side. "Diner's cook is dead. Do me a favor? Call an ambulance and local law enforcement. It's a circus here."

Benton swore so long he started repeating himself. "Find her."

"Can't." Vincent crouched next to the cook, noting the GSW to the head. "I can't leave the scene until the Sheriff arrives. Presently, I've got three perps tied up and waiting to be processed. Once the cops arrive, I'll give them an excuse so I can slip away." Benton hung up mid-expletive. "Then I'll track her down," he finished his thought aloud, though no one heard it but him. He peered out the back door and found it led to an alleyway. No Avery in sight.

So, she'd run. He wasn't surprised, nor did he blame her. She was a woman with something to hide.

And he'd kissed her. What the hell was wrong with him?

* * * *

When the fetid vapors from the back alley hit Avery, she was in shock, and autopilot took over. Images of Sam with a bullet hole in his head tormented her. And *Jim*. If ever a man deserved to die, Jim did. Yet, when she'd brought her foot down for that last strike, she'd aimed for Jim's head, not his neck. Sam deserved to be avenged. He did. But Avery couldn't do it. Experience taught her though vengeance was sweet, it ate your soul. Nothing could bring Sam back. Not even killing Jim.

She scrubbed unwelcome tears from her cheeks and told herself to stop crying. When that didn't work, she clenched her hands until her six rings cut painfully into her bruised and swollen skin. She'd been right to wear them all these years, instead of hiding them out of sight. They'd helped in the fight, helped her survive—gifts that kept on giving—but surviving had put her in a spotlight. *Quiet waitress, winning a fight with a knife-wielding druggie?* That was the headline, and it would go viral. People were looking for her, and this incident would help them find her. Find Millie.

She slipped her iPhone from her uniform's pocket, and saw it was eleven in the morning. She dialed her little sister. When the line connected, Avery told herself to keep her voice calm.

"Millie, grab the go-bag. Meet me at the bus station, just like we practiced, yeah?"

No arguments, no hysterics, Millie whispered "right" and then hung up. The station was three blocks from their crappy apartment, and she was there within minutes. Millie was already waiting, giving no indication of upset. No tears fell from her green eyes, because a crying child would attract attention. *She was ten*, sporting a long, blond ponytail hanging down her back, and she held a go-bag filled with thirty thousand dollars, one toothbrush, a package of wipes, a bottle of water, Tylenol, and a few granola bars. Millie *had* to leave by herself, because if the contract killers came here looking for them, they'd track a pair. Two sisters.

Avery stepped past Millie without comment and entered the convenience store to buy a ticket for the Greyhound bus idling at the curb. Neither she nor Millie asked where it was going. They knew it didn't matter. What mattered was Millie left this place. Avery handed her the ticket.

"Get off at the first station, and ask for a transfer ticket to Boston's South Station. Use money from the bag only when necessary, but be careful no one sees what you have. You're vulnerable, Millie. They'll try to use that against you." Millie nodded, looking at the blood on Avery's uniform. That look—stark terror—had Avery second-guessing herself. Maybe she should risk leaving together, but… Avery couldn't travel looking like this, and Millie had to leave now. It wasn't safe here.

Millie touched her hand, drawing her thumb over Avery's rings. "Maybe you could find a way to make him leave us alone."

Him. Her ex-husband. "The damage is done. Dante has set something in motion, and now he can't stop it even if he wanted to." And she suspected Dante didn't want to. The man was twisted, brutal, and without conscience. He wanted what he wanted, and Avery was a threat to his power. He wouldn't stop trying to kill Avery until she was under his control or dead. They had to hide, or kill him, and Avery wasn't a murderer. She wasn't. So, that meant running.

She glanced over her shoulder to see if anyone was paying attention to them. Jeremy, the college-kid clerk, was oblivious. She handed Millie her ticket and nudged her sister toward the exit. "Remember. *Boston's South Station.* My contact, Jason Chadwick, will find you. Remember that name. Give him the bag. Only him, okay? I'll meet up with you when it's safe, as soon as possible."

Millie nodded. "Yes."

Then Millie stepped on the bus, not looking back. The moment felt final, as if Avery would never see her sister again, and that scared her to death, because this was her fault. Eight years ago, something horrific happened. They'd been helpless, and everything dear and necessary to them was taken in the space of a moment. They couldn't recover, only react. Avery chose vengeance and was still paying the price. Millie, too. She was paying, too.

Trembling, drying blood made her arms and face itch, as Avery dialed her contact's number. He was her backup plan, that she'd hoped never to use. When the line connected, she didn't wait for Jason to say hello. "Millie will be at Boston's South Station Greyhound terminal in four hours."

"I'll be there." She believed him, because he knew Millie had the money, and he knew Avery would hunt him down otherwise. She hung up without comment, watching Millie's bus pull away from the curb.

Time to make Patty Whitman disappear.

* * * *

Vincent found Avery by following the trail of people gossiping along Main Street. Apparently, a waitress covered in blood wasn't a common sight hereabouts…and people noticed. Go figure.

"Patty?" It felt weird to use that name, but she'd never corrected him, so *Patty* it was. He held the storefront's door open, more relieved than anything else to find her inside. She was alive, safe. He'd take that as a win.

She had her back to him, buying a bus ticket from the clerk. Vincent saw the blood stains that started at her neck, and ran down her uniform to her legs, covering the white shoes with spatter. After seeing what she'd done to Jim with his knife, Vincent supposed most of the blood wasn't hers, but it was a small consolation. He felt pangs. Many pangs of guilt that she'd had to fight Jim alone, and that she'd been injured because of it. He told himself there'd been too many guns, too many potential targets to control the situation completely, but there was a niggling of fear that he could have done better by her. Should have. He'd had one mission in that diner, and that was to keep an eye on her. Sure, things went to hell, but Avery had survived that diner disaster without his help. He'd carry that guilt for life.

"Patty." She was ignoring him, acting as if she weren't covered in blood. He suspected she was in shock. He'd seen enough of it to recognize the symptoms. The clerk caught Vincent's gaze, and then widened his eyes, not hiding his unease that his customer was bloody and seemingly oblivious to the fact. Even *the clerk* knew her behavior was odd. Why didn't Avery? *Definitely* in shock.

She took the ticket and stuffed it into her purse. "Thank you, Jeremy."

From the looks of Jeremy, he was all of seventeen. Vincent flashed Jeremy his credentials so he wouldn't have to explain. Avery turned and saw them, and he saw her eyes. They weren't dilated, so she wasn't in shock, and his FBI credentials didn't even warrant a twitch of fear. That meant she wasn't running from him, and either had nerves of steel or was suffering from amnesia. She had to *suspect* he was here because of her ex-husband, right? Then he remembered the knife pinning Eric's hand to the shotgun, and Jim, the junkie, bloody on the floor. So…nerves of steel. Good to know. She was trained and unflappable. Dangerous.

"What are you doing?" He made sure to keep his expression puzzled and worried. The moment their interaction became about controlling her, he had a feeling he'd lose even the small amount of goodwill he'd managed to build between them.

Avery walked passed him. "Who's asking?"

"Huh?" It wasn't as if he could pretend he was anything but the FBI Special Agent she'd seen in action at the diner, but he could pretend that his status didn't matter. After all, Feds went on fishing trips, too. "I was worried about you." He kept pace with her as they walked down the sidewalk.

"How did you find me?" she said.

"I *could* say when local law enforcement arrived on scene, I explained the prime witness disappeared, so I went in hot pursuit."

"But that's not the real reason?" She seemed to be weighing his words.

"Like I said—" He gave her his version of puppy dog eyes. "I was worried about you."

That seemed to mollify her, but she didn't slow her gait. "You still didn't tell me how you found me."

She was interrogating *him*. And wasn't that just a fine how do you do, he thought.

"A blood-covered waitress meandering through town? You've started rumors of a zombie apocalypse." She kept walking, eyes front. "Stop and talk to me, will you?" She was strung so tightly he feared forcing the issue lest she see it as an attack, and she'd been hurt enough. He didn't want to upset her more. "I'm worried about you, Patty." Yeah, he needed to keep her under his thumb, but he wanted her injuries checked out by a doctor, too.

Her expression softened, making him think he was making headway with her. "Thank you," she said. "That's sweet. I'm sorry I worried you."

"But?" He could tell she was exerting herself with her pace, because her cheeks were flushed, and the pulse at her neck was visible and racing.

"But—" She threw him an impatient glance. "I'm sore, I'm upset, I want a shower, to...to... Listen, I want to *go home*." Vincent couldn't allow that. Not until Benton texted him the surveillance cameras were up. He needed a delay tactic.

"First you have to be checked out by a doctor. You could have internal injuries or something." When he caught her glance of distain, he threw his hands up in the air. "What? I'm not a doctor."

"No, you're a Fed."

"So, you don't like Feds?"

She pursed her lips. "I like Feds that tell me they are Feds before they try to get in my pants."

"If I'd told you, you never would have given me a second look. Despite what you might think, working for the FBI does not make me a chick magnet. They always think of their unpaid parking tickets when I want them to be thinking of me." Her cheek kicked up with a smile, but she didn't slow down. "Now you might be saying to yourself, but the FBI has nothing to do with parking tickets."

She glanced at him. "Is your punch line that you date only stupid women or women who illegally park?"

He chuckled. "I'm a gentleman. I'd never say such a thing."

"Listen, it's been fun, but, I got to go." She scanned the street and sidewalk, and walked faster, clenching and unclenching her fists, drawing her thumbs across her rings, as if they irritated. Maybe they'd swelled so much, her rings were cutting off circulation. Her right hand had it the worst; split knuckles, red and purple bruising.

"Patty, let's have the EMTs look at your hand, at least. Okay? It looks really messed up." He lifted it so he could get a better look. She winced, and pulled her hand from his grasp, then hid both hands in the pockets of her uniform's apron.

"I'm fine." No. She was limping, and the growing bruise on her knee looked angry.

"Did you fall?" He pointed to her knee.

She shook her head. "I aimed poorly, and kneed Jim's belt buckle during the fight. I think I pinched a nerve, but it's fine."

"*Fine*." He arched his brows, wondering if he should just shut up. Nope. "I think you need to rethink what *fine* means, because you're never going to see a picture of a person in your shape listed under a definition of the word *fine*. But…if you say so." He shook his head. "Fine or not, the sheriff is waiting for your statement. You shouldn't have left the crime scene. Don't you watch *Law & Order*?"

She glanced at him, and he saw a return of her unease. "I wasn't thinking."

She'd run from a crime scene and bought a ticket out of town. Seemed pretty clear-headed, if not premeditated to Vincent. "What about *Rizzoli & Isles*? Or *CSI*, or *CSI New Orleans*, or—"

"Really?" She was out of breath from walking so fast. "Are you going to list all the television shows I haven't seen?"

"How could you not have seen them?"

"No cable," she mumbled, not slowing down.

"Not even *Netflix*?"

"No Internet. No computer. I'm a waitress in a small town. Tips aren't that great." If she was telling the truth, did that mean "the files" were in paper form? He found that hard to believe. Not in this data age, but no Internet? He found that hard to believe, too. She had to have them on a flash drive, tucked away in her apartment. "I have my iPhone, of course, but who wants to watch a show on a phone?"

"Well, if you *had* watched those shows, you'd also know ignorance isn't a defense. Most of the time, anyway. I think if you come *quietly*," he said with a smile, "you know, not give me anymore of a hard time than you already have—"

"What?" She gave him a flirty smile. "You pulling out the thumb screws already?"

He laughed. "Just let the EMTs look at you. Don't make this a big deal. And yeah, you must give a statement, or the sheriff will come looking for you. Come on." He tilted his head in the direction of the diner. "They're all back at the crime scene. Let's go."

"I don't want to." She shuddered and kept up the fast pace. Her reaction read authentic. The diner upset her, and she was having a hard time processing. Now he felt like a jerk for forcing her to go back there, but he couldn't risk her seeing the task force wire her street for video. Too much time and energy went into this operation. Vincent's bleeding heart would have to go into storage.

"Unfortunately," he said, "it's nonnegotiable." Even his ears picked up the regret in his tone, probably because it was real. Yup. He was a jerk, but for a good cause.

She stopped walking, glaring at him. "If I give my statement, will you leave me alone?"

No. "Yes." He indicated the road that would lead them back to the diner, and after a heavy sigh, Avery pivoted and walked in that direction. "Where'd you learn to throw a knife?" he said.

That got her attention. Her annoyance fled, and her eyes widened as she covered the slice at her neck. When her fingers connected with the seeping injury, she winced a little. "I don't know what you're talking about. After Jim dropped the knife, I threw it. I didn't want him using it on me again."

Bullshit, but informative. She sliced and diced Jim before throwing it at Eric. No one accidentally threw with that accuracy, or with the strength to pin a man's hand to the stock of a shotgun. Her denial told him she was still invested in her role as Patty, and that meant she still thought there was a chance that Vincent was an unwitting dupe.

"I'm sorry I wasn't able to protect you." He *was* sorry. Guilty, too. He'd replay what happened in that diner for many years to come, looking to see how he could have done better, ended it quicker. Less dead.

Avery glanced at him, her brows and pursed lips giving him some indication of her annoyance. "I protected myself. I didn't need you." Then she squared her shoulders and winced. Her limping grew more pronounced.

"No," he said. "You did not."

She stopped, putting her fists on her hips. "What exactly were you thinking, by the way? Putting your weapon on the floor when so many guns were in play? Yours was the only gun we had on our side, and you put it down."

He scoffed. "I didn't put it down. I pretended to—"

"Did you pretend to put our lives at their mercy, too? Because you did. Eric could have pulled the trigger at *any* moment." She gave herself a little shake and then started walking again. Vincent couldn't suppress a little annoyance at being called out like that.

"I had a plan. It worked."

She scoffed. "They were a bunch of drug addicts. Addicts that had already killed a member of their own group, and… They'd killed Sam. You were going to *comply*, risking our lives in the hopes they'd be merciful."

She was working herself into a frenzy. Her cheeks were flushed, and her eyes were flashing. Vincent found he preferred her mad rather than upset, and that made him smile. She noticed and narrowed her eyes, glaring at him.

"I wasn't going to put it down," he said. "What I did is what we call in the biz a bait and switch."

She turned her eyes front, shaking her head. "I don't believe you."

"That's okay." *He didn't believe a word she said either.* "Still true."

"Hmm." Her grimace was ripe with annoyance, and she stayed that way, even when they'd arrived back at the diner, and when he'd arranged for her to step into the witness line leading to the sheriff and his men. Her annoyance, in fact, seemed to occupy the part of her brain that had been devoted to fear. He was glad of it, because she was so delicate-looking, and he felt like he should have protected her better. One good guilt-trip, and he feared being played like a drum. Women did that to Vincent. It was their superpower, so he was always on the lookout, but Avery didn't seem interested in his sympathy.

The sheriff and his officers took copious notes, but after a half hour, Avery had told her version of the events, and he had no more excuses to keep her occupied. She'd frequently surveilled the road, and milling crowd, during and after her interview. He could see she was antsy, and got the impression she wanted to be gone so badly that if he'd tried to stop her, she'd have lashed out, so Vincent didn't insist she see the EMT on site. Benton's text arrived soon thereafter, declaring the cameras installed, and the team gone. By then, Avery was already heading to her apartment.

He watched her walking away as the white surveillance van parked across the street from the diner. Vincent knew the van contained a socialite, an impatient, beat-up team leader, a bruiser, and a fish. They'd want him to back off, dangle her as bait for Coppola's contract killers, so the cameras could give them probable cause to rush into her apartment and find the files. But Vincent didn't have the stomach for that anymore, not after what he and Avery had just been through. She was injured. What if Coppola's men arrived and they got to her before Vincent and the team could? He couldn't risk it.

Sure, she was a liar. Sure, she'd filleted Jim and stuck Eric. And yeah, she was pretending to be someone she wasn't, but he hadn't expected her to be a Girl Scout. She was the ex-wife of a crime lord. He didn't trust her, but she had something he wanted, and it was in both their interests to keep her safe.

He followed Avery, instead of crossing the street to get in the now open side door of the van. When he'd walked passed the van, the side door slowly closed again as his iPhone vibrated in his pocket. Benton or Deming, most likely, was attempting to micromanage him. Vincent ignored his phone.

When he reached Avery's side, she rolled her eyes but remained silent. Then there was no conversation, no eye contact, nothing until they reached her front door. It was directly next to a Chinese restaurant, whose aromas made his stomach growl, because fucking Eric ate his cheeseburger.

After a fake smile, the kind that said *eat shit*, Avery extended her beat-up, cut, and swelling hand for a shake. Intending simply to hold it, he extend his hand, but Avery gripped it hard enough to make her rings bite into his palm. Then she pumped his hand up and down once before releasing him.

"Thanks for the walk home," she said. "It was like having my own bodyguard, and after what happened at the diner, I'm a little shaken up. It was nice not to have to worry." He didn't believe a word she'd said. Her tone was right, but this woman fended off a meth-head with a knife. She didn't need a bodyguard, and her gaze suggested an impatience to see him walk away. Avery Coppola was about to disappear, if she had anything to say about it. "It's been nice knowing you." She unlocked the door and was about to leave him on the sidewalk. Vincent stuck his boot out, stopping her from closing the door in his face.

"Invite me in," he said. She grimaced.

"I'm tired. I'm gross. I know you're on vacation, but I'm not." Rubbing her face, she looked every bit as weary as she'd professed to be. "I've got things to do."

"Please." He did his best to cajole, lifting his brows, donning a hint of a smile. "Invite me in." He was coming in whether she wanted him to or not, but he'd prefer she want him inside. It would look better on his report if he tripped over some evidence he wanted to use in court. "I could use a cup of coffee and the company of someone that won't ask me if *I'm* okay." Did he attempt to make her feel bad about not once asking if he was alright? Sure. Hopefully, it would work, but he was coming in one way or another.

She sighed, nodded once, and then turned her back on him, taking the stairs up to her apartment. "Just a cup. Then you have to go." Two steps later, she was wincing in pain.

Vincent couldn't handle it. Without a word, he lifted her, cradling her in his arms. With a nudge of his foot, he closed the door behind them, shutting out the daylight and leaving them in mostly darkness. Then the stairwell lights flickered on, and he saw Avery had flipped a switch.

Her arms encircled his neck, and she stared into his eyes, looking puzzled. "Who the hell are you, Special Agent Vincent Modena?"

He met her gaze for a moment, and then shrugged before climbing the stairs quickly. He saw her distrust, but that just meant she was smart. "Still figuring that out, Patty. Still figuring that out."

Chapter 4

Avery found it painful to be taken care of, especially the way Vincent did it. Carrying her relieved the stress on her knee, but his arm pressed on her bruises, *and* kept the injured knee bent. Ugh. Bending the knee was why climbing the stairs hurt. So she was basically in hell, and couldn't say anything, because the man was trying to do right by her. Was she stroking his ego by not complaining? Maybe assuaging his obvious guilt by allowing this act of gallantry? Hopefully. It might make him leave quicker.

When they reached the stairwell landing, and were face to face with her faux forsythia wreath hanging from her door, she gave herself a mental pat on the back. So far, she'd managed not to betray her pain—no grunts, no groans—decreasing the chances he'd hustle her to the emergency room.

Digging out her key from her purse, she wiggled. "You can put me down now."

Vincent didn't seem like he wanted to, but he did, steadying her as her legs bore her full weight. Blood smears now marred his arms and neck, reminding her that she was covered in the stuff. She quickly unlocked the door and hurried inside, giving the living room a once over. Millie hadn't trashed it before leaving, so it looked much the same as it did when Avery left for her morning shift. Worn, used furniture, cheap mementos from their lives resting on a few surfaces. A mug from a restaurant here, a cheap vase with a wooden rose there. No pictures. Nothing to indicate who lived here. It was safe to allow a stranger…an FBI Special Agent into her home.

Vincent closed the door behind them, and then put his hands in his jean pockets, looking around, not hiding his interest. "How long have you lived here?"

"Three years. Listen…" She bit her lip. "I really want a shower. Would you mind making your own coffee? It's in the cupboard over the coffeepot."

"Sure. You want a cup?"

"No, thank you. Hey, I appreciate the lift up the stairs." She held his gaze, gave him a nod. "I do."

"All part of the service." He adopted a bright smile, teasing.

"Privacy isn't part of that service?"

He pressed his lips together and averted his gaze. "Not when you could be in shock," he said. "I'm not leaving your side until I know for sure. What if you slip and fall in the tub? Most accidents occur in the home—"

"I'm fine!"

"Maybe." He lifted his brows, stepping into the galley kitchen. "You should have let the EMT decide that, but you didn't, so I'm here." He opened the cupboard above the coffeepot and pulled down a can of Folgers.

She frowned, folding her arms over her chest. "For how long? You moving in?"

"The time it takes to drink a cup of coffee." He threw her an easy smile. "Don't worry, I'm not a long-term kind of guy."

She could believe it. "More of a love 'em and leave him, huh?"

He chuckled, filling the coffeepot using the sink. "Take your shower, and then I'll take you out for lunch. Deal?"

She shook her head. "No. That's extortion, and I don't like the idea of—" She shut up, not knowing how to say *being naked in the shower with you in my living room unsettles me.*

"Of what?" He pulled filters from the cupboard, and stuffed one into the machine's coffee grounds funnel.

"Forget it." She pressed her lips together, unwilling to go there.

He glanced at her. "What did I do now?"

"Did anyone ever tell you that you're like a dog with a bone? No means no. You get that, right?"

He leaned against the counter. "And when, exactly, did you say no to me?"

Point, set, match. He chuckled when she just stood there, eyes narrowed, then waved down the hall, the only other place to go in her apartment. "You do your thing." Then he pushed the coffee machine's button, and left the kitchen. He walked into the living room and sat on her worn, Goodwill-purchased couch. "Go. I don't mind waiting."

She glanced at her television directly across from him, the one Millie always complained about. "I told you. I don't have cable."

He lifted his iPhone. "I'll check my mail."

"No Wi-Fi." She took a step back from him, having run out of excuses, but still not liking that he was in her apartment. "But then, you probably have plenty of data, being a Fed and all."

"If not, I'm sure the restaurant will have Wi-Fi." His smile widened.

Lunch. Hmm. "I am hungry. After lunch, though, I have things to do. It's good-bye." He nodded, but she didn't believe him, and decided to devise a plan to ditch him before she headed back to the Greyhound bus station.

"The shower will make you feel better," he said.

Vincent was doing a good job of acting as if he were a welcomed guest. It irritated the hell out of her, but it was the sympathy she saw on his face that convinced her she was probably making more of this than necessary. She and Vincent did experience something horrible together. They'd survived. Shared trauma was a powerful bond, and he'd already inferred that he was hiding from his peers' sympathy.

"Fine." She turned and hurried into her bedroom, gathering her clothes, and the stuff she'd take with her when she left on the bus. So, basically, her ticket, license, and debit card.

Changing her identity, hiding in a tiny town, keeping her head down, nothing she'd done over the last three years had protected her and Millie as she'd hoped. She should have known better. A person got to be one of two things in life, and one of them wasn't a bystander. That left the role of player or victim, neither of which she had any interest in being, not that life ever cared what she'd wanted. Avery and Millie had been steeped in victimhood for so long their fingers were pruned from it, but her choices had kept them alive, so there was hope of a future not dictated by whether Dante Coppola wanted them dead.

Lifting her face to the shower's spray, she dreamed of the day when she could feed off something other than hope, when scrubbing off the taint of violence wasn't in vain. There were things she wanted in life, ambitions, for her and Millie. They weren't big, like being an astronaut, or a rock star, or physicist, though if Millie wanted those things, Avery would do her best to position her to do so. No, Avery's ambitions were more about walking to the store without having to look over her shoulder, or maybe have a job that allowed her to afford Disneyland. Millie would love to go there. She wanted little things like that, the things that people took for granted, the memories that people looked back on with fondness. For Avery and Millie, memories carried fear, and were the reason they needed to hide. There was no room for happiness to muscle into their lives, and until things changed, all they had was hope. So, hope would have to suffice.

She lingered in the shower mostly because the hot water did ease her aches and was helping with the swelling, though her jaw still clicked when she opened her mouth. Jim's sucker punch was no joke. By tomorrow, she'd have a colorful bruise to show for it. The water stung as it washed over her abrasions, but it soothed the long ridge of bruising from when Jim slammed her against the counter. By the time she was soaped and rinsed, she'd logged all her injuries and decided she'd live. She was tired, though, and hungry. *Real* hungry.

The smells from the restaurant below made her mouth water. The bus ride would be long, so best to have a full belly when she embarked. Unfortunately, the food in her cupboards required cooking, so that meant eating out. No way was she going on the run *and* cooking. Vincent offered lunch, so she'd take him up on it, and then ditch him afterward.

Leaving the shower still feeling sore, but clean, she wrapped herself in a towel and then stepped into her adjoining bedroom. A wave of disorientation had her looking around. Everything seemed…wrong. Her bedspread was mussed, though Millie could have done that if she'd watched television in here. It would also explain why the nick knacks on her side table weren't quite where Avery had left them.

None of it matters anymore. Millie was gone. Her days of messing with Avery's stuff were over until they set up house somewhere else. What mattered was Millie was safe, and soon, Avery would be with her. Until then, she needed to focus on shaking Special Agent Vincent Modena, FBI.

She dressed in her black T-shirt, jeans, and Doc Martens, then pinned her wet hair into a messy bun on the top of her head. She found Vincent in the kitchen, drinking coffee, and balancing a bag of peas on his knuckles. His punching hand didn't look much better than hers.

"Great idea," she said. He lobbed the bag of peas to her, which she easily caught. "I'm sure there's another one in the freezer."

"Big pea eaters in this house?" Somehow, he'd found a way to use the existence of frozen peas in her house to ask if she was living with someone. Impressive.

"I've been known to like a pea or two."

"Do you live alone?" Good to know. If subtly doesn't work, the Fed came right out and asked. Eyelids lowered, he peered at her, pretending to be jealous, yet he was clearly making a joke out of it, and just as clearly wanted an answer. It was laughable. They barely knew each other, for one thing, and for another, it wasn't his damn business. Yes, he was sexy as sin, and yes, in an alternate universe where Dante wasn't desperate to kill her she'd jump Vincent's bones and stay in bed for a weekend, living off love. But life wasn't that simple. She owed Vincent nothing. Certainly, not the truth.

"My boyfriend won't be home until later, if that's what you're asking. And yes, he's jealous, and yes, he won't like that you're in my apartment, but I think I'll be able to keep him from killing you if you keep your promise and walk away after lunch." Nothing makes a man bail faster than being disqualified as a bed mate. *Do you live alone?* She wondered if he interrogated all new acquaintances this way. "You done with your coffee?" She didn't wait for an answer, but rather went to the door and opened it. "You said you'd feed me, and no, I don't consider a bag of frozen peas food."

Vincent glanced at the bag she continued to clutch. "You taking that with you?"

"Why? Will it embarrass you to be seen with me holding it?" Not that she cared. Her knuckles had swollen so much her rings were pinching.

"No." He walked to the door and motioned with a hand, indicating she step through first.

Avery didn't move. Not until she took one last look around the apartment. She and Millie had made a life here. This was where they'd schemed and planned for the day when fear was behind them, and freedom was something they could take for granted. They'd survived here, hadn't had much of a life, but it was theirs, cheap and shabby though it was…

She wouldn't miss it.

Clutching the frozen peas, she walked out and used the banister to ease the weight off her bum knee. Though her descent wasn't pretty, it was at least under her own steam, and lots less painful than being lifted. A glance behind her caught Vincent staring at her ass. An ass man. She felt relief, because that meant he wanted her, and his pursuit was about getting in her pants, not her head. Oddly enough, knowing that allowed her to enjoy his gaze. It felt like a caress, and sent arousing tingles throughout her body. The man had the naughtiest smile.

"You seem jumpy." He kept pace with her down the stairs, looking lazy and patient. Happy, apparently, to while away his time checking out her ass.

She reached the bottom of the stairs, opened the front door, and turned off the stairwell lights. "You have that effect on a woman."

Before stepping out onto the sidewalk, she scanned the street, automatically searching for familiar faces…faces that *didn't* belong in North Conway. It was a habit she'd developed over the years, but now that her face was probably all over social media, it became more important than ever to remain vigilant. Dante's men would find her here, the only question was, when?

She pressed the peas to her swollen knuckles, knowing it was past time to get out of Dodge. She stepped out onto the sidewalk and waited for Vincent to close the door behind them.

"Food." She was dying of starvation. Vincent used his hand to indicate the bistro seating of the Chinese restaurant next door. Though pleased with his choice, because it would be quick, she worried it wouldn't be quick enough. Her bus was leaving in a half an hour.

He pulled out a black cast iron chair from beneath a small, intricately designed cast iron table. "Sit. I ordered when you were in the shower. Hope you're in the mood for General Ghau's chicken."

She was. The restaurant door opened as Avery sat and Vincent sat across from her. Wan Gamon, the daughter of the restaurant's owner and Avery's landlord, carried a takeout bag under her arm and clutched two glasses filled with iced water. She was smiling, petite, her dark hair in a low ponytail, and she wore a Boston Red Sox cap. "Hey, Patty."

"Hey, Gamon. How you doing?"

Gamon placed the food and drinks on the table. "Heard about the ruckus at the diner. People are saying you won a knife fight with a killer?"

Avery laughed, and then rolled her eyes. "I don't know where you're getting your information, but no. That didn't happen." She showed her cut up neck. "I was terrified. He held a knife to my throat. I didn't win." Gamon oohed and awed, looking at Avery's neck.

"That's horrible," Gamon said. "It's a miracle you lived."

"It's a miracle I got a day off for my trouble. You know James. He hasn't even called me yet, but if it wasn't a crime scene, you know he'd be on the phone, telling me I was still on the clock." She smiled, ignoring the odd look Vincent threw her way. He wouldn't understand why she'd downplay her role in the diner's troubles. Winning a knife fight with a drugged-out killer would bring her attention. Her one play here was to create conflicting rumors, otherwise, it would be a red flag for her ex-husband. He'd send his goons here to check out the knife-fighting waitress.

Vincent handed Gamon a fifty. "Keep the change."

"Thank you." Gamon gave Avery a wink and a nudge, as if she approved of her date, and then disappeared back into the restaurant.

"You certainly impressed Gamon." Avery threw him a smile, and then opened the bag. She was so hungry her stomach hurt. "Thanks for this. It was shopping day and I was down to canned foods."

"But do I impress you?" He used his hands to indicate their surroundings. People walked by, ignoring them mostly, and cars passed at a slow crawl. "Only the finest venue."

"Do you ever not dig for compliments?" She set aside her frozen peas, and pulled chopsticks from the bag, laughing.

He took her implied criticism in the vein it was given, as a gentle ribbing, then saw the chopsticks, and it was his turn to laugh. "Good luck with that." He pulled two plastic forks from the bag, placing one before her. He was right. Her knuckles were too swollen to manipulate chopsticks.

After she'd devoured a few bites, and her stomach was no longer punishing her for neglect, Avery decided Vincent could satisfy her curiosity, if not her other, more neglected needs. "How come you're not at the diner with the cops?" she said. "I'd think a Fed would be all over what happened back there, exchanging stories, writing up reports. Isn't that what men like you get off on? Instead, you're babysitting the waitress. Two murders, Vincent. This is a small town. They could use your help." *And she could use him gone.*

"Sheriff took my statement." He shrugged. "I'm on vacation, remember? Not in charge, thankfully. The paperwork on this morning's shit show will take them all night to complete. I'd rather spend this time with you."

She speared a medallion of chicken with her fork. "You smell like fish, and you're wearing Jim's blood. The feeling isn't mutual."

He finished chewing his lo mein, and then licked his lips before replying. "If you'd invited me to share your shower, I'd be prettier."

"Any prettier and you'll be impossible to be around." She kept her smile prim when he barked out a laugh.

A carton in one hand, his fork in the other, Vincent's smile still seemed genuine, but it had grown subdued. "It could have been a hundred times worse back there at the diner," he said. "You know that. Right?" She nodded, thinking of Sam, and his grieving family.

"Could have been way worse." She'd thought herself dead more than once with Jim. "We survived, though."

"Thanks to you," Vincent said.

She licked the sweet sauce off her lips. "And you. You were impressive back there. I saw how you took out that guy in three moves. The silent one. Not many people can do that."

"Yeah? So, I've finally done something that impresses you." He smiled, winking. Then he leaned back, propping his feet up on the chair next to him. Spearing his fork into the carton, he twirled it, his gazed fixed on her mouth. Try as she might, she couldn't stop licking her lips. When his smile grew naughty, she suspected he was thinking of their kiss back at the diner, like she was, only she was the one blushing.

Avery filled her mouth with chicken, and told herself to stop screwing around. She was leaving this town, leaving him. Soon, he'd be someone she used to know. "You're staring," she said.

His smile grew. "Am I?"

"Yeah. You've been staring since we met." She leaned toward him, took his carton of lo mein and ate some, before handing it back. Then she picked up the chicken carton again.

"I'm sorry if I'm making you uncomfortable." No, he wasn't. If he was, he wouldn't be sporting such a shit-eating grin. She was attracted to him. He knew it, and she hated that he knew it. An FBI agent, for heaven's sake. She obviously had a death wish.

"I already told you I have a jealous boyfriend. What do you think you'll get out of this?" She waved her fork between them, indicating them as a couple. She really wanted to know, because she wasn't an idiot. She'd already declared sex off limits, and he was a player. There was no love at first sight going on. So, what the fuck?

He gave his head a little shake, and seemed a bit wistful, as if he too wanted the answer to that question. "Something about you, I guess. I don't know if it's that look in your eyes, or that you're so damn sexy, or maybe it's because there doesn't seem to be anything you can't do." He smiled suddenly, lifting his brows. "Can you yodel? I've tried. It's not so easy."

She laughed. He was so good at flirting. No, she couldn't yodel. In fact, her skill sets were extremely narrow. Even laundry seemed to elude her. If it wasn't for bleach, she'd have all pink socks as red items inevitably found their way into her whites.

"Exactly what look do I have in my eyes?" she said.

Vincent's smile faded, though he continued to stare. "Like you're caged." His words seemed to shock even him, and then he was the image of regret. "I'm sorry. That was unkind."

That was the thing about honesty, she thought. It wasn't always kind, but in this case, his words couldn't have been truer. Her family was killed eight years ago. The price of justice had been high, and part of that price was waitressing in North Conway, New Hampshire. The alternative was Dante finding and killing her and Millie.

"Patty, I'm worried about you," he said.

About *her*. Not any of the other customers in the diner this morning. Her. She was the only one he tracked down, followed home, waited until she'd showered, and then fed Chinese food. She believed him when he said he was worried. No one was that good of an actor. And she wasn't receiving a danger vibe from him, but still his focus worried her nonetheless.

Vincent was FBI. Just knowing him brought unwanted attention, and she was sitting with him, eating a meal with him, in full view of the town. It wasn't the smartest thing she'd ever done.

"Well," she glanced at her watch, "stop worrying. I'm not your responsibility." She had twenty minutes before her bus left, so she tried to relax and enjoy this free food. The chicken was delicious, and it would probably be the last time she'd eat at this restaurant. This, she'd miss.

"Good food, huh?" he said. She nodded. "I bet there are other restaurants in this town that have good food, too. Maybe we could hang, spend the day together, go on a pub crawl tonight to let off some steam." She shook her head. "Stay, Patty. Don't leave."

She frowned, chewing. "I'm sitting here, aren't I?"

"The bus ticket. I know you're going. Anyway, if you won't stay for me, stay for the sheriff. He might have follow-up questions. The least you could do is make sure he knows how to reach you."

"I gave him my phone number."

He avoided her gaze, as if he were being shy. It was adorable. "Maybe I'll want to reach you."

She rattled off her phone number and he smiled, all puffed up and satisfied as he inputted it into his contact list. This concession meant little to Avery. She'd memorized all her important numbers, so she'd lose little when she destroyed her phone's SIM and GPS cards on the bus. A new phone could always be purchased at a CVS or Walgreens.

Vincent dialed a number on his phone and seemed surprised when Avery's rang.

"Trust issues?" She sipped some water, hiding her smile, ignoring that her phone suddenly went silent.

Vincent groaned, but with humor. "You have no idea."

A van's sliding door opened across the street. Three people in business suits hopped out, looking official. Could have been Dante's men, but Avery's brain tagged them as Feds, because if they'd been Dante's, they'd be shooting already. When they walked toward her and Vincent, holding up their credentials, she looked away, praying they were here for Vincent, maybe looking for a debrief on the diner dustup. She put her fork down and prepared a pretty goodbye, hoping to leave Vincent to it and get on with his life.

He sipped his water and then wiped his hands on a napkin. He seemed curious to see their approach, but not concerned. "The jig up?" So, he did know them.

A tall, manly, black-haired and blue-eyed Fed stepped forward, still holding out his credentials, but aiming it at Avery. It read *Special Agent John Benton, FBI.* Serious as death, the man locked eyes with her. "Avery Toner Coppola, the jig is definitely up."

Chapter 5

Benton didn't wait for Avery to respond, not that she looked as if she had a response at the ready. Her face flushed red, and her glare couldn't have been more toxic, but she remained silent. "Change of plans," Benton said. "We're taking Mrs. Coppola to the sheriff's office."

Benton directed his words to Vincent, but kept glancing at Avery, as if expecting trouble. He understood Benton's concern. She was glaring like she was calculating their demise.

"Just as well," Vincent said. "I searched her apartment pretty thoroughly and didn't find anything. If it's in there, she'll have to tell us." He heard Avery's gasp and ignored it. Benton was in a rush for a reason. "What's up?"

Deming tucked her ID back into her black suit jacket pocket. "We've confirmation Coppola's men are in the area, and there are more of them than anticipated. They've good as found her, Modena."

Vincent did his best to push down his anger, not wanting to show team discord in front of Avery. "We've been sitting here fifteen minutes, easily. It would have been nice to have this intel." He glanced at Deming. "Sooner."

"Maybe someone should answer his phone," Deming snapped back.

"Get the witness into the van," Benton said. He, Gilroy and Deming then hustled across the street to the van, leaving Vincent to deal with Avery.

He tilted his head toward the van, waiting, wondering if she'd give him a hard time. Surprisingly, she didn't. Instead, she followed the agents at a fast clip, looking both ways, hopping inside the van without fuss. Vincent supposed hearing Coppola's men were in the area had a way of reshuffling her priorities. Whatever got her to move was fine by him, because he had an itchy feeling between his shoulder blades, like a laser scope was aimed, a rifle locked and loaded, like he was taking his life in his hands by staying in the open.

The sun reflected off Special Agent Gilroy's silver West Point college ring as the man jumped into the driver's seat. Benton, Deming, and Vincent followed Avery inside the van's interior and took seats in front of the computer monitors on small tables affixed to its walls. It was their mobile HQ in here, and now Avery was an inner, huddled against the far-right corner, eyes lowered, hiding in plain sight. He wished things could have worked out differently. There was no reason he couldn't have groomed her more, got her to open up to him, maybe prompt her to ask for his help, but time, and events, were having their way. The FBI now had to be the hammer to Avery's nail, and knowing what he did about her, it was going to be messy.

Hunched, feeling cramped in the back, he focused on her, looking for a way to move past what she had to think was a betrayal. "We're on your side," Vincent said. "It might not feel that way right now, but we are."

"We're the good guys," Deming said. Sitting across from him, the profiler was studying Avery like a chemist might a boiling solution in a beaker. He was almost positive Deming had no idea how intense she was being, and if she did, he suspected she wouldn't have the slightest interest in changing her ways. Deming was Deming. She was a damn fine agent, smart as a whip, and perceptive.

Avery ignored them all and managed to project the image of a waif, bruised and battered. He wondered how much of that image was true, and how much was a mask Avery hid behind. She pulled at Vincent's emotions and made him want to hold her, and tell her everything was going to be all right. *Which was ridiculous.* She was a job. She had to be. And Vincent needed to pull his shit together and focus on the situation at hand.

"Deming, where's Coppola's men now?" Vincent drew his gun, checked the clip, and then chambered a bullet. Avery's gaze focused on his gun, making him wondered if she was thinking about snatching it from his hand the way she'd snatched Jim's knife. "Any updates?"

"There are no updates." Deming inclined her head toward the driver. "Gilroy has a snitch and he said Coppola's men were spotted five miles outside downtown."

Vincent glanced at Avery, hoping to see a reaction. Nothing. She was keeping things close to the vest. At the diner, faced with crazed killers, she'd revealed plenty emotion. She'd been scared like the rest of them. Now? Stone cold. He wondered if she was disassociating, then decided it was more likely she was planning her next move. It was the team's job to convince her she didn't have one...unless they sanctioned it.

Soon thereafter, Gilroy parked the van at the sheriff's building. Not in the lot, but at the curb outside the entrance. When Gilroy jumped out, he opened the sliding side door, his gun at the ready, surveilling the area. Vincent took Avery by the arm and hustled her out onto the sidewalk, and retained his hold as he walked her toward the building, just in case she had ideas of running. Thankfully, she didn't resist, because whether she wanted to admit it or not, they were saving her ass. The last thing he wanted was to fight her to do it, and if she played this smart—and there was no doubt in his mind that she was smart—she'd take their protection as the gift it was, and live.

Guns drawn, the agents escorted her to the building. Benton took point. Deming rear. Gilroy stayed with the van, keeping a watch out. Once inside, Vincent chose the stairs instead of the elevator, because long ago, he'd chosen differently, and when the elevator doors opened on their destination floor, so did a barrage of bullets. This building had two floors, so the climb was of little consequence. It wasn't until they reached the top floor and Avery's limp became pronounced that he'd realized his choice had caused her pain. By then, it was too late. The damage had been done.

The sheriff was waiting for them in his outer office. Ten deputies were retrieving rifles from gun lockers behind a caged room off to the left. Admin people were at their desks, some on phones, hopefully coordinating with neighboring town's law enforcement, seeking backup. Fear was palpable in the room. Avery said they were small town, but he hadn't imagined they'd be so young. Facing a worst-case scenario, something they'd trained their whole careers for, he didn't blame them for being afraid.

Avery was busy checking out the surroundings, probably hoping to game the system, see her best route to escape. That's what he'd be doing. The office was sectioned off by shelves that separated desks and paralleled the walls. Black metal shelves. They were mostly filled with files, some lay bare, or had legal tomes stacked in neat rows. The whole place wasn't big, wasn't much, certainly wasn't enough. Not nearly for what was coming. Yet, he glanced at Avery, and saw she seemed detached from fear, and the frenzied activity. He wasn't sure why he was surprised. She'd already proved she had nerves of steel.

Vincent caught the sheriff's attention in the crowd, and indicated Avery with his thumb. "Where can I put her?" The sheriff pointed across the room. Holding. It was a small, white, Plexiglas-fronted room, with a caged door, located next to the sheriff's office in the back of the main area. As he escorted Avery there, he saw an older admin wearing a floral blouse. She lifted a phone receiver in the air.

"Sheriff?" the admin said, looking beyond Vincent. "It's Sam's wife. She's arrived to view the body and we need to coordinate with the coroner."

Avery stumbled, and he had to tighten his grip to keep her upright as the sheriff took the call. Lips compressed, pale as paste, she kept walking as she looked over her shoulder, attempting to listen to the sheriff speak to the cook's widow. Vincent suspected her anguish was the first authentic emotion he'd seen from Avery since she'd discovered he was a Fed. She'd obviously cared for the cook. It made Vincent suspect she was more *Patty, the waitress* than Coppola mob wife.

He told himself it didn't matter. There was little she could do to convince the task force she wasn't complicit in her ex-husband's sins. She'd stolen syndicate files, for shit's sake. She knew the syndicate was a criminal enterprise, that she'd benefited from its blood money. Who she was now didn't matter, beyond being the FBI task force's weapon, because they were going to use her to bring down her ex-husband.

"If you'll excuse me," the sheriff called out to Vincent. "I need to… I'll be back as soon as I can." He handed the phone back to the admin, looking harried, and then was soon gone, out the office's door. Vincent didn't envy the sheriff's task. Not at all.

Vincent led Avery into holding and then shut her in the room. A uniformed officer locked the door, and then left after giving Vincent the key. She stood where he'd left her, in the white, ten by ten-foot room, her back to the office, to him. Was she scared? She'd be a fool if she wasn't, because it was as if someone was turning a Jack in the Box lever. Only in Avery's case, *Jack* represented a shit load of contract killers with one goal. Kill Avery.

He slipped the key into his pants pocket, and tracked down Benton in the center of the room. About twenty feet from holding, far enough away to speak without her overhearing them, they gathered around an empty desk. He and Benton, staring silently at Avery as she remained standing, ramrod straight, fists at her side.

"Look at her," Vincent said. "That foolish woman would run, given the chance. She knows killers are out there just waiting for their chance to find her alone, unprotected. Why doesn't she know she needs us?"

Benton waved Deming to his side. She'd found the coffee machine and was walking toward them with cup in hand. Benton indicated Avery with a glance. "Shouldn't she be freaking out? She's been in hiding for three years, on the run from a psycho ex-husband who has now found her. What the hell is going on in her head and how do we use it to our advantage? If she doesn't want our protection, we have no leverage to negotiate for the files."

"You don't know she doesn't want our help." Deming shrugged, tucking a blond lock behind her ear. "What you're seeing might just be an over-developed defense mechanism. People deal with stress differently, and you said it yourself. She's been on her own for three years. Taking care of herself is what she's used to."

"She's no wallflower," Vincent said. "I've seen her in action. She's got skills, and it was a ballsy move to steal her ex-husband's files. Stupid, but ballsy."

"So, why'd she do it?" Deming said. "Stupid, but ballsy was probably predicated by necessity."

"Huh?" Modena said.

"She left a pretty cushy lifestyle," Deming said. "She was safe. Think about it. Her family was massacred. Safe matters to her, so why'd she leave? Why'd she do something so ballsy and stupid as run away with stolen files that would assure her dangerous and powerful ex-husband would search to the ends of the earth to find her?" Deming sipped her coffee. "If she took the files to hurt Coppola, she could have released them on the Internet, or sent them to reporters, the law, rival syndicates. She had any number of ways to screw with him. Instead, she's in exile, waitressing in a quiet town. That's not vengeance. It's certainly not justice. So, why?"

"Détente?" Vincent said. *Leverage to keep her safe?*

"Her husband put a hit out on her," Deming said. "How is that détente?"

"She's alive, isn't she?" Benton said, his blue eyes flashing. "Enough guessing. The files are solid evidence." He folded his arms, causing his suit to bunch up around his shoulders. "We need those files."

Vincent exchanged uneasy glances with Deming, then felt a moment of panic. "Where's the kid? The sister."

Deming's eyes widened. "Millie. Shit. She's only ten."

"She hasn't been seen since yesterday," Benton said. "Gilroy is directing local law to canvas the town." He frowned at Vincent. "Avery give you any hints about Millie's whereabouts when you were schmoozing over Chinese?"

Vincent shook his head. "She did a fine job pretending she didn't have a sister."

Deming watched Vincent over her coffee mug, and he could tell she was trying to be subtle. It was something she did. Her profiler thing. He found it annoying as hell.

"Vincent, why aren't you in there talking with her?" Deming said. "You looking for an invitation?"

He grimaced, narrowing his eyes at the profiler, before turning his gaze back toward Avery. "I don't have a handle on her yet, and she's pissed. I don't want to screw this up." Everyone else looked at Avery, too, watching as she sat on the built-in platform that served as holding's chair and bed. All evidence of her earlier anxiety was gone.

"We don't have time for nuance." Benton shook his head, clearly struggling to rein in his impatience. He looked exhausted, and the bruising around his split lip had grown more colorful; dark purple, with green, and yellow on its edges. "I need answers."

"Look at her," Vincent said. "She looks like a coed, but she's as calm as a lifer. Most people collapse under this kind of pressure, but not her. How exactly am I supposed to force her to do anything? Even if I were willing to scare her, I'm not sure I could. She's tough."

"She survived marriage to Coppola. Survived the diner. How is she alive?" Deming said. "I heard that meth head, Jim, put a knife to her throat."

Vincent nodded. "And she didn't just survive Jim, she sliced him to ribbons, and left him with a fractured skull." It seemed impossible to imagine Avery, so delicate and pale, being the one who'd done that, but he'd seen the evidence close up and personal.

"Stop." Benton lifted a hand, dismissing their concerns. "Deming, she's alive because Modena saved her ass." A young man, clipboard in hand, approached and Benton barely hid his impatience as he scrawled something on the form. "Modena, your quick work saved everyone in that diner, and Avery Toner Coppola is alive thanks to you." He handed the clipboard back, and scowled at Vincent. "Be sure to remind her of that when you ask her for the files."

Vincent knew better. Without Avery's well-timed interference, everyone in that diner might have died this morning. Every one of them. "I guess."

"The files," Benton said. "Right now, that's all that matters." He turned to the admin. "We good here?" The young man nodded, hurrying off, leaving Benton to exchange glances with Deming, before smiling at Vincent. "That form I just signed allowed me to use Coppola's men in the vicinity to buy us FBI backup. They'll arrive within an hour." He narrowed his gaze. "I did my part, now it's your turn. Offer Avery Coppola a deal. Anything. Just get us the files and do it quickly. In one hour, we'll have enough personnel to transport her to the safehouse to be processed by Federal Marshals. We'll want her to testify, Modena, but we'll settle for the files."

Deming continued to sip her coffee, frowning at Avery, ignoring the people rushing about. "I'd suggest using her sister, Millie, as leverage, but I'm thinking Avery has her tucked away somewhere safe, or she'd be climbing the walls. They're obviously very close. More mother and daughter, than siblings."

"Gilroy's on Millie Toner. Only so many places to hide a ten-year-old girl," Benton said. "This town isn't that big."

Deming shrugged. "Control Millie and you'll control Avery." Then she glared at Vincent. "Is there a reason you're not in there talking to her yet? Stop second-guessing yourself, or is this you fishing for compliments?" She waved a hand toward holding. "You're amazing at what you do, so go do your magic, Modena, and be quick about it."

Vincent smiled, winking at the profiler. "Not the first time I've heard that."

Deming narrowed her eyes, her lips thinning with irritation. "Don't be stupid. You know what I meant. Charm her. Make her think you're on her side."

"Get the files." Benton nudged Vincent toward holding. "Whatever it takes. Understood?" Vincent nodded as he navigated his way past the officers and admin people. Deming caught up with him, and handed him a file she'd lifted from a nearby desk.

"I had one of the assistants print these photos. They might help. Also, this," she pointed to a thin file inside the thicker one, "is what we have on Avery Coppola. Most of it you've seen before, so you know it's not much."

Vincent nodded, took the file, and reached into his pants pocket and retrieved the holding door's key. Once inside, he waited until the lock clicked behind him, then he moved deeper into the room. The Plexiglas wall muffled the sounds in the office beyond, so it was a bit of a relief to be in there, and it was exciting. For the first time since they'd met, they were having a one on one, as themselves, rather than Patty and some random hiker who'd wandered into her diner. His body grew taut with anticipation as he approached her on the platform.

She lifted her chin, adjusting her seat, crossing her legs. "I have a bus to catch," she said.

He sat next to her, recognizing her anger. So, no more flirty smiles, licking her lips, lingering gazes raking over his body? He'd miss them. He'd enjoyed them. Vincent put the file on the platform between them, and flipped through the pictures inside. "Your bus will have to leave without you."

"Charge me or release me," she said.

"Charge you?" Vincent shook his head. "Avery, you're a hero. I want to give you a medal."

"Let me go," she said. "You can mail it to me and we'll call it even."

"You saved a lot of lives today."

"Yours included, so do a woman a solid and unlock the door," she said. They both knew that wasn't happening.

"Coppola's men are on their way." And they wanted to kill her. She had to know that.

"So, you say. I wouldn't know. I have nothing to do with my ex-husband, or his business associates." Her expression remained unmoved, which impressed Vincent. They both knew how brutally efficient Coppola contract killers were. If they wanted her dead, nothing would stop them from trying to get at her.

"No, you're right. It's *family* business," he said. "Right, *Patty*?" He winked, as he kicked up a cheek, giving her a half smile. "Avery Toner Coppola. Daughter of the last boss, ex-wife of the current boss." She averted her eyes, but otherwise, didn't move a muscle.

He threw down a picture of her family in happier times. A crowd of smiling faces at a well-to-do family reunion celebration. Vincent was disappointed to see no reaction from her beyond a glance at the photo. Did she see herself in the picture? She was in it, just turned seventeen, and her little sister, Millie, who was two at the time, was also in it. Held in her mother's arms, a woman who looked like a slightly different version of Avery; red hair, strong jawline, but her lips were thinner, whereas Avery's lips were more like her father's.

Vincent forced himself to look away from Avery's stalwart expression, and focus on the picture. The sun was shining, setting the scene, and everyone was smiling, happy, and seemed normal. They weren't. They were the Toners, a crime family that ran a syndicate that controlled a large swath of the illegal drug and gun business along the east coast. But that was eight years ago. Things had changed. Dante Coppola had taken over and ran things now.

"If this is about Dante, I told you, I haven't seen him. Three years ago, I divorced him," she said. "I can't help you."

"Yes, you can, and you will."

"No. I can't. So charge me or release me." He threw down the material witness warrant. She flinched, obviously recognizing what it was, or at least, suspected. "Why are you doing this?" she said.

"You're a witness," Vincent said. "The cook, Sam Rutherford is dead. Charlie Humphrey is dead. Murdered, this morning. You were a witness to all that and this piece of paper allows me to keep you here for twenty-four hours." Now *that* got a reaction. She flushed and glanced out the Plexiglas window, seeing all the curious gazes staring back.

Her outrage shifted to resentment. "My tax dollars at work."

Vincent kept his smile in place. "Would that be Patty Whitman's tax dollars or Avery Coppola's tax dollars?"

Her eyes flashed with anger, and then just as quickly he saw her shut it down. The woman looking back at him now was composed, and if anything, mildly amused. "Twenty-four hours will come and go and I'll still have nothing to say. About anything."

"We'll see." The Feds weren't the only people who would benefit from tearing down the syndicate. Why didn't she recognize that she had something to gain? Avery was smart. He had to assume she *knew* the Feds were her one shot at a life after Coppola, so why the resistance? What did she know that the Feds didn't? The potential answers to that question unnerved him. She'd stolen the syndicate files. Maybe they held some truths that weakened the Fed's hand.

"I've been authorized to offer you freedom for the files you stole from your husband. Once they're verified as authentic, you can go. Hell, you might even make your bus on time." Unlikely with Coppola's men on their way, but she had to know that, and he had no doubt Avery knew how to negotiate. This was his opening offer. Vincent was curious to hear her follow up bid. It might give him some indication of where her head was at.

Avery pulled her lower lip into her mouth, biting it, avoiding his gaze. "I've got nothing to say."

He found it difficult to take his eyes off her lower lip, now reddened and damp from her mistreatment. "The bus won't wait for you." Her cheek kicked up, and Vincent saw the humor in her eyes. She seemed intent on dismissing these proceedings as simply an irritation.

"I can buy a new bus ticket," she said.

"Coppola's men are coming. Now." His composure slipped, and his tone hardened. Where was her fear?

"Let them come." Her contempt made him think her behavior was less about surviving and more about thwarting the FBI. They both knew time was running out, and waiting for the next bus was a fantasy. Hell, holding her here for twenty-four hours was a fantasy, too, but if she hadn't figured that out on her own, Vincent wasn't about to tell her. He wished he knew why she wasn't freaking out. What was the missing piece to this puzzle? Incriminating files, baby sister to protect, hiding from an ex, she should be *begging* the Feds for protection.

She stared back at him, giving him…nothing. Vincent supposed being married to a man responsible for hundreds of deaths, millions of dollars-worth of drugs and guns peddled onto the streets, had a way of making a person numb. Was that what he was seeing? Her inability to process the enormity of the danger she was in? He just didn't know, but needed to if he had any hopes of controlling her.

"Why did your ex-husband put a contract out on your life?" he said.

Avery's smile faltered, and her shock pleased him, because it meant she either hadn't known her husband wanted her dead, or was horrified to discover that Vincent knew. Either way, it gave him leverage, he just had to figure out how to use it to make her give up the files.

Chapter 6

"What do you mean, a contract?" Avery purposefully said it as if she'd never heard of the word, widening her eyes and doing her best to project an affable innocence. They didn't know her, though they obviously thought they did, and this conversation was being conducted for one reason only, to help the FBI, not to save her sorry ass, so she knew to do the exact opposite of anything they told her to do. He said "up," she'd say "down."

Vincent didn't seem to believe her ignorance, not that she cared. If Dante's men were on the move, the Feds, the cops, and anyone in their way were screwed, too, and Vincent knew it. "You don't add up, Mrs. Coppola."

"Don't call me that." The name made her skin crawl.

"Well, I can't call you Miss Whitman. *Patty.* Because that's not your name."

"And you're not a backcountry hiker on vacation. You're a Fed." She leaned forward, making a big show of sniffing him. "The smell should have tipped me off."

Vincent threw a glare at the women standing just outside the room, the one wearing the expensive suit. Special Agent Deming. The blond was clearly amused and watching their exchange with great interest, reminding Avery to be on her guard. Vincent was so charismatic he kept making her forget they were in a Plexiglas fish bowl. The Feds were watching.

"We know you've been hiding from your ex-husband for three years, and you took something when you left. Something he's willing to kill you over. Give us those files so we can keep you safe." *So* reasonable, *so* smooth, as if he only had her interests at heart. Well, Avery wasn't so easily moved. She'd lived with Dante for five years, and *he* was a man who understood true coercion. His brutality had kept her with him long after she should have run. "I'm worried about you, Avery."

Her heart skipped a beat. "Were you worried about me when you kissed me?" She turned to look at his fellow agents' and saw reaction . It made her think they were either okay with Vincent playing with his food, or they'd whored him out, desperate for any leg up in a case against her ex.

"You liked it." His smile, and the memory of their kiss made her flush.

"You took it," she said. He'd kissed her when they'd realized they weren't going to die. And yeah, she'd like it. The man was thrilling. His *kiss* had been thrilling.

He leaned forward, resting his elbows on his knees. "*You liked it...a lot.*" A gentleman shouldn't force a woman to admit such things, but she suspected Vincent didn't identify as a gentleman.

Fact was, he'd deceived her from the start, and no, it didn't count that she'd been using an alias, too, and would do her best to continue deceiving him, because she wasn't the Fed in the room. She was the woman who couldn't seem to escape a syndicate life no matter how hard she tried. Why didn't that earn her points? Instead, she kept receiving punishment for her efforts.

"We're the good guys, Avery," he said. "We're the people who can protect you, put a stop to Dante Coppola. All we need is your compliance. Just ask, and we'll help you."

"You just served me a warrant." Avery stood, stepping away from Vincent and the platform, throwing a resentful glare at their audience of Feds. "You can't now say I have a choice." She slapped the door's casement with her palm, daring the Feds outside to ignore her. "Let me out." She locked gazes with the intense one, the guy with the black hair, and blue eyes, the guy who watched her like a hawk. He stood no more than three feet from her, returning her gaze as if they were in a primate house, and she was the gorilla on the wrong side of the glass. "If I have a choice, I choose freedom. Now." She grabbed the door's handle and rattled it, holding the blue-eyed devil's gaze. After a quick, exchanged glance with Vincent, the man walked away, and the blond Fed followed. *Shit.*

Vincent followed her to the door and leaned his palm on it, his face close enough to warm her cheeks with his breath. She saw strain around his eyes, and decided he wasn't feeling as cavalier as he behaved. The FBI had been dogging her family since they'd come into power in the 1950s, and there'd been plenty of snitches along the way. What happened to them acted as a deterrent to others. Avery wanted to be free of that life, but snitching was a death sentence. Vincent had to know the danger they were in, that her ex-husband's people were insane, or worse, intelligent without conscience. If Dante's contract killers were nearby, staying here was a death sentence for them all.

"Let me help you," Vincent said, his words a mere whisper. A lock of her hair had fallen from its bun, and draped next to her eye. He nudged it behind her ear with a tenderness that surprised her. Not that he'd done it, but that she'd allow the intimacy, and that it caused butterflies in her stomach. Her reaction indicated how rattled she was. "You're so fierce, Avery, and...delicate at the same time. I know you're tough, believe me. I've seen you in action, but you're flesh and bone, just like the rest of us. You need help. Let's help each other." He leaned closer, blocking her view of the office and its hustle and bustle. All she saw now was him. All she felt was his heat. Then he lifted his chin and inhaled sharply, as if smelling her, and his eyelids lowered a bit. That simple "tell" clarified much. He hadn't been pretending that he wanted her, *he did*. It was information she could use. "Just nod and I'll be your best friend, bodyguard, whatever it takes," he said. "I'll keep you safe until your bastard of an ex-husband is behind bars."

"Whatever it takes?" she whispered, her eyes focused on his lips. She wondered if he realized he'd just promised more than most did in their wedding vows. There was no mention of love, but she had a feeling Vincent had as much respect for that emotion as she did.

He bent his elbow, making his body press against hers, branding her with his hard length. They were still in a Plexiglas-fronted room, within full view of any that would look, but Vincent didn't seem to care. He was in full seduction mode, daring her to take him on.

His eyes lingered on her mouth. He bit his lower lip. Did that tempt her to want to kiss him? Sure. Would he welcome her kiss? He was giving her every indication that he would, but, *damn*, she wasn't an exhibitionist. What the hell was he doing? Did he believe a set of bedroom eyes would make her produce the files? If so, he was about to receive a hard truth.

The files didn't exist.

"Sweetheart." He tipped her chin up and held her gaze. "It's okay to be afraid." It could have been the intensity of his expression, or maybe his tone, maybe even the endearment, but Vincent's words triggered Avery, and not in a good way. She felt her chin quiver, she trembled, and suddenly she was fighting tears. Yes. She was afraid. But it was not okay. Fear weakened you, and when it came to her ex, weakness got you killed. It was being locked in this damn room that was freaking her out. His mouth tightened as she fought her emotions, then he swore under his breath, and pulled her into his embrace. Embarrassed, Avery hid her face against his chest. "Oh, Avery. What am I going to do with you?" She felt his warm lips against her temple.

"Me? It's you that you should be worrying about. They'll kill you." Her words came out in a whispered rush, muffled by his chest. "And I won't be able to stop it."

He made her look at him, and his expression was hard, unyielding. Whatever he saw in her eyes had him releasing her, and moving to the platform again, sitting. Using his fingertips, he moved through the pictures, until he found the one he sought, and slid it from the pile. "Sit." He indicated the photo with a wave of his hand. "Tell me about this."

A glance at the photo had Avery flinching. The last Toner family reunion. It had been a massacre, and this picture documented the moment that had defined her. Bullet-riddled bodies hung over tables covered with copious, overflowing bowls and platters of spilled food. The dead were everywhere, sprawled on the lawn, huddled together, mothers clutching children. Old, young, able, and ill. So much blood spilled that afternoon, that it covered the patio and bled into the pool, staining it red. The forensic photographer captured Avery's shock as she looked at the carnage, holding two-year-old Millie. Someone had draped a reflective blanket around her shoulders. That was the day Avery's eyes were opened to the real world.

She sat on the platform as memories buffeted her, not wanting to reveal that her legs were about to buckle.

"You lost your family, Avery, but you and your sister survived. That's a miracle. It's going to take another one to survive the men coming for you. You need our help. Give us the files so we can help you."

Bile tickled the back of her throat, and she found it difficult to remain calm. *It's a picture.* Just a picture capturing a moment out of time. That she relived it in her dreams shouldn't matter. *This* was just a picture. Lifeless and flat. It couldn't hurt her.

But Vincent could.

She glared at him. "Am I supposed to thank you for this walk down memory lane?"

Had he expected tears? Maybe rage, resentment? She glanced out of the room, seeking curious eyes, and caught Benton, sitting at a desk, staring at her. Those emotions were all alive and kicking inside her head, compartmentalized, never to be taken out, too dangerous to be unleashed lest they tear her apart. It didn't mean Vincent got to know that, that she was willing to give these Feds even that much. These *strangers* knew nothing of her, and she'd be damned if she changed that and beefed up their files.

"Their murders are still a cold case," he said. "No one claimed responsibility, and what witnesses survive remain silent, but we kept digging. The FBI didn't give up. Do you want to know who killed your family?" Avery wanted him to stop talking. She drew her thumbs across the smooth surface of her rings, hoping to still her mind as she weighed the odds of whether the Feds did know who killed the Toner family. She thought it unlikely. "All you have to do is ask me, and I'll tell you." His gaze became intense, no longer pretending to be sympathetic. He nudged the thick file toward her. "It's all there. Enough to curl your hair."

She didn't need to look. She already knew who'd killed her family, and she didn't care if the Feds knew or not. All that mattered was them releasing her from this room. That had to be her focus.

He pulled a slim file from within the larger one, and then opened it. "It says here, 'She married soon after the deaths of her family, and then nothing else on Avery Toner Coppola and her sister, Millie. They went missing five years after the Toner massacre—'" Vincent paused, studying her face. "That's the official name for what happened to your family. The Toner Massacre." When she didn't respond, he returned to the file. "'—they went missing five years after the Toner massacre, after a contract was put out on Mrs. Coppola.'" He grimaced. "A contract. Your husband put a contract out on you. What were you? Twenty-two at the time?" He lifted his brows, shaking his head. "One slim page with a few grisly photos. Kind of sad, but that's what we've got on you. *This,*" he held up the page and photos, "will continue to be the totality of your life if you don't allow us to protect you."

"Your warrant"—she used her fingernail to flick it away from her—"is bogus and you know it. Did the judge know you were using it to keep me here for an unrelated case? Your superiors okay with that?" Vincent glanced toward the blue-eyed man. Benton. Whatever secret signal was given had Vincent smiling.

Damn. She was going nowhere.

"I think three years ago you discovered your ex-husband was behind the murder of your entire family and you ran with your sister to escape him, taking the files as a safety net." Avery closed her eyes, feeling helpless. "And Dante Coppola didn't like being left, and felt threatened by the evidence you held over his head, so he put a contract on your life." When Avery opened her eyes again, she saw sympathy in Vincent's gaze. "Tell me what happened."

"Dante saved me and my sister when we needed to be saved. Our marriage didn't work out, so we divorced. It happens."

"He was your father's right-hand man." Vincent folded his arms over his chest, slouching back in his seat, studying her. If he wasn't so damn handsome, so sexy, he'd be intimidating. Large, muscular, she'd fought trained men his size. It took a special mixture of superior technique and ruthlessness to win, but it could be done. She hoped it never came to that between her and Vincent. He was an ass, but she liked him, and didn't want to hurt him.

"Dante saved us," she repeated. To admit anything else was to give the Feds something, and something would make them want more.

"Your marrying him was tantamount to a gold seal, and signaled to the syndicate that you believed he was innocent, that he didn't kill your family. Even at seventeen, you had to know that. It was a lie, but you married him anyway."

Was Vincent trying to understand her? If so, he was doing a piss-poor job of it, and she feared if she allowed him to flounder longer, he'd define her in a way that kept her behind bars. It was time to shake things up a bit, but how? Avery ran her hands over her face, trying to think, trying to buy time.

"Avery?"

"Stop. Just stop. It's not simple. None of it is simple." She fidgeted, attempting to find a comfortable position on the hard platform.

"Sounds simple enough," he said. "You married him, and then *you left him*." He said the words as if that was the worst thing she could do, and there was a flicker of something in his gaze... Was that hurt? As soon as she saw it, Vincent shut it down, which told her it was important. He'd been triggered. So... Detective Vincent Modena had been hurt by a woman who'd left him. Watching him closely, she tested her assumption.

"Yes," Avery said. "Sometimes we leave." He couldn't hide his discomfort. It surprised her a bit. Who would leave a guy like this? *A fool.*

"So, what happened?" Vincent said.

Avery would have loved to ask Vincent the same question, but she was nearly positive whatever had happened with his ex still baffled him. He didn't seem the type to do post mortems on relationships. "Like I said. It didn't work out."

"He put a hit out on you, Avery. Why?" When she didn't answer, Vincent pulled out more pictures and placed them in front of her. The first photo was of her ex walking into a restaurant with syndicate contract killers. She knew them all too well. "Coppola's men," he said. "They used to work for your father, and when he died, they stayed on and worked for your ex-husband. They're dead now, but I have a feeling you know that." The way he said it made her blood run cold, like he knew things he shouldn't.

"We had our forensic accountants pull their financials, so we know they were on your ex-husband's payroll."

"Yeah?" Accountants. They were relying on accountants to take Dante down. Ugh. Dante was playing chess, and the FBI was playing checkers.

"We believe these are the men that killed your family. Rumor has it *The Stinger* killed them."

"Rumors. Accountants. Next, you'll be telling me you've got a team of Ouija Board enthusiasts on your payroll. Are you being stupid on purpose?" Her words tripped off her tongue in one long ramble, because she was nervous. He'd taken her by surprise. She was almost positive Vincent was fishing, because *no way* he knew about *The Stinger*. Only two people did.

Vincent lined up six gruesome morgue photographs. "Six men. Killers. Stabbed in the shoulders and back of the knees, severing the ligaments, immobilizing them before the kill shot to the head." He watched her closely as she studied the photos. "Injured like that, those men were defenseless by the time they were shot in the head." Avery looked away from the pictures. "We have a credible source in the syndicate who is convinced these men killed your family. Does seeing them dead give you any kind of closure?"

Avery glared. "Excuse me? You think murder will give me closure?" She picked up the photo of the aftermath of the Toner massacre, and threw it at him. It floated to the floor, devoid of the fury that had propelled it there. "I don't get closure. There's no peace to be had for me. And the person who did this"—she glanced at the morgue photos of the men, taking a moment to control herself— "is a monster. No better than the men he killed." She swallowed hard. "I haven't seen Dante in three years. I have a sister to protect. Don't bring me into this."

"You brought yourself into this when you married him, when you stole incriminating files, and you have the power to end this. *Him*." He pressed his finger over the image of Dante walking into the restaurant with the killers. "Taking them down might not give you closure, but you could move on. You and Millie. That's not on the table while Coppola is out there, trying to kill you. I don't understand why you remain loyal to him, Avery. Help me to understand."

She wasn't loyal to Dante. She hated him. Vincent deserved answers, sure. He was just trying to do his job, to save people, to make the world a better place. She applauded that, but in this *one* instance, he needed to *back off.* Avery slapped her palm over the photograph, and her rings made loud clacking noises on impact.

"Stop acting like you know me," she said. It was making it hard to fight back.

"I can make this go away." His hubris was awe-inspiring and her composure was slipping. "Or I can convince a judge you're the one to hand us Coppola's head on a platter." In other words, the Feds were stirring a bee's nest and forcing her to stick around for the show. "It's not you we're interested in, Avery. It's your ex. We need the files."

The files. That the FBI even knew about them, and *The Stinger*, proved Vincent's assertion that Dante did have a snitch working on the inside. "You think you're being smart, but I'm telling you, you're going to get us killed."

"If you're so afraid of Coppola, why'd you marry him?" He said it like she'd had a choice.

"I told you. Dante offered protection."

"You were using him."

"Yeah. I used him." And he'd allowed it, reveled in it, in fact. The man gave her enough rope to hang herself and she'd jumped with enthusiasm. "He used me, too. *A lot.*"

Vincent flinched. "Give me the files so I can take him down, Avery."

"There are no files. Never were. Dante spread that rumor, because it gave his people the excuse they needed to kill Ralph Toner's little girl. *Me.* His ex-wife. That isn't an order someone can give unless there's something heinous to support it, like betraying the syndicate." That she told him information he hadn't already had was unfortunate, but he'd made it clear she wasn't going anywhere while they believed she had these files. Somehow, she needed to convince him of this truth.

"Your ex made up files to excuse ordering your death?" Vincent glared. "What did you do to piss him off?"

She refused to love him.

When she didn't answer, Vincent nudged the picture of the contract killers walking into the restaurant. "Tell me about *The Stinger.*"

She snorted. "He's like those monster stories people tell children to make them obey. A fairy tale. You obviously have a snitch, but he's fed you bullshit. Sure, these stories swirl around the syndicate, but that doesn't make them true. *The Stinger* doesn't exist. Never existed."

"Like the files that don't exist." Vincent's irritation spilled over. "This guy that doesn't exist killed these men." Avery glanced at the photo and felt and thought many things, none of which she was willing to share. "*The Stinger* disappeared after they turned up dead. In my circles, "disappeared" is code for dead. Coppola cleaning up?"

She shook her head, disgusted. "You know nothing, but jump in with both feet anyway, with what evidence? Some fairy tale." Desperate to make him understand, Avery took his hand, squeezing it. "I am not your solution."

Vincent squeezed her hand, too, and then ran his thumbs over her rings as she'd done herself more times than she could count. It disconcerted her, felt threatening. She pulled her hand from his grasp, saw his curiosity, saw that he knew he was missing something.

It made Avery feel trapped, cornered. She bolted for the door, found it locked. Still locked. *Of course,* it was locked! *She couldn't breathe.* Avery attacked the Plexiglas, unleashing all the frustration and fear she'd bottled up since the bell chimed over the diner's door and death walked in. She pummeled it, finding relief in the violence, and then kicked it hard enough to split the wooden casement near the locking device. Her foot went numb. Her battered hands pulsed with renewed pain, and *still* she was on the wrong side of the door.

Vincent grabbed her from behind. Avery head-butted him, knocking him onto his ass. Disoriented, his eyes watering, Vincent sat up and pinched his nose to stem the bleeding. Avery fell on him, and used her attack to hide her lifting the key from his pocket, and slipping it into hers. Outside the room, the cops and Feds rushed the door, distracting her. Vincent took advantage and muscled her onto her back, using his weight to restrain her, tucking his head, prepared for a fight. Avery happily obliged.

It took her thirty seconds of maneuvering to work off some steam while the cops got their act together and opened the door. Vincent was highly trained, so he countered her every move, and when she ran out of breath, and he had her good and pinned, she gave up, content to lose the battle when she knew she'd won the war.

She had his key.

All eyes were on them, staring from the other side of the open door. Vincent lifted his head, glaring at them. "No," he said. "Back off. I got this." When his weight shifted, she bucked her hips, dislodging his weight enough to turn on her side and get a breath in. She'd been moments from passing out. Vincent tensed, and she realized he thought the fight was still on, so he muscled her, attempting to pin her again. The officers surged forward, triggering Avery. She shrimped her hips to the side, grabbed Vincent's wrist, swung her legs over his chest, and within seconds, had him positioned for an arm bar. He slammed his palm on her leg, tapping her off, and jumped to his feet. Arms spread wide, he stopping the officers mid-surge toward her, allowing Avery to scurry away.

Crouched in the corner, teeth bared, she sucked in gasps of air, waiting to see what they'd do. Vincent kept them back, blood dripping from his nose. He smiled.

"You play for keeps," he said, waving the officers out of the room, keeping his eyes on Avery.

"You're a bunch of idiots." When the door was closed again, she sat back on the platform, resting her forearms on her knees, doing her best not to pass out.

His smile widened, and he was all charm, bloody nose and all. "Lady, where have you been all my life?"

She straightened her back, furious. "This isn't funny! Get on the wire. Tell everyone I've escaped and put a BOLO out on me."

"Why would I do that?" He shifted his weight, and sniffed, blinking past his watering eyes.

"They'll be monitoring the police frequencies. Stop Dante's men from showing up here. Buy time for backup to arrive." She saw the flicker in his gaze, and read it to mean he *didn't want* to buy time. He wanted to keep the pressure on, to force her to give up the files. "But you're not going to do that, are you?"

"Because I'm an idiot," he said, proving he was the only person on the planet that could make a broken nose look *that* sexy. The man was having too much fun.

"You're doing it again," she said.

"Doing what?"

"Putting your gun on the floor, hoping the shooter won't kill you. Eric. Remember him? Remember how well that ended? Remember who had to save your ass? This time, you're playing chicken with Dante. You won't win that game with him."

"Like I said before, that was bait and switch." He slapped his tattoo on his forearm. "Sniper, remember? I never intended to put my gun on the floor." He folded his arms across his chest, still wearing that flirty smile. "So. About those files."

In her mind's eye, Avery saw a prison cell closing on her forever. The FBI were digging. They would discover Avery trained with Dante's dead contract killers, all six of them, and that Dante was the one that named her *The Stinger*. They would discover the rings on her fingers belonged to those six killers, were proof of their deaths, a reminder of what had been done to her family, and that justice had been served. *Could* she burn the whole Coppola Syndicate down? Sure, but not without implicating herself. Vincent and his team had enough of the threads to unravel the whole skein. She had to make sure she was nowhere to be found when they did.

Not an easy task. She didn't know what to do, so she curled into a ball and leaned against the wall. Ten minutes later, still silent, unwilling to speak no matter the provocation, Vincent stood to leave, and she had a moment of panic. He'd need his key to get out, but luckily, the officers hadn't locked the door after her outburst. He exited, and allowed a passing officer to lock it after him.

So, she prayed, knowing she'd lost that right three years ago, but she did it anyway, because she was desperate. She prayed for that miracle Vincent mentioned earlier. Avery didn't know what else to do, and nothing short of divine intervention would save them, because Dante's men were coming. Death was coming, and she was afraid.

Chapter 7

"She's holding back," Deming said.

"You think?" Vincent rolled his eyes. Every time he thought he was getting through to Avery, she pulled back and shut down. "But she's right about one thing. We can't stay here anymore."

Benton grimaced. "The sheriff's men radioed in while you were chatting with Mrs. Coppola. Three black sedans with New Jersey license plates, filled with known Coppola associates, were spotted parked three blocks down the street. Luckily, ETA on our backup is better than we'd hoped. They should be here soon."

"Modena," Deming said, "did Mrs. Coppola give you anything new?"

"She doesn't like to be called that," Vincent said. Deming's blue eyes narrowed. "That's new," he said. "Hey, she's divorced. How would you feel—" He stopped talking when Deming showed him her palm.

"Don't get me mixed up with whatever is going on in your head," she said. "You're giving every sign that you're too close to the subject. You two kissed?"

Vincent smiled. "What can I say? Women like to kiss me."

"Let's stay focused," Benton said, catching Deming's attention. "Tell Gilroy that when our guys arrive we'll come downstairs, and get her out of here. The safehouse is preparing for our arrival, and the Federal Marshalls said they'll meet us there."

When Deming hustled to the exit, pulling her phone from her back pocket, Benton turned toward holding, staring at Avery through the Plexiglas. "She's the only thing stopping brass from shelving this operation. A year, Modena. I took a year of my life to bring Coppola down, and she's all I have to show for it." He caught Vincent's gaze, and held it with an intensity that made him worry. Deming claimed *Vincent* was the one too invested? Benton's eyes seemed dead, and hopeless. "She has to flip on her ex, or we're dead in the water."

"I know," Vincent said. "We'll get it done. It's soon yet. Give me time." Like Benton had said. They'd been on this a year. If they didn't get Coppola now, they'd get him some other way.

Benton nodded toward holding. "Get her ready to leave." Benton's phone rang, and when he saw who was calling, he held up a finger, silently indicating Vincent should wait. "Yeah?" He inhaled sharply, and then released it in a burst. "Don't interact, but keep close. Follow them in and keep me informed." Benton disconnected the line, and then pocketed his phone. "Two of the sheriff's men are watching Coppola's people, and they say they're on the move. I've ordered the officers to hang back. They're not trained to deal with this level of shit storm, and I refuse to lose lives today. You get all nonessential personnel out of the building, Modena. Go. I've got to consult with the sheriff."

Benton took off, and just as Vincent was about to follow orders, he took a moment to glance at Avery. She was leaning against her prison wall, staring back at him. Her glare held fear and accusation, and it occurred to him that she must feel vulnerable there, caged, waiting for contract killers whose sole objective was her death.

His instinct was to bring her with him as he followed orders, but Benton was in charge, and he'd never authorize that, so Vincent left her there… feeling as if he'd left a limb behind.

Chapter 8

It seemed like forever until the first gunshot had Avery on her feet, searching the holding cell for cover. It was a fruitless search, because there was no cover. She was a sitting duck. The cops in the outer office scattered, and Vincent was nowhere in sight, hadn't been for some time. She'd waited as long as she could, but if she didn't escape now, she might never get another chance.

She slipped her hand into her pocket and felt the key. A second, third, and fourth gunshot discharged in the distance, sounding progressively closer.

Three damn years. Why couldn't Dante move on?

Now the gunshots were constant. *Pop, pop, pop-pop-pop.* She licked sweat off her upper lip as she scanned the area. Some had taken cover in the sheriff's office in the back, so they were out of her line of sight when she opened the door and then low crawled out of holding. Hiding behind shelves that separated her from the entryway, she took a moment to gather her courage. The gunshots sounded as if they were closer, though more spaced apart. Was that a rifle? *Sniper?* She wouldn't be surprised to discover she was hearing Vincent's handiwork, and could imagine him lying on a roof, playing hero. Longer intervals of silence between gunshots passed as she continued to low crawl toward the main door, her one known avenue of escape. It made her wonder if the cops and Coppola's men had reached an impasse, or if attrition was giving one side the edge. Quite selfishly, she rooted for the cops.

She peeked under the shelves to her right, looking toward the door. Three pairs of dress shoes. Feds or Dante's men? The pant cuffs broke perfectly, and the suit was a familiar New Jersey brand, but that wasn't definitive enough to make an ID. Poking her head up a bit, she peeked between the shelves and saw men bottlenecking the room's entryway. They wore familiar pinkie rings. Damn. Unsurprisingly, Dante's men had cleaved through the cops outside like a hot knife to butter, though they did it faster than she'd expected.

A rifle's discharge came from the sheriff's office, and had Avery faceplanting on the cool tile. The bullet splintered a piece of the entryway's casement, and had Dante's men fall back. Someone in the sheriff's office was feeling frisky, she thought, and kudos to them. Even so, it told Avery she needed to find an alternate exit. Dante's men were probably moments from tossing a concussion canister into the room, and she didn't want to be here when it happened.

"I've got two counties sending reinforcements! Leave while you can!" The sheriff sounded confident enough, but Avery knew those police stations were five miles out. Full throttle, sirens blaring, would they be here in time to help? Avery didn't think so.

One of Dante's men, shotgun in hand, dropped to the floor and low crawled toward her. He hugged the shelving on his left, coming right for her. Flat on the floor, afraid to poke her head up, Avery felt around on the shelf above her, desperate to find a weapon. The man had eyes on the Sheriff's office, so hadn't seen her yet, though she couldn't count on that lasting long. She felt a paperweight, grabbed it, and lobbed it at the man's head. He slumped on contact, out cold.

Avery low crawled to his side and nabbed his shotgun. Firing it would announce her location, so it was a last resort option, but she certainly wasn't going to leave it behind. Instead, she crawled to the door closest to her, which was open already; a file room, with a small window high on the wall. Increased gunshots outside, and more in the halls, had her twitchy.

"Give us the woman," said an unfamiliar voice. Avery flipped him the bird, and wished he could see her.

Protected by the file room's wall, she stood, hoping this was where she'd find her escape route. Dante's men were evil, and they had one goal: whatever Dante last told them to do. Today, that was *kill Avery*. A "good" person would stick around and fight that evil, but Avery didn't have the luxury to cater to her conscience. Millie was out there, alone, waiting for her. Avery needed to live, so Millie could live.

Eyes on the small window across the room, she climbed the filing cabinet below it. As quietly as she could, shotgun in hand, she crouched on the cabinet, and opened the window. Peering outside, she contemplated the two-story drop with dismay. If she survived the fall without breaking an ankle, she'd have a barrage of bullets to dodge.

Avery sighed, glancing around the room. She needed a rope.

"Two minutes before you hear sirens," the Sheriff shouted, "and then the town will have more law enforcement than citizens. Go, now." If he was hoping to scare them away, he was wasting his breath. Avery had trained with men like this. Only the kill would stop them.

She hopped off the cabinet, and started lifting things, opening drawers, searching for anything that would ease her fall. She ripped an extension cord off the wall, and decided it would have to do, then climbed back up the cabinet, tied an end around a handle, and threw the other one out the window.

As predicted by the sheriff, sirens grew in volume and number as neighboring county's cruisers neared the building. The cavalry had arrived, and none too soon. From the looks of it, so had a phalange of FBI Special Agents. Avery could tell the difference, because the Feds were in huge black SUVs with tinted windows and sirens on their roofs. Did their arrival cut down on her odds of escape? Probably not. They were dismal even before, so she was no worse off.

Feet first, she squeezed the extension cord between her boots' treads, and used the friction to slow her descent, while hugging the cord to keep herself upright, but not suffer burns. It was a controlled fall until the cord length ended, and then she just fell, hit the ground, tucked, rolled, and then slapped out just like she'd been trained to do, never once losing the grip on her shotgun.

She hit hard, but didn't crack her head, or break her wrists, so called it a win. Laying there, staring at the drop she'd just navigated, she told herself to move. *Move, Avery.* The sirens goosed her into rolling onto her belly and scanning the street. She saw Special Agent Benton, and then Deming, guns drawn and shooting, taking cover around the corner of the building. Gilroy was running up the building's stairs, arm extended as he repeatedly shot at a man hiding behind a pillar.

Where was Vincent? She glanced at roof lines, but didn't see any rifle barrels.

More shots fired had Avery crouched, shotgun in hand, running from the building, the Feds, and the sound of guns. A block down, she stumbled upon an idling black sedan, with a getaway driver smoking a cigarette, leaning on the hood, watching the chaos. She huddled behind a tree, careful to stay out of sight. Gripping the barrel of the shotgun, she swung at the man's head like she was at home base and the ball had been pitched to her sweet spot. Avery hit a home run, and down he went.

His car was gorgeous, and idling. An Audi Sportster with a veritable arsenal in the back seat. Avery tossed the shotgun in through the open back window, and grabbed a Gerber knife from the pile, sheath and everything, tucking it into her boot. Her eye spied a Glock. She grabbed it, too, chambering a bullet, checking that the clip was full. Then she tucked it into her waistband before sliding behind the wheel. Gunshots grew closer; much closer than she'd have liked.

Vincent's face popped into her mind's eye, and she worried.

She told herself he wasn't her responsibility, and yet now that she had her chance to escape, she felt weighed down with a need to make sure he was safe. *Stupid man.* She'd warned him. But no.

Avery peeled out, hunching low in the seat, hoping to hide that it was she who was driving, and to lessen the odds of a stray bullet to the head. Things were out of hand. People were running toward the building, pointing, shouting. It made her want to stop and tell them to run away.

A black-suited contract killer jumped in front of the car, and everything happened at once. She felt the impact, automatically slammed on the brakes, and the air bags hit her like a ton of bricks. Emptying her lungs. She pulled her knife and deflated the bag in time to see the man's body slide down the hood. Bullets hit her door, forcing her to duck as she tried to regain her breath. Rounds peppered her fender, and she feared they'd shoot out her tires, so from a slouched position, she lifted her foot off the brake, not knowing what else to do. Coasting, not wanting to step on the gas without a visual, she took a chance and peeked out the window.

That's when she saw Vincent, off to her left. Both arms straight, firing his Glock, he aimed at something beyond her car, as he ran down the federal building's stairs at a fast clip. He didn't get past the sidewalk out front, before he clutched his side, spun in the air, and fell amidst shots peppering the area around him.

Avery was out of the car, laying down cover fire in the space of a heartbeat, emptying her clip behind her as she ran toward Vincent. *He's dying. He's dying. Was he dying?* She didn't know. Please, please, not one more death because of her. When she reached his side, she grabbed his shoulder, afraid she wasn't strong enough to drag him to the car, shoot the gun, and not die.

Then he grabbed her hand, hopped to his feet, and dragged *her* to the Audi, both shooting at Dante's men who all seemed to converge on them from all angles.

"Go, go, go!" He reached the car first, saw the guns in the back, and grabbed a rifle from the pile. He cocked it, and shot three rounds at the corner of three buildings. One of Dante's men fell from the rooftop, dead when he hit the ground. Then the second, and third shooter fell from neighboring buildings. Three shots. Three kills.

Avery never stopped shooting as she reached behind her for the Audi's door handle, as Feds spilled from their black SUVs, laying down cover fire. Then someone grabbed her leg, aimed his gun at her from the ground. Avery aimed back, squeezed the trigger, but her Glock was empty. Panic flushed her system as she saw a familiar face smiling up at her.

Joseph "Fingers" Pinnella. His normally slicked back hair was now in his face, and his brown eyes were bloodshot. He lay on his side, his revolver aimed at her belly. Oh, how she hated his smile, and his tobacco-stained teeth. She'd hit him with the car, and his leg was busted, bone on display. Somehow, the bastard had found the energy to crawl to the side of the Audi. *Please, powers that be, please don't let it be "Fingers" who ends me. He's such an asshole.*

"Never thought I'd see you again," he said, then pulled his revolver's trigger. The firing pin hit an empty chamber. His gun was empty, too. Avery stomped "Fingers" in the face. Twice.

"Get in the car!" Vincent was still shooting his rifle, scanning the building, laying down cover. Avery jumped in as Vincent got in the back with the guns. She saw Benton waving from behind a parked car, catching their attention.

"Get out of here!" Benton said.

Avery stepped on the gas as Vincent climbed into the passenger side seat, his rifle discarded, replaced with a Glock. Vincent was a big guy, so the move wasn't graceful, he knocked her around a bit, caused her to hit a few parked cars, but reinforcements were here, speeding by in the form of big, black, siren-blaring, flashing SUVs, so her errors went unnoticed. Three blocks down, she pulled over, out of breath and nauseous.

Vincent clutched his side, and blood oozed from between his fingers.

"You're hurt. Get out." She leaned over him and opened the door, shoving him. "The cops will help you." He needed a hospital. Vincent grabbed the door and slammed it shut again.

"Just drive." He pulled his shirt up, wincing as he assessed his injury. Even she could see it was just a graze, but an inch or two more, and the bullet would have blown through his liver. "I'll live."

He'll live. They'll live, for now.

She drove. Then she started to shake, and then ugly sobs escaped her lips and she was blinded by tears. Furious that she couldn't control herself, she started slapping him with her right hand, eyes on the road, other hand on the wheel, all the while shouting every expletive she knew.

Vincent didn't parry her slaps, but instead tugged on the wheel until they were on the road's shoulder, and then slammed his foot on the brake. Shifting into park, he pulled her onto his lap, holding her so tightly she couldn't move, and it hurt her neck. She tilted her chin up, to ease the pressure, and found she'd wedged her face into the hollow of his shoulder, just above his T-shirt's collar. His skin was hot, and wet with her tears. Soon her thrashing died a sad little death and she went limp in his arms.

"It's okay, baby. We're okay, baby. Avery, honey, shh." He kissed her temple, rocking her in his arms. Soon, her sobs quieted, and her brain worked enough to know she should be embarrassed, yet, still she sobbed, swallowing hard, struggling with emotions she couldn't suppress. "I, I, I was…"

"Afraid. I know. It was scary. You should have stayed with the sheriff. I came for you, and you weren't there. How did you get out and past the shooters?"

"It doesn't matter." She clutched him close, knowing she shouldn't. She had things to do, and catering to her weakness wasn't one of them. Millie was out there, waiting for her, and if she needed a reminder of how determined Dante was to destroy her, it was just delivered with the efficacy of a slap to the face. Anyone close to her was in danger. She had to get rid of Vincent, and then find Millie. First, she had to stop holding him. She had to give up his tiny kisses and murmurs of comfort.

Avery pushed off his chest and sat behind the wheel again, wiping her cheeks.

Vincent opened the glove compartment, and rooted around until he found a first aid kit. "Drive," he said. "Take the first left after that bend in the road. I have a nearby cabin we can hideaway in while things cool down. No one knows it exists but me and the town assessor's office. We should be safe enough there." He pressed a large square bandage over his wound, periodically glancing over his shoulder toward the sheriff's office. The gunshots were escalating now that more law enforcement had arrived. "Now, Avery."

She reached into the back seat, retrieved a new, full magazine, and exchanged it for her Glock's empty one. Then she pressed the gun's muzzle to Vincent's temple. He went still, lifted his hands, palms front.

"Get out of the car," she said. He might not know what was good for him, but Avery did. *Far from her.*

Vincent's eyes narrowed. "If you wanted me dead, you would have left me back there."

"True." Not wanting him dead was why he had to leave. She lowered the muzzle to his knee, pressing hard enough to make him flinch. "But I need you gone." And she needed to escape. "So maybe I wound you instead."

"You need me." He wasn't backing down.

She admired that about him. She admired a whole hellava lot about him. That didn't change anything. "Nothing personal." She arched a brow. "Go." She tilted her head toward his door, sniffing. Her tears were still dampening her cheeks, but her hand didn't shake. Her goal was clear.

"You don't want to do this, Avery."

Like he knew what she wanted. All his talk of "files," his assumptions, his surety, the man acted like he knew her. He didn't know her at all. Nor could he know what she was capable of, though one look in the mirror should have told him. His poor broken nose was swelling, and the bruises were migrating to under his eyes. Funny how it didn't detract even an iota from his beauty.

In another world, she'd want Vincent to know her. Want to know him. His constant courage under fire mixed with his heroic agenda was a powerful thing, a pleasure to witness, and it wasn't a huge leap to assume the guy was amazing in bed. One kiss and she was a believer, but it wasn't to be. She ground the muzzle of the Glock into his knee. He grimaced, but otherwise didn't move.

"You need me," he said.

"I don't *need* anyone." She loved Millie. Hell, she'd die to defend her, but that wasn't need. To need was to be vulnerable. "Get out, Vincent." She steeled herself to pull the trigger. It would be for his own good.

He must have seen her intent, because he tensed, squinted, as if preparing for the pain. "I can help you," he said. "Let me keep you alive."

She gouged the Glock harder against his knee, forcing herself not to care that it caused his teeth to clench against pain. "I'm trying to keep *you* alive. Stop making me hurt you! *Get out!*" She shoved him with her other hand, but he wouldn't budge. He kept his hands in the air. "Why are you being so stubborn?"

He flinched as another round of gunfire was exchanged behind them. "It's my job."

"I hope your medical insurance is good, because you're gonna need a new knee."

He narrowed his eyes. "You can't run forever, Avery."

"I don't need forever." She told her finger to pull the trigger. "Open your door, so when I shoot you, you'll fall out. Put your hand up to protect your head. I don't want you breaking your neck. Can you do that for me?"

Still, he refused to move. "Dammit, Vincent!" Aiming the Glock at his center mass, she leaned back, using her door for leverage, and then kicked at him, but still he didn't budge. "Get out!"

He caught her ankles, ignoring her gun, and pulled her over the center console, forcing her legs to straddle his waist. Then he lunged forward, draping himself on top of her, sandwiching her body with the seat. Then he grabbed her wrist, forcing the gun to aim at the car's ceiling. Face to face, her knees bent, spirit broke, Avery knew she wouldn't shoot him, and from the look on his face, she suspected he knew it, too. After a moment where neither of them moved, he sighed, released her wrist, and then rested both elbows on either side of her head, contemplated her. Then he lowered his lips to hers, nuzzling them.

"You can trust me," he whispered. "Let me help you." His weight pinning her, and her lost control, should have freaked her out, but instead, she felt safe…and aroused.

"You say *help,* but you mean *use.*" She was no person's dupe.

"Dante Coppola needs to be stopped, Avery. His victims deserve justice. You deserve justice for what he did to you and your family." He dropped a light kiss on her lips. "I mean to deliver it with your help or not." His earnestness was a spike to her heart. His head turned, and she saw him glance out the window. He ducked low, his body tensing. "Two more black Audi's coming our way."

Dante's men. If they drove close enough, they might see their car wasn't empty.

Avery wrapped her calves around Vincent's, and pulled his chest flush to hers, then she clamped her arms around his neck to keep his head down. He complied with no resistance. She pressed her lips to his ear. "Please stay down. Stay quiet. Please, please." If he played hero, they'd both be dead quick.

His heat touched her everywhere, and she could feel his erection pressing between her thighs. So, he felt it to, she thought. He wanted her, as she wanted him. Vincent's hand slid down to her hip, sending shocking tingles through her. Then his fingers bit into her thigh, steadying her, locking their hips, before he took her Glock.

"Loosen your arms from around my neck," he said. "I need to see if they've driven past, or are stopping to investigate."

Reluctantly, she loosened her grip. He peered out the window, only to duck his head quickly, then his lips were near her temple. "They're driving by. Almost on top of us."

She couldn't stop herself from squirming beneath him, because his arousal was pressing on her sweet spot, making her breathless. "They have to wonder why this car is unattended."

He peeked out the window again, surging his hips forward, grinding against her. She gasped, squeezing her eyes closed as a jolt of desire had her trembling. When he ducked his head down again, he rested his elbows on both sides of her head, nudging the tip of her nose with his chin. "Hey. Open your eyes. They've driven past, and the shooting has stopped." Her eyes opened, and saw his lazy grin. "You're afraid," he whispered, "but are you afraid of me?"

Terrified. She cupped the back of his head and pulled him to her kiss, threading her fingers through his hair, welcoming his tongue, marveling at his ability to make her lose her mind as he licked and sucked, showing her what a man could do with a tongue when prompted. She moaned into his mouth as his hips slowly moved on her, jean against jean. Her hips rose to meet his, arching upward, creating a glorious friction that had her shuddering with want. The day's stress, her fear, all the scary emotions that stood between them dissolved with this kiss.

Life. They had it. Maybe not for long, but they had it now, and she wanted to kiss him.

Still resting his weight on one elbow, he tucked the Glock in the back of his waistband and then proved his one hand was more effective than most men's two. It was everywhere, under her shirt, cupping her breast, and his kisses were heady, enlightening. She'd never experienced the like. Certainly, not with Dante.

When she slipped her hands under his T-shirt, raking her fingertips across his muscular back and then down his side, she felt his bandage, it sobered her instantly. She broke the kiss.

"You have to let me go, Vincent." He shook his head, bumping their noses. He winced, and sniffed. Though it had stopped bleeding long ago, it was definitely broken. "Find a doctor. Get patched up."

"Stop trying to get rid of me." He dropped his forehead to hers. "You're in over your head. Admit it." She was having a hard-enough time admitting she liked his weight on her, but she did, so hugged him tightly while she could, because she couldn't keep him. Vincent could die just like anyone else, and people died around Avery all too often, so she needed to bail on him as soon as she could. For his own good. "You deserve more than the life you're settling for, sweetheart." He nipped at her lower lip. "Let's clean house and give you a chance to live in peace. Don't you want the killing to stop?"

She went limp beneath him, out of energy and out of fucks to give. *"Of course, I do."*

"Then we want the same thing." He gave her an encouraging smile. "It's as simple as that."

"Simple, huh?" She shook her head. It was anything but simple.

"You have information we need," he said.

If given a gun, she'd have gladly shot him.

Two steps forward and one step back. Vincent didn't believe her when she said the files didn't exist. Considering he was still sporting a raging hard-on, and she was wet and swollen for him, the moment was beyond awkward.

"You're too good-looking," she said. It was affecting her judgment. "I should have shot you when I had the chance." She told herself to stop worrying. At the rate he was going, he'd be dead before he discovered her secrets. She pushed out from beneath him and sat behind the wheel, scanning the road before them, and then in the rearview mirror. The other black Audi's were nowhere in sight, but she couldn't count on that continuing. "I'm his *ex*-wife. I know nothing. The files were a fabricated rumor, and I have no information that can help you or the Feds. So, go away."

"Okay, let's say all that is true." He adjusted his pants to sit more comfortably, if that was possible with what he was sporting. "So why is Coppola trying to kill you? You know something, and it scares the hell out of him. Help us. Help *me*, Avery." She was convinced he was insane. "Say yes."

No. But she did need someplace to hide out and formulate a plan, and just before she'd threatened to kneecap him, he'd mentioned a cabin. It would have to do. "Yes."

Vincent laughed, as if he'd won something, and then leaned toward her, kissing her again. Lots of heat, and no less wonderful for its brevity. "We're making a commitment here. You and me."

His excitement was catchy, even knowing it was based on a lie. She'd use him to escape Dante, but that was it. The first opportunity she got to run, she'd run to Millie. "Sometimes, Vincent, a kiss is just a kiss."

He didn't seem convinced. "You need me. You don't want to admit it, but you do."

She visualized cracking him upside the head, and then dumping him out of the car. Instead, she shifted gears and hit the gas. "Where is this cabin?" They'd already stayed in one place too long. If Dante's men didn't find them, the Feds would.

Vincent pointed. "Take that road."

She drove, and forced herself not to think beyond escaping Dante's men. Too much had happened in too little time, and she felt fried. Her one consolation was Millie wasn't here. She was on her way to safety. Grinding her rings against the steering wheel, it was hard to ignore that she'd lost focus. She liked Vincent, liked kissing him. Had, in fact, risked her life more than once to save him. A Fed. *Shit.* If she died saving Vincent, who would save Millie?

Avery needed to be smarter. She needed to bail on Vincent.

Chapter 9

Vincent's phone rang as he was checking their six, making sure no one was following them out of town. "Benton, it's about time you called me back. Is everyone else safe? No one is answering their phones."

"We're fine. Well, Gilroy got hit on the arm. A graze. He's mad as hell on an ambulance heading to the nearest hospital, wherever that is. Deming? Do you know where they took Gilroy?"

Vincent frowned, thinking of all the other personnel that had been left in the building. "Anyone else hurt? I got as many out as I could, but then the shooting started, and I thought I was of better use on the roof, using a scope."

"We got one dead, an assistant deputy, shot through drywall. Crap luck. A few other minor injuries. Where are you?"

"On the Kangamangus highway. Want to meet up?" Vincent glanced at Avery, and didn't like the look of rebellion on her face. He suspected she was planning a coup.

"It's not safe. Hole up somewhere," Benton said.

"That was my thought."

"At least for a few hours and I'll call you when I'm ready for you. Coppola's men have scattered, or are either dead, or in critical condition, heading to the hospital under guard, but I have one guy alive. Says his name is Pinnella."

"We saw two more of Coppola's cars drive into town as we were driving out." Vincent felt no guilt about omitting that he'd been kissing Avery as he'd witnessed their arrival, nor did he regret the kissing. The woman revved his engines like no one had ever done before, and he wanted to kiss her again, preferably under more auspicious circumstances.

"Our agents are giving chase," Benton said. "We'll get them all, but until we do, we have Pinnella. I'll call with an update after we interrogate him. You, make use of this time to make her give up the files, Modena. Make all this worth it." Benton hung up.

Tall order. Vincent stared at the phone, frustrated, because he knew there was little in life that made senseless violence worth it. A man died today at the hands of a brutal killer, because another man wanted Avery dead. There was no making that balance out. He pointed ahead. "Take this turn."

He led Avery down roads simply to prevent being followed. Backtracking, turning left when they should turn right, it took longer to arrive than necessary. His late grandparents' cabin was his "bug out" hiding place, deep in the woods, not even on the Feds' radar. He wanted to keep it that way. He'd almost told his ex-wife about it, but she was a city girl, so it never came up. It felt weird bringing anyone here, but Coppola's men were looking for her, and once word got out, every reporter looking for a scoop.

When the pavement turned into dirt road, and he knew the cabin was up ahead, Vincent felt his body release tension. Maybe it was the woods, its solitude, whatever, he needed this place now, and a glanced told him Avery felt it, too. Going into hiding with a hot, sexy, kickass woman wasn't all that shabby, either. Just thinking about the mischief they could get into had his smile widening, pulling on his nose. He winced, sniffed ineffectually, and had to blink through the pain.

"You broke my nose," he said.

"Yup."

He arched a brow, glancing at her. Eyes fixed on the road, she seemed without regrets. He wondered how much of her attitude was bluster, because she was pale and seemed exhausted. It made him glad they were heading to the cabin. It wasn't the Ritz, but it had an outhouse in the back and a water pump in the front. Plenty comfortable for their needs.

"A half mile more," he said, "there'll be an unmarked private drive on the left. I'll point it out when we're closer." Soon, he was pointing. "There," he said. "Take this turn."

Pine, maple, and beech trees lined the private dirt drive, and dense, overgrown wild grass slashed at the Audi's paint job as she barely slowed the car, despite the uneven surface. They arrived within minutes, and then Avery parked in front of the one room, cedar shake cabin. When she turned the engine off, she rested her forehead on the steering wheel, eyes shut, the image of dejection. Vincent felt bad for her, and didn't know what to say. He couldn't pretend everything would be okay, because he honestly didn't know if it would. She'd agreed to help. That was something, but a lot about their circumstances depended on things beyond their control; Coppola's reaction to his men's failure to kill Avery today, the status of their RICO case, and any backlash over what happened at the sheriff's office. These were variables neither he nor Avery could control, but they were effected by them. They'd just have to wait and see how things shook out.

Avery lifted her head, blinked a few times, and then was out of the car, looking around. He got out, too, and joined her. She didn't seem all that impressed with his grandparents' cabin, and soon shifted her attention to the back seat's cache of weapons. By the time she was done arming up, both her boots, her belt, and her waist had knife sheaths in place. She'd done it quickly, and efficiently, making him suspect he'd just witnessed her ritual. Which begged the question, why was a pampered mob wife turned waitress so versed in knives?

Nothing in her file suggested Avery was trained, but he was convinced it was true. He'd fought her on the ground. He'd seen her skills at the diner, and then later, at the federal building, she'd handled a gun like a pro. No, not a pro, because a professional killer—a murderer—wouldn't have hesitated to shoot him in the car when she'd wanted him gone. So, she was trained, but for defense. He supposed it made sense. Though daughters and ex-wives of syndicate bosses didn't usually need to see to their own defense, Avery's family had been massacred. That meant she wasn't like the rest.

He found it interesting that she preferred knives. They were messy, up close bloody. Vincent was a gun man, and this back seat treasure trove was like Christmas. He rubbed his hands together, wondering what goodies he'd find. "Will you look at this baby?" he said, picking up a small Smith & Wesson revolver from the pile. It even had a strappy ankle sheath. Vincent checked its cylinder, saw it was loaded, then strapped the sheath on his calf, just above his hiking boot. The revolver slipped inside snugly. Next, he chose a *gorgeous*, mouthwatering Ruger semiautomatic handgun. He checked the magazine, the chamber, and then donned its accompanying shoulder holster, before holstering it. His Glock was back at the bank, on the sidewalk, probably logged into evidence by now, so these babies were a welcome sight. He pulled another Ruger from the pile, checked the chamber, the magazine, and then held it out to Avery. "You might like to try this one." He felt like a teenage boy, sharing his Magic Cards.

Avery dismissed the Ruger with a roll of her eyes, and patted the 9mm Glock already tucked in her waistband. "I like my guns to shoot." Vincent tucked it into his waistband. Then she indicated the rest of the stash with a tilt of her head. "Is it safe to leaves these here, unattended? Any neighbors?"

"No neighbors. Not for miles. But let's put everything into the trunk just in case I'm wrong." Together they transferred the guns, knives, and accessories. It was distracting, because Vincent kept finding beautiful pieces he needed to admire, and Avery kept taking them from his hands and stacking them on top of the others in the trunk.

"How long are we staying?" Avery said.

"Benton will call when he's ready for us. Your guess is as good as mine." He picked up an HK semiautomatic handgun. Its serial number had been filed off. Totally illegal. He tossed it on the pile as Avery hauled a duffle bag from the back seat. She dropped it on the ground next to the trunk, at Vincent's feet, then unzipped it. She pressed her palm to her chest, and gasped. "What?" he said.

Avery pulled out bundled money. "This is at least a hundred thousand dollars," she said.

He agreed. "Payment? Half upfront, half when the job is complete?"

Avery threw him side eye, as if she thought he was being obtuse. "That's not how it's done. This is for incidentals, but wow, this would have come in handy these last few years. Just thinking of what I could have done with this money makes me weepy." She used her thumb to flip through the bills. She looked like she'd won the lottery.

Back in the day, his wife had always been a big fan of telling him he didn't make enough money. That was before, when he was a grunt in the Army. Now, he suspected she'd have no complaints with his income. "What?" He frowned at the bag. "You want expensive clothes, or a fancy car? There is more to life than things."

She snorted, but kept her eyes on the money. "Food is "things." Braces for Millie is "things." Paying the gas bill. Is that "things?" Yeah, I want "things." She zipped the bag up again and threw it in the trunk. "It's blood money."

"You don't spend money with bad juju?"

She looked at him as if he were crazy. "That money doesn't care if it's used to finance my death, or my sister's dentist. That money doesn't care at all, but I care. Finders keepers, that's what I say."

He almost laughed, but then realized she was dead serious, and it didn't seem the moment to explain the concept of government asset forfeiture, so he let it slide. That discussion could happen later, when things became…less dicey.

Vincent locked the car and then opened the cabin. There was always a risk of break-ins when you had a cabin in the woods, either by desperate hikers, looters, or kids looking for a place to drink or get laid. It looked much the same as when he'd left it a month ago. Musty, but clean.

Avery didn't hide her trepidation about entering. He wasn't sure what she'd expected, but from the look on her face, it wasn't what she found; a one-room, hardwood-floored studio, outfitted with bed, dinette set, and wood-stove. The cabin had never been intended for anything beyond a hunting lodge, but his grandmother had insisted on a few niceties.

"It's kinda nice," she said, sounding surprised.

"I'm glad you like it."

"We're safe here. That's what counts." Then she pulled her Glock from her waistband. He tensed, only to feel foolish when she lay on the bed, and then rested it on her chest. He wasn't sure what he should think about assuming Avery was always a heartbeat away from pulling a gun on him. He supposed that episode in the car with her gun to his knee would take some time to move on from. She lay on the bed, ankles crossed, and stared at the knotty pine ceiling as if it might reveal some answers. "I need to think," she said.

He closed the screen door, and then opened the four windows, hoping to air the cabin out. "This place is good for that. That and hunting." She grimaced. "What did I say?"

"*We're* being hunted, Vincent."

He thought about that for a moment, and then decided she was splitting hairs. "It's temporary. We'll get you to a safehouse—"

"And live happily ever after." Avery grimaced again. "Cue the canned laughter."

Vincent pulled the Ruger from his waistband and lay next to her, resting the gun on his chest. "Can you imagine someone stumbling into this cabin right now and catching us like this? Armed to the teeth. They'd think they'd walked into a horror film."

Avery chuckled, weakly, and then groaned. "They wouldn't be far from the truth. What's wrong with us?"

Us? Vincent didn't marry a monster and runaway with incriminating files. "What do you mean?" He turned his head to the side, admiring her profile. She was...*arresting* to look at. Not a conventional beauty, by any means, and the bruise on her jaw had swelled and turned blue, challenging even that claim, and there was a definite look about her eyes that always seemed to be saying *fuck you* without even trying, but he liked her face. Her eyes...so green, with the speckles of gold. Her soft red hair. Yeah. Arresting.

Avery turned her head and met his gaze, causing their breath to intermingle. "Somehow," she said, "we've both made life decisions that resulted in us landing in this bed. Right here, right now, guns on our chest in a remote cabin in North Conway, New Hampshire. It's insane." When she put it like that, their situation did sound crazy.

"My wife left me," he said. "That nudged me here." He was embarrassed as soon as the words left his mouth, but it was true. Madeline leaving him made his career take an abrupt left turn back to the states. "I had some misguided hope I could win her back." He looked at the ceiling again. There was something about Avery that prompted him to confess, apparently, because that's all he seemed to do with her. She kept him off-balance, whether because he wanted to kiss her or protect her, he wasn't sure, but he was positive he wasn't thinking straight. "If Madeline had been faithful, I might still be in the Army, maybe dead, but not here."

"Sniper. You killed for a living."

"*This We'll Defend.*" The sniper motto. He glanced at her, saw her eyes were closed, and thought maybe she was on the verge of nodding off, but then she took a deep breath and opened them again.

"Why did your wife leaving make you discharge from the Army?" she said. "Most people would cling to the familiar."

"It was time." It was only later, when he'd gotten therapy for his PTSD that things started making sense.

"And you didn't win her back."

"No. She was the one person in the world who I'd thought loved me, supported me, sacrificed with me, and she *betrayed* me. Even if she'd agreed to try again, the marriage would have failed, because I stopped trusting in people."

"In your judgment, you mean."

"Maybe. I'm stronger for the experience." Now he knew not to trust anyone, so when they *didn't* screw him, it was a nice surprise.

She gave a little nod, staring at the ceiling. "I left my husband and he's been trying to kill me ever since. Trust issues don't seem like the worst reaction a man could have to divorce."

He grinned. "Good point. Compared to your psychopathic ex, my damage seems junior varsity."

She smiled a sad smile. "I understood why Dante did it. I didn't like it, but I understood." She opened her mouth, working her jaw with her palm, making him think the bruising and swelling bothered her. "No one likes to be left behind. No one likes to be alone."

He studied her profile again, and wished she'd look at him, maybe let him kiss her again. As unprofessional as his desire was, it was consuming him. "I'm here with you. You're not alone."

She didn't turn her head toward him, but her smile lost its sadness. "Have you met me? I'm the ex-wife of a crime boss. You should be afraid, not turned on." Then she did turn her head, and he shared her amusement.

"Stop defining yourself by the worst attribute of your ex-husband. You're a lot of things, Avery. A lot of things that most people admire. A hardworking waitress. A doting sister. A phenomenal martial artist, sharpshooter, and knife thrower."

She blushed, looking away. "I'm a horrible cook."

"That's what restaurants are for." He knew he was embarrassing her, but couldn't stop smiling.

"Can't do laundry to save my life."

"I send mine out to be cleaned," he said.

She glanced at him, and he saw her shyness. It was new. He'd never seen Avery shy. Ever. And he'd been studying her photos and available videos for a year now. She was feeling shy, and it made him feel funny inside, as if her insecurity was now his.

She licked her lips, speaking barely above a whisper. "I can drive most anything that has an engine, though."

"That's impressive," he whispered back. "I can't wait to see you in action."

"Yeah?" She bit her lower lip, peeking at his eyes, and then looking away quickly.

"I have a friend who owns a Model T, pre-1919. Now that is a hard car to drive."

Her smile widened, and though she didn't laugh, she looked as if she were on the precipice of happiness. The sight floored him, and emptied his mind of all but her beauty. "Challenge accepted," she said.

His gaze dropped to her lips, and try as he might, he couldn't make them politely look elsewhere. "I want to kiss you."

She did laugh, then, and put her Glock on the side table before turning on her side, facing him, hand pressed between her cheek and the pillow. "You are such a flirt. How many girlfriends do you juggle back wherever you come from?"

He put his gun on the side table and turned to face her, forcing himself to keep a half foot between their faces, rather than risk her backing away. "Boston. And none. No girlfriends. I work too much to romance anyone."

"Who are you kidding?" She laughed deep in her throat. "All you have to do is walk in a room, and women swoon. I know. I was one of them."

"I'm serious. No relationships since my ex-wife tossed me to the curb."

She lifted her brows. "Gun shy?"

"Guns seems to be the only thing I'm not shy of. All work, no play, until you." Her expression told him she did not in fact believe him at all, but it was the truth. He propped himself on his elbow. "Now all I can think about is you, Mrs. Coppola." As soon as that name crossed his lips, he winced, hating that he'd slipped up so badly when her mood had finally lightened.

"Don't call me that." A shadow crossed her expression.

"I'm sorry."

"I divorced him. I started over. I don't even want that part of him touching me." She pressed her face into the pillow for a moment. When she'd readjusted her head on the pillow, she'd composed herself, but she looked at him with sadness now.

"It slipped out." Dante Coppola was twenty years Avery's senior, at seventeen she must have been very desperate to marry the syndicate boss. "I'm assuming you didn't know he was behind your family's massacre." Otherwise, Vincent couldn't fathom her decision to marry him, no matter how desperate she'd been.

He saw a flash of temper, but it didn't leech into her tone. "Remember when I said you don't know anything? Well, this is one of the things you don't know." He thought for a moment that she was going to leave it at that, but instead, she sighed. "Dante had nothing to do with it. It was a coup within the ranks of my father's people. Dante found out soon after it happened, but didn't have the power to do much beyond rebuild the businesses by then. The contract killers didn't like that my father was pulling the syndicate out of illegal activities and going into legitimate business. He was essentially putting them out of a job."

"Who needs contract killers if you're not a criminal enterprise?"

Her eyes lost focus, and whatever thoughts tormented her, they were familiar enough to shrug off. "My father should have foreseen what eventually happened, and taken steps to prevent it. He didn't, and now my family is dead. All but me and Millie."

"So how does Dante fit in?"

Her eyes focused on Vincent's face, and she frowned. "He took over because he was the only one left who could without creating a range war, so people got behind him. I married him. He protected me and Millie." She seemed defensive.

"And hired *The Stinger*?"

"Stop. If you won't believe what I tell you, why do you keep asking me questions? I told you. *The Stinger* doesn't exist."

"Hmm." She was lying. He could tell. She had a tick on her right eyelid that gave her away every time. "Okay. Fine. I'll back off."

"I don't want to talk about Dante. I'm tired." She curled up, bumping knees with him. "Let's talk about you. What do you do for fun?"

Vincent couldn't repress his smile. "I could show you." Then he nudged a curl behind her ear.

Avery laughed and pushed his hand away. "I thought you don't have time for romance."

"That doesn't mean I don't have fun." He flopped onto his back, tucking his hands behind his head. The afternoon was getting old, and the sun was dropping. This deep in the woods, it got dark sooner because of tree cover, so he'd light a fire soon, if only to see by. "I read. I run, go to the gym, and there's poker night every Thursday with the team." He glanced at her, expecting a smirk, or some level of derision. He saw interest.

"That sounds like a nice life. Lonely, though."

"What are you talking about?"

"Reading. Done alone. Running. Alone. Gym? Maybe that could be considered a group sport, but I don't see you as the guy that works out with friends. You probably do your sets with earbuds on and head home an hour later."

That was about right. "Poker is a group activity."

"With coworkers makes it an extension of work." He must have revealed a bit of irritation, because she pressed her hand on his arm. "Don't get me wrong. I understand. You have poker and I have Millie. Having a ten-year-old forces you to do things. School activities. Playdates. I'm around people all the time, but I'd rather be reading."

He frowned. "You work out. I know you do. I saw your moves at the diner. The meth head—"

She covered her jaw with her palm. "I thought I was dead six times, at least."

"You've trained with some seriously skilled people, Avery. *You* are seriously skilled."

"I don't deny it. After what happened to my family, I felt vulnerable and didn't like it. It crippled me, actually, so I trained."

"With who?"

She bit her lower lip, and for a moment, he thought she wouldn't tell him. "Dante's contract killers."

Vincent sat, staring down at her. He didn't know what he'd expected her to say, but that wasn't it. "Tell me the six that killed your family weren't involved in your training." She wouldn't meet his gaze, and seemed unwilling to answer, so he nudged her.

"Well, obviously, I didn't know what they'd done," she said. "Not when they were training me."

Obviously? He didn't know what to say. A person couldn't be that mind-fucked and survive, could they? "And I thought my ex was Satan."

She covered her face with her hands. "I shouldn't have told you. I knew you wouldn't understand."

He pulled her hands off her face. "Make me understand."

She flopped on her back, then she grabbed her Glock, resting it on her chest again. He took it as a sign that she was feeling threatened.

"I was desperate," she said. "I'd stopped sleeping. I thought whoever killed my family would come after me and Millie." She wiggled on the bed, adjusting herself. "You can't imagine, Vincent. The level of fear I lived with." She shook her head. "My family was massacred at a family reunion, where I should have been completely safe. I would have been dead, too, if I hadn't gone upstairs to check on my sister. We spent an hour cowering in a closet. Millie kept crying, and I knew if she was heard, we'd both die. Ever since then, my life has been centered on keeping Millie safe."

He'd seen the pictures. He knew what happened that day, and knew what she'd found when she'd left that closet. "I'm sorry, Avery."

"I didn't know it was them. That the people that killed my family were training me. I didn't. I just knew I needed to be more, be stronger." Her chin quivered and tears spilled over her lashes. "Being vulnerable is intolerable."

"But Coppola married you, promising protection."

"I knew it wouldn't be enough. I'd had my father's protection. That didn't save anyone, so I made Dante promise to have his men train me. That way, if anyone tried to hurt me or Millie, I'd be prepared this time. I would never have to cower in a closet again. I would be in control. They'd cower before me."

Vincent couldn't even imagine what the undercurrents in those training classes must have been like. "You might not have known, but they knew. Why did they train you?"

She shrugged. "Dante told them to."

"But they killed the last boss."

Sniffing, she gave him an impatient glance. "I explained that."

"Job retention?" Hard to believe.

She shook her head. "It's about power. Control. Most things are."

He wasn't sure he bought that story, but she seemed to. "I just can't visualize you training with those killers."

"For five years. I began the day after I married Dante." Avery rubbed her thumbs against her rings. "They beat the crap out of me three times a week and called it "training." It would have been more frequent, but Dante feared the pace would kill me. I think they believed if they were brutal enough, I'd give up. They underestimated my fear, and I had no idea they'd killed my family, so there was that. If I'd known, I would have been too afraid, but I learned, persisted, became better. When I won sparring matches, more often than not, and could shoot and throw knives as well as them, my "training" ended. I ran with Millie soon after."

"When did Dante tell you they'd killed your family?" He saw her surprise, as if she hadn't seen that question coming. It surprised him in turn, because it seemed the most important question.

"After they were dead." She pursed her lips, and her eyes lost focus.

Vincent couldn't wait to put the whole damn lot of them behind bars. "I'm sorry," was all he could force past his lips.

She sniffed, blinking. "Dante had to know if I'd found out, I would have left him, so he kept it from me. No way I could have stayed with them around all the time."

"So, he killed them for you? Trying to keep you there?"

Her eyes slowly focused, and her expression hardened. "Nice try, but no dice. I don't know who killed them." She sighed. "Anyway, Dante isn't so romantic. They were his men. Why would he kill them? They had their uses, and it takes a long time to train one. I should know."

"That means *The Stinger* must be from a rival syndicate." He saw she wanted to deny it, so stopped her before she could speak. "Someone killed those six men, Avery, and our forensics people say it was one person, same time of death, so one after the other. Do you know someone skilled enough to do that? You trained with those killers. You'd know if one of Coppola's people were capable." She shook her head, denying any knowledge of such a person. "*The Stinger* has to be from a rival syndicate."

"I can't think about this anymore. It's too much." Curled up, she grabbed the pillow and hugged it, seeming more a little girl, than an exhausted warrior. When she closed her eyes, he told himself to allow her to rest. It didn't matter that what he needed was to take her in his arms and make everything better. That was his burden, and not his job. He gave himself a mental shake and then he rolled off the bed, afraid if he stayed there, lying next to her, he'd kiss her and set in motion events that he wouldn't be able to take back.

Like making love with her. Like growing more attached to her. Like losing his last shred of objectivity, which was already shaky, at best. Instead, he set about building a fire, determined to pretend he had everything under control.

Chapter 10

Avery woke in the dark. Achy, and cold, she could only make out the outline of furniture as moonlight peeked in through the windows. She wanted to sleep, be oblivious again, but her muscles were cramping so badly she couldn't ignore it, and when she yawned, her jaw clicked, reminding her that an asshole had sucker punched her at the diner.

Vincent's arms encircled her, pulled her close, spooning her. She sighed with relief as his heat eased her muscle pain. He'd taken his shirt off at some point during the night, so her cheek pressed to hot skin when she turned in his arms, cleaving to him, her lips now against his neck. She felt a little bad about splaying her cold hands on his back, dragging her palms up to the back of his neck, threading her fingers through his hair. But he was so warm, and she needed his heat to sleep.

He shifted his body, lying on his back, bringing her with him, so she didn't even have to try to touch him. She was draped on him, splayed, dead weight, and when he turned his head and his warm lips pressed against the hollow of her neck, it felt right. She sighed, lifting her knee and dragging it up over his naked belly, curling around him so more of her could touch him and benefit from his warmth. When his lips moved left and right along her neck's hollow, she didn't think much of it, beyond that it felt nice, relaxing, because she was drifting off again.

His hot hands splayed on her back, his fingers bent and gently kneaded her, easing the ache of strained muscles as her mind took note of serenading bugs and frogs outside. She heard the crackle of a fire, and remembered they were in Vincent's cabin, on borrowed time. She didn't have to do anything, be anything, because it was that limbo point after midnight and before dawn when the world stopped and expectations ceased. Avery could just be. She could allow this small pleasure with Vincent. Him, easing her sore muscles, his lips moving against her neck.

She found the strength to loll her head to the side to give him better access, and then he was tugging at her T-shirt's neckline. The shock of his tongue touching her skin wasn't enough to open her eyes, but she stopped breathing for a moment, and then sighed as its drew a line up the band of muscle from her shoulder to her ear. There, he lingered, having left a cool dampness behind that he used as a marker to return to with his open mouth. He nuzzled her neck, sucking, tasting her, driving her crazy as tingles of desire laid waste to her body. Overwhelmed, more aroused than she'd ever felt before, she found it impossible to think past his mouth on her, and how he made her feel.

Avery's hips arched, rocking, as delicious tension twisted up her belly. It took a moment to recognize her rhythm matched his kisses, and another to recognize it felt right. Necessary, like breathing. Her chest rose and fell, and tension nudged aside sleepiness. She wanted Vincent.

Her first tiny moan startled her. The second came after Vincent's kisses prompted a spike of arousal so powerful, her eyes open. Then she saw him beneath her, the fire to the left, its flickering light dancing around the cabin, as they lay there, her hand pressed to his chest.

She should stop this.

She should, yet her eyelids drooped when his teeth nipped at her neck, and another wave of desire hit her, making her tremble, urging her hips to move harder against his. Vincent's palm moved to her waist, and then to her waistband, teasing its edge, slipping under the fabric. Then he reversed direction, and his hand moved under her T-shirt, between their bodies, even as he teeth grazed the sensitized skin near her throat. He cupped her breast, his thumb brushed its tip, and her body arched toward him, seeking more.

This is wrong. *She* was wrong. Avery was uniquely *wrong* for Vincent. She could ruin him. Get him killed. He had no idea what she'd done.

She had to stop this.

Vincent turned them onto their sides, and then his kisses, licks, and nibbles moved from her neck to her breasts, mouthing her through her T-shirt, leaving damp marks where he covered her nipples and sucked. It was one of the most erotic experiences of her life. Vincent seemed starved for her, and it was intoxicating, made it hard to think, to feel guilt, to resist him.

When her hand found its way to his fly, she felt his arousal straining against the fabric. Vincent covered her hand, stopped her caress. "I'll explode," he said. The words seemed to burst from him. "This is out of control." He guided her hand to his chest, holding it there. "My fault."

She pressed her face to his neck, forcing herself not to taste his hot skin. She'd just…lay with him. "Go to sleep," she said, knowing it was impossible. It felt as if she'd never sleep again.

"Yeah. Sleep." He rolled her onto her back, and settled his weight between her thighs, pinning her to the mattress. "Kiss me good night, sweet Avery." Elbows resting on either side of her head, she looked up at him, but his face was in shadow. "Kiss me." He lowered his head, brushing his lips against hers. She told herself one kiss…one more kiss. Then he swept his tongue inside her mouth, and their kiss was hot, and wet, and lingering, banishing all thoughts on what she *should* do.

She grabbed his ass with both her hands and arched her hips higher, needing him closer. "What are we doing?" Out of breath, out of her mind. This wasn't right. *She didn't deserve a man like Vincent.* "We have to stop."

He rolled off her, eyes squeezed shut. "Stopping. We're stopping."

"Good night, Vincent." She stared at the ceiling, blinded by her failures as she curled up, facing away from him.

If he learned her secrets, he'd hate her. How could he not? Yes, she'd allowed him to worm his way into her…what? Heart? Head? She needed to protect herself, be strong, where she was weak. A few more moments of kissing, and she'd have begged him to be inside her. Even now, swollen and pulsing, her panties wet, Avery feared she still might beg.

But some instinct told her that if they made love, he'd never let her go. He'd use that intimacy to excuse his "protection," maybe even force her to deal with the Feds. She shuddered at the thought.

She'd come to care if Vincent lived or died, and that caring made him a vulnerability. This man, this *Fed*, made her vulnerable. He could destroy her, *would* destroy her if he knew the truth, so why the hell was she playing with fire?

* * * *

Something woke her abruptly, and she didn't know if it was the sunlight, birds chirping, bugs clacking, or the chill in the air. Vincent's warm arm was draped over her side, and he was spooning her, his hand tucked just inside her unzipped waistband, as if poised to slip into her panties and cup her heat. The thought had her lady parts clenching. She turned her face against the pillow and suppressed a groan.

Vincent tensed, and then his arm twitched, making her recognize what had woken her. He was having a nightmare. She looked over her shoulder, at his face, and saw a furrow between his brows, his jaw muscles flexing and releasing. He was suffering. Pressing her hand to his forearm, she snuggled close, seeking to give solace where she could, because she sympathized. It was rare she didn't suffer nightmares. Dante had hired a counselor just after they'd been married. He didn't like her thrashing about in bed, crying as he attempted to sleep. Her nightmares eventually chased Dante from her bed, so they were a welcomed plus in the end.

Vincent tensed again, so she tightened her hold on his arm, feeling the need to keep him company as he waged his internal battles. Soon, his breath no longer caught, as if poised to shout, and his arm no longer squeezed her close. Twenty minutes later, he was smacking his lips and nuzzling the back of her neck. She couldn't help but smile as she felt him pressing his erection against her ass. Her warrior, randy after winning the battle.

She turned toward him, propping herself up on her elbow. Her hair had completely fallen from its bun, so now draped over her shoulder, pooling on the pillow. He smiled back at her, looking sleepy. It occurred to her that she must look a fright, that the bruise on her jaw had to be spectacular, but consoled herself that Vincent didn't look much better. Swollen nose, purple bruises under his eyes, there was a line of scabbing across the bridge of his nose.

"Hi," he whispered.

"Hi." It felt as if the bubble they'd been living in since last night still encapsulated them, and the real world was held at bay. "I'm sorry I broke your face. You used to be pretty," she said.

His shoulders shook as he chuckled, still struggling against sleep. "Who you kidding? I'm still pretty."

He certainly was. "You're the only guy I know that can pull off a broken nose and two shiners and still be sexy."

"Sexy is good." He inhaled deeply, and released it with a moan, his eyes focused on her lips. "Why do you say it like it's bad?"

She swung her legs over the bed's edge, sitting, keeping an eye on him. "Stop digging for compliments and tell me where the bathroom is." She had to pee.

He'd closed his eyes, and was lifting his brows as if struggling to open them. "No bathroom." He tucked his hands beneath his head, and created a feast for her eyes; his corrugated abdomen, thick arms, broad shoulders, not to mention his hard-on from heaven. "There's an outhouse in the back." As he spoke, his stomach tightened—as a stomach is want to do when a person speaks—but Vincent's abdomen was not like others. His rippled with muscles, and had the effect of forcing the air from her lungs.

"*Damn.* Are you doing that on purpose?" The man was gorgeous. Did he have any idea how he was affecting her? When she could look away from his body, their eyes locked. He winked. So, he did know what a turn on he was, laying there, tempting her to touch him. She licked her lips, totally tempted.

"Didn't you say something about having to go to the bathroom?" he said. Yes. Right. "Is the outhouse nasty?"

"Define nasty."

"Lie if you have to," she begged.

"Expect turf wars with spiders, but you're tougher than they are."

"Which part of that is a lie?" She held his gaze, telling herself not to look at his body.

He smiled back, offering himself up for her viewing pleasure. "I don't want to lie to you."

Her stomach clenched, because his words sounded like the truth, and she wasn't a hundred percent positive they were still talking about the outhouse. "If I use the woods, I'll have to fight mosquitoes."

He nodded, his gaze lingering on her breasts, her belly, and the jeans he'd unzipped last night. "Some of life's biggest decisions are between two evils."

Dante killing her or life in jail. Truer words were never spoke. "Spiders it is."

Avery grabbed the sheaths and knives that he must have stripped from her last night, because they were on the floor, and she didn't remember him taking them off. Yes, that unnerved her as she strapped them into place, and then retrieved her Glock from the side table. Tucking the gun into the back of her waistband, she headed for the door to kick some spider ass.

Vincent's phone rang as the screen door slammed behind her. It reminded her that there was a world outside of the cabin, and it wasn't friendly. She didn't stop to eavesdrop. She preferred to delay bad news, and it had to be Benton, and he was probably calling to give them the all clear. Their borrowed time had expired. Too bad, really, because she'd liked it here, liked being alone with Vincent, her sexy beast. She absolutely loved that her hardest decision was choosing between spiders and mosquitoes.

The outhouse proved easy to find. As promised, the small structure had its share of spiders, and they'd died beneath her boots. She took her time, because she still had no idea how to escape her sexy beast, and the Feds that pulled his strings. They thought she was the pot of gold at the end of the Coppola Syndicate rainbow, so their grip was tight.

Fact was, they wanted to believe Dante's lie, so nothing she could say or do would convince them otherwise. Human nature, she supposed, but it forced her to run from them, and she had a feeling they wouldn't be as easy to escape as Dante's men. The FBI task force was smart. Maybe smarter than Dante. Definitely smarter than her.

Barely a high school graduate, Avery had abandoned thoughts of college when she'd married. There was Millie to raise, and she had other training to keep her busy. These federal agents probably spent most of their lives in school, probably studied people like Dante in a classroom. Maybe people like her, too. They probably thought they had her number, a fleeing ex-mob wife with evidence they wanted. They'd smarten up soon enough, so Avery needed a plan while the Feds remained in the dark. If she didn't make them her bitch now, they'd make her theirs soon.

Entering the cabin, she froze, causing the screen door to hit her ass. Vincent's expression screamed bad news. "What?" she said.

"That was Benton."

She'd assumed as much. "And?"

"They're interrogating one of Coppola's men from the sheriff's office. He's asking for you. Says he'll only speak to you."

"His name?" Her anxiety ratcheted up.

"Pinnella. Know the guy?" Vincent was studying her, as if he knew the answer already, but wanted to see if she'd lie.

Yes, she knew "Fingers." He'd tried to kill her after she'd hit him with the stolen Audi back at the federal building. "He's one of my ex-husband's men." Pinnella hated her, and would do his best to screw her with the Feds. There was no upside to speaking with the contract killer. At the very least, he would sidetrack her efforts to escape. "I don't want to talk with him."

Vincent nodded, as if he understood. "Benton's thinking if you won't flip on Coppola, maybe Pinnella will." He shrugged. "This might be your way of deflecting the FBI's attention. Could be a win for both of us. All I'm asking is for you to think about it."

That was crazy talk. Pinnella wouldn't snitch. There was no one more loyal to Dante than Pinnella. "You can't trust a thing he says."

"Of course not, but it's something. Maybe he'll give something up without meaning to, or we could make a deal. He's looking at life in prison. Murder one. He'll want a deal."

Pinnella knew too many of her secrets to completely ignore this problem. Her choice was bleak. See him, and risk Pinnella messing with her plans to meet up with Millie, or ignore him, and risk him data dumping to the Feds everything he knew about her. "It's a bad idea."

"If we can't use Pinnella, Benton will want to use you. Make a decision. What do I tell him?" He tossed his iPhone in the air and caught it. "He's expecting a return call ASAP. He says if you won't talk to Pinnella, he expects you to tell him where you're hiding the files."

She forced herself not to growl at him, but she wanted to. "The damn files."

"It's not about the files, Avery." He slipped his phone into his back pocket and approached her. His pants were still unbuttoned at the top, though he'd zipped them. That little detail didn't make him any less sexy, because his waistband sagged low, giving her a tempting view she wanted to explore. He wrapped his arms around her hips and pulled her into his embrace. She leaned back, resisting with two palms to his warm, hard chest, inadvertently positioning them groin to groin. He smiled, all sexy and sweet.

"It's about taking down Dante Coppola," he said. "We both want that, don't we?" He inched his hands up her back, pulling her chest closer to his, hugging her. He pressed a kiss to her temple. "The files will do it."

"Meaning it *is* all about the files." His shoulders sagged, and his hands moved to her hips, giving her a pang of regret that she needed to disappoint him, but damn, the Feds wanted something that didn't exist. Hell, Avery wanted something that didn't exist. A life beyond her involvement with Dante Coppola, but her ex just wouldn't leave her alone.

Pinnella didn't want to talk with her. Dante ordered him to kill her, so he wanted her dead. She replayed the memory of him at the federal building, lying on the ground next to the Audi. Gun aimed at her, his leg all broken and shit. Pinnella had to have been in extreme pain, and yet his one thought was to end her life. He would have, too, if she hadn't lucked out, and he'd been out of bullets. His goal didn't change simply because he was in a hospital, his pain dulled by meds. She'd be crazy to meet with him, and even if she did, she couldn't speak to the guy with the Feds in the room. She had too many secrets.

Avery groaned, and buried her face against Vincent's chest, hiding her indecision. His heat, his smell, reminded her of the feelings she'd enjoyed last night. She wanted to feel that again, but this time, without her worries of him scratching at her heart. *Just a sliver of happiness.* Was that too much to ask? A sliver would go a long way to soothing her unease, and maybe it would help her solve this problem.

Millie was in Boston, afraid, waiting for her, and Pinnella was looking for trouble, possibly poised to spill the beans on her. And Dante, damn him, was probably still asleep, probably nestled with a lover, dreaming of her execution.

Avery needed to escape Vincent and get her ass to Boston.

He tilted her chin up with a fingertip. "Hey." He compressed his lips, and donned puppy dog eyes. "Stop it. You keep acting as if you're alone. You're not. You've got me."

A Fed. She'd be a fool to trust him. "We're not a team, Vincent. We're not even on the same side. You want to take Dante down. I want to escape him."

Vincent frowned. "Is this you warning me not to trust you?"

"Of course not," she said. "That would be a waste of breath. We both know you don't trust me. But know this, Millie comes first, before the Feds, Dante, you, even me. Keep that in mind, and you just might have a future."

She pushed out of his arms, averting her gaze as she hurried outside. The woods, the locked car, was a splash of reality. She was trapped here, and couldn't leave unless Vincent drove her out. Frustration had her kicking the car's tire.

Not soon enough, he had the cabin locked up, and was at the Audi's driver's side door. Avery had worked herself into a frenzy, worrying about a confrontation with him, but he seemed calm, absently tossing and catching the keys in the air.

"So? Where're we going, Avery? The hospital or to pick up the files?" He leaned his forearms on the Audi's roof, peering at her, his expression devoid of emotion. He was hiding something, and she suspected it was glee for giving her two bad choices. Both were win/win for the Feds, of course, Pinnella or the files, but they were lose/lose for her; one wanted her dead and the other didn't exist.

"Let's see what that pissant has to say," she said.

At least, Pinnella existed. It seemed the safer risk, less likely to invite the fury of a thwarted FBI. Didn't mean she was happy about it, so Avery didn't hide her resentment. It was real, and she saw no benefit to hiding it. Not that Vincent seemed to care. After a quick call to Benton, he turned on the radio, smiling as he shifted into gear. *Smiling.*

He wasn't going to be smiling when she gave him the slip, or when she drove off with the trunk full of weaponry and money. It was happening. Avery just needed to bide her time.

Chapter 11

Avery was silent for the whole ride, despite his attempts to carry a conversation. She was sulking. He tried to keep things light, but she was having none of it, and kept up her silence through the whole drive to the hospital. It was hard to believe she was the same woman who'd flirted with him yesterday over a diner counter. *Patty* seemed young, a little bored, and looking for something. Avery, not so much.

When they'd stepped through the hospital front doors a half hour later, they received more than their fair share of interest from the staff. Upon seeing them, the elderly receptionist's eyes widened in alarm, then she lifted a phone receiver to her ear. When he and Avery stood before her, she set the receiver back in its cradle, clearly frightened. Vincent glanced left and right, wondering when security would arrive. He didn't blame the woman for being alarmed. His two shiners and broken nose, plus his blood-stained flannel shirt was off putting, and Avery wasn't looking as if she'd just attended a tea party, either. She looked rode hard and put away wet.

Deming arrived before a word was spoken, saving him from having to interact with the pearl-clutching receptionist. Vincent flashed his FBI credentials to soothe the woman's fears, nodded, and then followed Avery and Deming down the hall. Benton met them at the open elevator, and then fed Avery a list of questions he wanted her to ask Pinnella. Riding up two floors, Benton was relentless.

"I want dates," Benton said. "Anything he says that can't be verified is useless to us."

"Yeah, yeah, okay," Avery said, eyes front, avoiding their looks. "I know what you want, but you're cracked if you think he'll squeal on Dante."

When the elevator doors opened again, she walked into the hall first. "He got me here, so he's already won."

Benton indicated the hall to the right, and led them toward the room with the uniformed officers milling out front. "How has Pinnella won?" Benton said. She shrugged.

Vincent caught her arm, making her stop. "What do you mean, he won?"

She narrowed her eyes, glaring at his hand on her upper arm. She tugged once, and he released her. "I'm saying that he used you to drag me here. Mission accomplished."

"That's obvious," Vincent said. "He's promised us information for a chance to speak with you. Are you saying he brought you here for a different purpose?" She shrugged again, acting as if she had no idea, but he didn't believe her.

"The moment I step through the door and he sees me," Avery said, "he has no incentive to tell *you* anything." She walked away from them, walking toward the guarded door.

Benton and Vincent exchanged glances. "She doesn't want to see Pinnella," Vincent said.

"He tried to kill me," Avery snapped, glancing at him over her shoulder, but she didn't slow her gait. They caught up with her at the door, and greeted the uniformed officers.

"No one is going to kill you," Benton said. "We'll be in the room."

"And when he says he won't speak unless he's alone with me?" She arched a brow, meeting Benton's gaze, then Vincent's and finally Deming's. "You'll sell me out quicker than a junkie jonesing for a dime bag."

She glanced at the two uniformed policemen bracketing the door, as if calculating their effectiveness in battle. It made Vincent wonder what she feared? Pinnella was in his sixties. Sure, he was evil as shit, but more likely than not was in a leg cast, and hopped up on pain meds. He wasn't a danger to anyone, least of all Avery, who was scary skilled.

Benton seemed to pick up on the same vibe Vincent had. Something wasn't right here. Deming noticed, too. She was doing her profiler voodoo thing. He expected a data dump after this interview, and couldn't wait to hear her analysis.

"Let's get this over with," Avery said.

Benton nodded to one of the policemen, who opened the door, then he and Deming walked in first. Avery followed, and Vincent pulled up the rear. Deming immediately sat on a chair in the corner, pulled out a small notepad and pencil from her suit jacket pocket, and did her staring thing:

blue eyes laser focused on everything and everyone, seemingly unaware that she was being rude.

Pinnella's brown eyes narrowed as he glared at them all filing into the room. His dark hair had been slicked back, he was clean shaven, and his johnnie seemed freshly laundered. He was pale, despite his swarthy complexion, and seemed frail lying in his hospital bed, his leg hooked up to a metal device that elevated it above the mattress. If Vincent wasn't mistaken, the devise was attached to Pinnella's leg via metal screws, and had to be painful. Strangely enough, Vincent didn't feel an iota of sympathy for the contract killer.

"You're not wearing cuffs," Pinnella said to Avery. His New Jersey accent was pronounced. "So, you're a snitch, you piece of—" He didn't get to finish his sentence, because Avery's fist connected with his nose. Pinnella's hands covered his face, but it didn't stop the blood from pouring down his chin and staining his white hospital gown.

Avery stepped back, eyes still on Pinnella. "Show me respect, little man, or I'll feed you your front teeth. We clear?" She shook out her hand, making Vincent think she'd reinjured it. He took it, and though she tried to pull it away, he wouldn't let her, needing to make sure she wasn't bleeding. She wasn't. The rings probably protected her, as well as added more oomph to her strike. As soon as his grip relaxed, she pulled her hand back, giving her full attention to Pinnella, who was now wiping the blood off his mouth with his thin cotton blanket.

"You always were a bitch." Pinnella pressed the blanket to his nose.

That's when Vincent saw his pinkie ring, a replica of the six Avery wore.

Vincent made a mental note to ask her about the significance of the rings later, then stood back to watch the show. Avery and Pinnella were both Coppola Syndicate. One active, and the other…something else. It was rare to have this opportunity to view inners discussing syndicate affairs, and he was kind of excited to see what was said. Born to the syndicate life, a crime lord's granddaughter, daughter, and his successor's wife, Avery was royalty. Pinnella, however, was a relative newcomer, having worked his way from the ground floor up. His rap sheet was long. Pinnella chose the life, whereas Avery was doing her best to get out of it.

"You got her here," Benton said. "Now talk."

Pinnella glared at Benton. "That bitch assaults me in your custody, and you don't see nothing. I'm sure my lawyer will make plenty hay with that, maybe even make you lose your job. That the "talk" you looking for?"

Avery caught Vincent's eye, then shook her head and averted her gaze to the ceiling, the image of frustration. He could tell she had zero patience, which made him think she expected nothing from this interview. It made him think Benton should have given Avery's opinion more credence than this piece of shit, Pinnella's. The guy was a known killer, with no willingness to help the Feds. The longer Vincent stood there, watching the man tend to his bloody nose, the more he felt as if they *were* wasting their time.

"Assault?" Vincent lifted his brows, meeting Benton and Deming's gazes. "You two see any assault?" Deming shook her head, and turned to Pinnella, weighing his reaction.

"This nose don't lie," Pinnella said.

Avery snorted. "Then it's the only part of you that doesn't. You've got ten seconds to tell me what you want to say, and then I'm leaving."

Pinnella's expression morphed from victim to cagey predator in a heartbeat. "I don't think so. You're going to want to know what I have to say." Then he turned to Benton. "But I won't say it in front of the Feds." Avery turned to leave. "It's about Millie!"

She stopped at the door, her hand white-knuckled as she gripped the knob.

"What about Millie?" Vincent had wondered if Pinnella dragged Avery here to threaten her, and now he knew. What had Avery called him? *Pissant.*

"Tell them to leave, Avery," Pinnella said, "or I'm not saying shit." He wrinkled his nose, as if trying to sniff, but nothing happened.

Avery surprised Vincent, surprised them all, especially Pinnella, when she threw open the hospital door and walked into the hall. Vincent followed, and shortly, so did Benton and Deming. They huddled around her, frowning, as Avery leaned against the wall, her arms folded over her chest. Vincent studied her face, searching for a hint of what she was thinking. Avery didn't give much away, but he had to assume she was frustrated, maybe frightened.

Benton waved off the two uniformed policemen guarding the door. "Go take five, grab a coffee down the hall. Just give us a minute to talk in private." The policeman and policewoman nodded, and left without a word. "Listen," Benton said, "I know this is hard to hear. He's basically threatened your little sister, but I can't leave you in there alone with him." Benton pressed his lips together, unwilling to bend, but Vincent could tell he was sympathetic. "I'm sorry. Truth is, I don't trust you. If something happens to him while in my custody, that's on me. If you kill him, you'll have done the world a favor, but you'll go to jail, and my career and this case will die, too. So, you in there, alone with him, is not happening."

Avery glared. "I don't kill people."

Then she pushed off the wall and stepped toe to toe with Vincent, grabbing his T-shirt, pulling him close. Resting her forehead on his chest, she trembled, and he thought she was crying. He didn't think twice, just wrapped his arms around her, but Avery shook him off and stepped back.

She moved so swiftly, so unexpectedly, none of them saw it coming. Then she was in Pinnella's hospital room, door locked behind her.

"Well," Deming said, "she's a quick study."

Vincent glared at Deming, while Benton banged on the door, looking left and right, presumably seeking someone with a key.

"Quick study? What the hell does that mean?" Vincent said.

Deming stepped to Benton's side, stopping him from banging. Then she put her ear to the door, listening, shooting Vincent an irritated glare. "You know exactly what I mean."

And he did. Avery had played him. Played them all. To make matters worse, she'd done it openly. She'd warned Vincent that nothing would keep her from Millie, that if he or his team, or anyone for that matter, got between her and her sister, she'd wreak havoc and take names later.

"Stand back." He'd kick the damn door in.

Benton shook his head. "No." He pointed down the hall as the officers stepped into view. "They have a master key." He waved them over. "Hurry up! I need this door opened now!"

* * * *

"Talk," she said. "That door won't stop them for long."

Pinnella smiled. "I don't need long. Mr. Coppola has a message for you."

"Yeah? What does my dear ex-husband have to say to his long-lost wife?"

"He says, 'Jason Chadwick is dead.'" His gaze dripped malice, as his nose dripped blood, smearing his tobacco-stained teeth. It gave him a ghoulish quality.

In the past, she'd "sparred" with "Fingers," won some, lost some. They'd beaten and battered each other to a draw more often than not, and he hated her, but he wouldn't dare to speak for Dante and lie, because it would inevitably get back to her ex. It would be cause for dismissal, and in their world, that meant a bullet between the eyes, so she didn't bother to call him a liar. His expression told her he wasn't bullshitting.

"Prove it," she said, struggling not to show her fear.

Pinnella's smile widened. "It's easy enough to verify. We left his identification on the body."

A tinny ringing in her ears competed with the sound of scraping metal on metal. It took her a moment to notice a key had inserted in the door's lock. Everything seemed to move in slow motion, and it felt as if time were endlessly stretched before, so she curled her fingers into fists, felt the bite of her rings like an old friend's embrace. Then she showed him her rings, wanting him to see the truth, because it would scare him, as he was scaring her.

"See these?" His eyes widened as he read the ring inscriptions, the initials. "Before I die, I'll have yours, too." He knew what she meant, knew what these rings implied, and she saw his fear. But it wasn't enough. Not nearly enough.

She punched him. Then she punched him again, wiping his shocked expression off his face, and saw it turn to fear. Cuffed to the bed, he lifted a hand, attempting to parry her blows, but her rage blew through his defenses, and she landed punch after punch. He was just the messenger, sure, but he was an evil fuck.

The door burst opened. "Modena, get her out of here!" Benton said.

Too soon, she felt Vincent's arm encircle her waist and drag her from the room. "Fingers" was unconscious, but she hadn't noticed until she was in the doorway. If she was lucky, he'd stay that way until she escaped the Feds. Now, Pinnella was even more dangerous, because she'd told him something only she and Dante had known. In federal custody, he'd sing, and use that information to negotiate. Not about Dante. He'd never snitch on the syndicate's boss, but he'd squeal like a pig about Avery.

"Stop!" Vincent threw her against the wall, and only upon impact did she realize she'd been fighting him the whole way out of the room. Her chest heaved. She couldn't catch her breath. Bending at the waist, hands on her knees to support her weight, Avery focused on her bloody right hand. "What were you thinking?" Vincent was shouting. "You'd better hope he survives, or there's nothing I can do to save you!"

Deming's expensive shoes clicked on the tile as she approached, moving within Avery's line of sight. "She's having a panic attack," the profiler said.

"She almost killed him!" Vincent sounded furious.

"I suspect, if she'd wanted to kill him, he'd be dead," Deming said.

There was sudden silence, as if Deming had dropped a truth bomb, and everyone was processing what she'd said. All Avery heard was blood racing past her ear drums, she felt her heart beating a mile a minute, and her lungs burned as she struggled to breath. It was hard to focus.

Vincent grabbed her by the shoulder and stood her up, forcing her to meet his gaze. "What did he say to you, Avery?"

She swallowed. "Jason Chadwick." It was hard to get the name out, but she managed to push it past her locked teeth. She felt on the cusp of throwing up, and the only thing stopping her was sheer willpower.

"What did she say?" Deming stepped close.

"Jason Chadwick," he said, never taking his eyes off Avery. "Look him up in the databases. Avery," he gave her a little shake, "who is Jason Chadwick?"

Deming groaned. "Did you know him?" She looked up from her phone, and Avery felt herself crumbling under the surety that she'd been right, that "Fingers" wouldn't lie about something like that. "He was found beaten to death yesterday in a condo in the Back Bay of Boston. Who is Chadwick to you, Avery?"

He was her contact, the man she'd trusted to keep Millie safe. Dante had Millie.

Her vision narrowed, and the ringing in her ears grew louder.

"Catch her, Vincent. She's fainting," Deming said.

Just as Avery was about to protest, to tell the Special Agent she'd do no such thing, her knees collapsed, Vincent swung her into the cradle of his arms, and she fainted.

* * * *

"Hey," Vincent said.

Avery was exhausted, but managed to open her eyes a slit. She heard a beeping and the back of her hand felt cold. They'd put her in a hospital bed and hooked her up with an IV. Vincent held her weapons on his lap. When she looked at them and raised her brows, he cracked a smile.

"The nurses took them off and threw them at me like they were poison. Takes all kinds, I guess." He tilted his chin toward her. "How you feeling?"

She smacked her lips. "Thirsty."

"Yeah, they said you had low blood sugar and were down a few quarts of fluids. I guess I'm not a good babysitter. You were starved and dehydrated. They say it's a miracle you'd lasted as long as you did."

"Don't be stupid." Her words lacked heat, because he was right. She'd neglected her health, lost time, and Millie was in danger. "This is my fault."

"I ordered us a burger and fries. It should be here soon," he said. She nodded, though food was the last thing on her mind. Millie had to be terrified right now. "Pinnella woke up."

She felt a jolt of adrenaline, and from Vincent's expression, he noticed. "What did he say?" she said.

He shook his head. "Lawyered up. Why don't you tell me what happened in that room? Who is Jason Chadwick to you?"

"Just…someone I know. "Fingers" told me he'd died. I was just making sure the pissant wasn't lying."

"He dragged you to his hospital bed to tell you a mutual acquaintance was murdered?" Vincent didn't hide his skepticism, and she didn't have the energy to convince him otherwise. She had other problems. "He said it was about Millie."

"He lied," she said.

"I don't believe you."

Avery nodded, irritated beyond tolerance. Yeah, she was lying, but *really*? *She* was the one he didn't believe? Didn't the last two days buy her any leeway? "You believe Pinnella when he says it's about Millie, but you don't believe me when I tell you he lied." She nodded again, pressing her lips together. "That's some weird twisty shit trust issues you have. Is it because we'd kissed? Because you just don't trust women? Or is it because it's in your interest not to believe me?"

He stared, seemingly without emotion. "So, it wasn't about Millie."

She closed her eyes, and told herself not to hit him. "You know… whatever. It doesn't matter. Believe whatever you want to believe."

He inhaled sharply, showing the first crack in his composure. "You say that too much. It's lost its meaning. *Everything* with you, Avery, matters, or you don't notice it. Pinnella told you something that upset you so much you fainted. I've seen you in action. You've nerves of steel. What could that man possibly have said to you that is worse than a drugged-out killer holding a knife to your throat?" Jim, at the diner, had threatened Avery. Dante threatened Millie. It was a whole 'nother ball game. "And so help me—" He closed his eyes for a moment, taking a beat to control himself. "If you say it doesn't matter again, I'll go apeshit on you. Now talk."

She needed to get on the road, and there was no way they'd let her leave this hospital unless Vincent and his team were in tow, so she needed to work them. "I'll take you to the files."

Vincent leaned back heavily in the chair, looking as if she'd whopped him on the back of the head. "Files. That you claim don't exist."

She had to work with what she had, and the files were the only thing they wanted from her. Begging them to help her rescue her sister would give them leverage, and she had no illusions they'd use it to force her to testify against Dante. At least if she went head to head with her ex, she had a chance of survival, maybe negotiation. She and Millie could then run away again, and maybe build another life, farther away this time. If she partnered up with the Feds, she'd be no better off, back on Dante's hit list, and Millie still on the chopping block.

"It's the only way to end this," Avery said.

"Tell me where they are."

"Jersey," she said.

"I'll order plane tickets. We could be—"

She shook her head. "Dante has snitches in the FBI. You, me, driving. Or no deal."

His eyes narrowed, and from his grimace she got the impression he was far from happy, but she was confident Benton would give her plan to drive the green light. The man was obsessed, and would give his left nut to take down Dante. Normally, she'd be rooting for him, but her ex was too dangerous. She needed him dead, or free, not captured by the Feds, and squealing on her. Nope, she needed Dante left alone, and her and Millie off the grid. Her best bet to do that required a road trip, ditching Vincent along the way, and setting up a meet with her ex to negotiate Millie's release. She forced herself not to think of the "price" she'd be asked to pay for Millie's return, because she knew Dante, and she feared fainting again.

Vincent compressed his lips and nodded. "Fine. I'll talk to Benton, but you're not going anywhere until you've eaten and the doctor says you're okay to leave."

Three hours later they were in the parking lot of the hospital, standing next to a beige Ford Escort. Vincent was giving her an impatient and expectant look. "So?" he said.

They'd just survived a testy argument with Benton, who'd reluctantly agreed to allow Avery to keep her weapons. Vincent was the one that had convinced him with a snarky, *do you really think she needs a weapon to kill anyone?* Thinking to help, she'd mentioned she only used weapons when her opponents used weapons. That information had Benton lifting his hands in the air in disgust, and turning his back on them, walking away.

She'd shouted after him, "I don't kill people!" Then glanced at Deming, qualifying her statement with, "on purpose." Deming had snickered and followed the team leader down the hospital's hall. Vincent hustled her to the parking lot, where he'd then handed her the knives, their sheaths, and her Glock.

"*So*, what?" she said. Adjusting the last of her sheaths into place, she then tucked her Glock in her waistband.

"You're the only one that knows where we're going, Avery. Where are the files in Jersey? Sooner or later, you'll have to tell me."

"Later is better." She had to play him nice and easy. Less information meant she was less likely to be called on her shit.

He tilted his head, narrowing his eyes. "What if I promise not to tell Benton where we're going?"

"I wouldn't believe you." She gave him an overly bright smile.

"What about if I promise only to tell them when we arrive?" He unlocked the doors and opened the driver's side.

She slipped into the passenger's seat. "Let me think about it." The longer they lingered arguing, the more time Millie was with Dante.

Her ex had started a negotiation when he'd killed Jason and took her sister, so they started at Avery's unconditional surrender. She had to counter that offer with something tempting enough to save Millie, and not die doing it. She feared her four-hour drive to Jersey wouldn't be long enough to devise this Hail Mary pass.

Vincent gave her side eye as he slipped the key into the ignition. "When are you going to start trusting that I'm on your side?"

"I do trust you, Vincent." Mostly. She trusted him to be consistently in the Fed's corner. That meant she could trust he'd do what she predicted, and that made him relatively safe. "I just don't trust your team, or the Feds that work behind the scene, so I'm keeping the details close to the vest. For now." When he frowned, as if about to argue, she lifted a hand to stop him. "I don't know them. Don't ask me to put my life in their hands, and we'll get along just fine. We both want Dante stopped, and the files will do it, so we go to Jersey."

His irritation and stubbornness faded, and he nodded. He believed her. Enough, anyway, to be useful to her. He believed she trusted him, and because he was a good guy, he thought that meant on some level he could trust her. He must be thinking they'd had some sort of a personal breakthrough back at the cabin, and then at the hospital, because he was ignoring his instincts. Truth was, he shouldn't trust her, and if he knew this trip was about saving Millie, he wouldn't. He wouldn't allow her anywhere near New Jersey. He'd see it as too dangerous, and a mission creep, because his priority was taking down Dante, not saving Millie.

"Okay, we'll play it your way," he said, "but know this…expect the leash to be short. You've used up all your leeway with Benton, the team, and yeah…*me*. Don't test our patience." He shifted into gear and pulled out of the parking space.

"Leash? I'm not a dog." She folded her arms over her chest and sulked.

Normally, she would have dug in deep and tried her best to make him feel bad for the illusion to a pet, but she was feeling too guilty about her deception, even though the cause was good. Millie's life was on the line, and she still didn't have a plan to save her. Should she offer herself up in exchange? Dante might take that deal. Her death for Millie's freedom?

Other than the obvious drawback of *dying*, that plan had other flaws. Avery wasn't the teen he'd saved all those years ago, the teen he'd corrupted and then some. He knew she was dangerous, and wouldn't trust the offer of exchanging her life for Millie's. He couldn't understand that kind of sacrifice and wouldn't believe it. And Avery wasn't the same person who'd left him three years ago, either.

She couldn't kill Dante, couldn't kill anyone, no matter how much they might deserve it.

She'd spent the last three years not being *The Stinger*, and she didn't want to survive if it meant becoming *The Stinger* again.

Chapter 12

Vincent donned earbuds for privacy, and speed-dialed Benton as he drove. Soon he heard the click of the connected line. "We're on our way."

"Don't lose her. She'll cut and run at first opportunity." Benton's tone was clipped and irritable, making Vincent wonder when the last time the team leader had slept. Like the rest of them, he'd been living off coffee and adrenaline.

"We have to drive, but you don't. Take a flight," Vincent said. "Grab some shut-eye. Eat something, Benton."

"Yes, mom. Gilroy is harassing me, too, so don't worry. I'm eating my vegetables. What about you?"

"Do I have to eat my vegetables?" Vincent smiled.

"No." He went silent, and for a second, Vincent thought the line had disconnected. "Do I have to worry about you?"

Vincent nodded. *Probably.* He was getting an odd feeling about this case. "Don't worry about me. You're the one who's burning out. You should have taken time off before jumping back into the game, Benton. Did you even debrief with the Special Agent in Charge?" Vincent knew what Benton had sacrificed to spend a year inside the Coppola syndicate, and he knew Benton closing this case was the only way the team leader felt justified for making those sacrifices.

"I wrote up my report and handed it in yesterday," Benton said. There was a slight pause. "Listen, got to go."

"See you in Jersey," Vincent said.

They disconnected the line, leaving Vincent worried and tense. Worried, because after a year undercover with the Coppola Syndicate, Benton was too enmeshed in the RICO case to walk away. It was distorting his judgment, maybe making him see things not there, investing man hours chasing incriminating files that Avery said didn't exist…and now said they did. Both assertions couldn't be true, yet the case would succeed or fail depending on where the truth landed. He hated that level of uncertainty, especially with this shroud of secrecy Avery added with her refusal to tell him *exactly* where these files were. Damn, he just didn't trust her, though he wanted to. The *wanting to* is what made him nervous.

He glanced at her next to him, and saw she was deep in thought, her gaze on the road. Her clothes were rumbled, and spattered with blood, as was his. He was a guy mid-op, so didn't care, yet Avery professed a reluctance to retrieve the files. Wouldn't she seek the delay of cleaning up, and finding replacement clothes? He was suspicious. Him and Avery seemed finally on the same page, yet it was just too good to be true.

He got onto the highway easily enough. Traffic was light. He settled in for the long drive, kicking in cruise control. He could feel her watching him, but he kept his eyes on the road, because she was giving him the vibe that she was in the mood to argue. When her fingers drummed impatiently on the console between them, he glanced at them, and sighed.

"Why do I feel sorrier for your hand than I do for Pinnella's face?" He lifted her poor, bruised and battered hand, and kissed a spot that didn't look like it hurt.

"Because he's a pissant." She pulled her hand from his grip, dragging the rings against his palm.

It reminded him of something. "I wanted to ask you about those rings earlier. I saw that Pinnella wore one, too, and I remembered seeing photos in the bureau's files. I researched them again, when you were unconscious, and discovered they're popular with some of Dante's men. Not women. Only men."

She kept her gaze directed out the windshield. "My father had them specially made."

"Mementos of your father? *Six* of them?" For symmetry's sake, maybe. Vincent wasn't into fashion, so didn't know, but this was Avery. Her reasoning probably had something to do with self-defense, or offense. Pinnella's face certainly suffered from her wearing them.

She bit her lower lip, and looked as if she'd ignore him, until she didn't. "I've grown…*sentimental* since my family was murdered. I wouldn't recommend it." When he didn't respond, she threw him side eye before slouching in her seat. "It comes with a cost."

So, the rings were probably from family members that died at the massacre? That was something not in her files. A bit morbid to wear them, but understandable, and their history was explanation enough for why she didn't want to talk about them. He decided to drop the subject of the rings, feeling the necessity to pick his battles. *Not* because he'd lost his objectivity, as Deming had accused.

Avery wasn't playing Vincent. He'd studied her just as Deming had, and knew her history. Her agenda was clear. Run with her sister, because she was afraid of her ex-husband's mania. That he sympathized with the shit Avery lived through made Vincent *human*, not Avery's chump. Once she handed over the files, everyone would get what they wanted, except for Coppola. He'd go to jail and Benton could finally relax. They'd rescue Millie, and Avery would be free. And Vincent? He'd keep on, keeping on, just like always.

He sniffed, grimacing, feeling an unease he didn't want to explore, so he blamed it on Deming's fish assault yesterday. It was a gift that kept on giving. Not that Avery seemed to mind the smell. She'd fallen asleep, so he turned off the radio and settled in for the long drive, telling himself not to think of tomorrows. They were unreliable, and sometimes they didn't come.

* * * *

It was the heat that woke her. It certainly wasn't dreams of her and Vincent, pawing at each other like animals. Despite the air conditioning blasting in the car, she'd sweat through her clothes and her face was sticking to the car's leather seat. That would wake anyone.

After a few blinks and a yawn, she got her bearings and saw the Accord was parked at a TD bank off the I-95 exit to Hightstown, New Jersey. Her iPhone said it was 8:00 a.m. They'd driven through the night. That didn't account for all of the time, so Vincent must have parked and slept behind the wheel at some point. Where was he?

Smacking her lips, feeling parched, she grabbed the bottled water in the console's drink holder, and took a sip. The AC blasted, and the engine hummed. He'd left her alone in a running car, asleep. She frowned, a little pissed, then felt a jolt of adrenaline that had her screwing the bottle's top back on and tearing at her seatbelt buckle.

This was her shot to escape.

Vincent opened the driver's side door and sat next to her. "You snore." He tossed a money bag into the back seat.

"Blow me." Her heart skipped a beat, as anger—at herself—flushed her system. She'd missed a prime opportunity to escape. She wanted to scream. Worse yet, she worried that she'd *unconsciously* done it on purpose.

"If you need to use the bathroom, do it now," he said. Avery grimaced, opening the door, but in truth she was excited because she saw this as her mulligan. Maybe she could slip out a window, steal a car, or hitchhike. When Vincent turned the car off and followed her up the paved walkway to the bank, her heart sank, despite the cool and moist air, the blue sky, the birds chirping in the trees. A perfect day, if not for the colossal shit show of her life. She was due the universe cutting her slack. *Why couldn't Vincent have just stayed in the car?* "I'm going to want a location on the files before we leave here," he said.

Avery kept walking, eyes front. "I've known you for three days now, Vincent, and I think you've said the word "files" a million times already. You're a broken record."

"It's called message discipline."

"It's called a pain in my ass," she said under her breath.

She walked into the bank hoping the bathroom might give her a way out. But nope. No window, and Vincent was making a big production of waiting outside the bathroom door, so there would be no slipping away. The man wanted a location for the files, and she had none to give him.

She peed, finished up in the stall, and then went to the sink, feeling dejected and a mess. Splashing water on her face, she did her best to clean up, and fix her hair. Face dripping water, she stared at her reflection in the mirror, wincing when she saw her colorfully bruised jaw. What the hell was she supposed to do now? A discrete knock on the bathroom door told her she'd been in here too long. Vincent was getting antsy.

Fine, she thought. When in doubt, go shopping.

He'd taken money out of the bank. She'd make him spend it. They smelled, so even Vincent couldn't argue the delay. Shopping also gave her an address to plug into the GPS, without showing her true plan to the Feds. She was close now. Millie was within reach. If she could just play Vincent a little bit longer, her sister might yet survive.

Drying off, she left the bathroom, ignoring him as he followed her back into the parking lot like a duckling. Once inside the car, she programmed the Accord's GPS for a hotel in Jersey City. Vincent was all eyes.

"The files are at a hotel?" he said.

"We need clothes, a shower, and a meal for where we're going."

"Why?" He seemed confused. Was she the only one that could smell them?

"We're disgusting, Vincent. Where we're going, we need to clean up. And no, I still won't give you the exact location of the files, because you'll tell Benton, and then Dante's snitches will know where to find me."

"Oh, ye of little faith." He didn't look happy, but he started the car and drove off, leaving Avery to count her blessings.

A half hour later, he pulled into the hotel's lot as Avery retrieved the money bag in the back seat, opening it. Over ten thousand dollars was inside. She took out approximately one thousand and held it to him. "Get us a room. I've got some shopping to do."

Vincent took the money bag and returned the money to the bag. "I'd never see you again."

That was the whole point. "Foiled again." She stepped out of the car.

Walking into the familiar lobby together, Avery stopped a moment and faced the atrium of various stores. It was loud, the stores expensive, and the hotel's concierge was behind them. Last time she'd been here, she had money to burn, and was in the dark about most things about the syndicate. That Avery, the one with the husband and platinum credit card, didn't exist anymore. She'd been retired much like most of Avery's past identities, no more real than the one she used now, with Vincent. Avery had become good at being who she needed to be to get what she wanted. Yesterday, it was dutiful wife. Today, she was schemer, double-crossing snitch. And the only thing those two identities had in common was someone was bankrolling her. Today it was the Feds.

Avery led Vincent to the most expensive store in the mall.

An hour later, weighed down with bags of clothes and accessories, Vincent arranged for a room using fake identification and cash. A bellhop took Avery's bags and led them to the elevator. The fifth floor arrived, and soon they were in their room, and Vincent was tipping the man.

"Dibs on the shower," Vincent said.

He stripped on the way to the bathroom, and Avery stopped what she was doing to look, memorizing everything; where his hands went, what his fingers looked like as he undid his belt. How he gripped the hem of his T-shirt before he pulled it over his head. By the time he was in the bathroom and the shower was on, she was swaying on her feet, replaying his striptease.

Vincent poked his head out of the bathroom and crooked his head to the side, indicating he wanted her to approach. "Come on." She noted the twinkle in his eye. "You can either join me under the water or sit on the toilet. Your choice, but I'm not letting you out of my sight."

His smile told her his preference, and if it were another world, and she were another girl, she'd have taken him up on it. "I'm not a voyeur." She wasn't sure she'd survive watching him take a shower.

His smile widened. "Then be a participant. You can soap me up."

"No!" She waved him off, hoping he'd see reason.

"Get in here." He looked as if he were about to hunt her down.

"Are you naked?"

He chuckled. "Do you doubt it?"

She narrowed her eyes. "Well, get in the shower first, and then I'll come in."

"Get in the bathroom first, and then I'll get in the shower."

She didn't argue anymore, because it was clear he didn't trust her to stay put, which he shouldn't, but it was still irritating. "This is ridiculous. Get in the shower. Come on, hurry up." She stepped into the bathroom, keeping her eyes averted as he laughed, yucking it up. He soon stepped into the opaque glass-fronted shower stall, and under the shower's spray, and no, Avery couldn't resist the urge to watch. She voyeured her ass off.

She wasn't sure which was more arousing, watching Vincent soap up, or watching him rinse his nooks and crannies. The man was thorough. She had to give him that. Soon, she was sweating, and it was hard to breathe, and her lips were so damn dry she gave up licking them, and simply kept her lower lip in her mouth. By the time he spoke, she was wiggling on the toilet seat, and physically restraining herself from busting into the shower stall to molest him.

"Benton's chomping at the bit," he said. "Wants the location now."

"Where is he?"

"Down the hall—"

"What?" Panic distracted her from her swollen nether regions. "What happened to keeping a low profile?"

"—and our backup team is down one floor."

"If this hotel is crawling with Feds, Dante will find out, and soon. The news will travel like wildfire." Her tone should have been sharper. She should have devoted more time and effort to chastising him for going against her directives, but *damn*... She couldn't seem to care about anything but what she was seeing behind that shower stall glass. It would replay in her dreams tonight, for years to come, but now, it was testing her control. The man was too damn sexy.

He turned off the water and opened the door, triggering Avery to stand and pivot out of the bathroom. Naked, wet, and willing? *No way* she couldn't reach out and touch him.

She upended the shopping bags on the bed and stared at their contents until they came into focus, and she was no longer imaging Vincent's hot body. Black everything. Jeans, leather boots to replace Vincent's sneakers, underwear, shirts, and leather jackets to hide their weapons. These clothes would allow them to blend where they were going.

Vincent walked up behind her, a towel wrapped around his waist. His bandage was gone, revealing an angry-looking, scabbed wound on his side. "They look expensive."

"They are."

"It will look horrible on my expense report."

"We need clothes." He smelled of soap, and stood so close she felt herself swaying toward his heat. He stepped closer, until his naked chest pressed against her back, and his breath warmed her cheek.

"Clothes are overrated," he whispered, then rubbed his lips against her temple. When her breath caught, he chuckled and stepped to her side, lifting the men's leather jacket. "Nice."

Simple. Quality. They'd blend, and that's all that mattered.

"My turn to shower," she said.

Vincent dropped his towel, and reached for his clothes. She squealed, pivoting toward the bathroom door. "I'll order breakfast."

His amusement shaded his tone, but she was beyond caring. She needed to hide, so she slammed the bathroom door behind her, and leaned against it. Flushed, heart pounding, she told herself not to open the door again, yet, she wanted to see what she was missing.

Him. Naked.

She turned, palms against the door, the one thing standing between her and ecstasy. Then her gaze fell on her rings, on the bruises and cuts on her knuckles, and she immediately knew *one* thing didn't stand in her way. A lifetime of being on the wrong side of the law stopped her. What she had to do to rescue Millie stopped her, but most of all, what she'd done, what Dante made her... That stood between her and Vincent more than any door could, more than anything, and like that jackass chasing the carrot on a stick, Vincent would always be out of reach.

Hot and bothered, Avery turned on the shower and stripped to her skin, forcing herself not to replay the images of Vincent naked. She kicked her clothes into a corner, and then stepped under the warm spray, scrubbing and soaping until she washed away the dried blood and sweat, and it swirled down the drain. Her bruises and cuts had bloomed over the last couple of days. They ached and were still sore to the touch. Water stung her abrasions, and her jaw still clicked from the sucker punch. She'd grown rusty since she'd left Dante, mostly because she'd tried to pretend she wasn't the person he'd helped to create. That meant she'd stopped training. It had been a mistake and these injuries were the result. Three years ago, no one could have touched her…and survived.

When she could no longer control her thoughts, when she not only thought of Vincent naked in the shower, but thought of how it felt to be in his arms, his lips on her neck, on her breasts, holding her, bringing her so close to climax… She turned off the warm water and blasted herself with the cold. Soon, she could think again, and ended her frigid shower feeling more able to handle what was on the other side of the door.

She wrapped herself in the terry cloth robe hanging from a hook on the wall, and then opened the door, stepping into the bedroom. She smelled the food before she saw it; eggs, bacon, home fries, toast and there was coffee on a tray. It rested on the bed, where Vincent ate, fully dressed. She accepted the coffee from his outstretched hand, and sipped as she sat on the bed's edge. "Thanks."

He bit into a piece of toast, lounging, and then wiped his hands on a napkin. "Nice robe." He wiggled his brows, glancing at the belt, hinting she could take it off and give him a show. Like he'd given her? Avery wouldn't survive the attempt. Though heaven knows she was tempted—extremely tempted—but her cold shower had woken her to more things than an ill-advised romp in a government paid hotel room.

If Avery couldn't give Vincent the slip, he'd become collateral damage in this battle between her and Dante. In fact, the guy was doing his best to position himself for that fall, urging her to include him in her schemes, her confidence. She needed to resist harder.

He was splitting her allegiances.

Millie had to come first. The Feds and Vincent had to be an afterthought, and that meant Avery had to resist Vincent's siren call to trust him, no matter how tempting.

"You look nervous." He was smiling, looking naughty.

She sipped more coffee, and then put it on the tray, picking up a fork. "You make me nervous."

His smile widened. "In a good way?"

"Maybe nervous isn't the right word." She shoveled eggs into her mouth, telling herself to shut up. Yes, she wanted Vincent. Wanted him enough to think about long, lingering sex. In the shower, on the bed, standing against the wall…anywhere, really. Avery couldn't remember the last time a person made her feel this way, because nobody ever had, and he did it effortlessly. "You make me want things I can't have."

Damn. She'd said it aloud.

Suddenly, Vincent wasn't laughing. He was staring. She held the robe closed at her throat, and bit into a slice of bacon, fearing she'd open her mouth again. There was something about Vincent that made her default to honesty, and it scared her, because telling Vincent the truth could get them both killed.

Chapter 13

He noted Avery's shaking hand with dismay. Delicate, battered, she seemed to collect bruises. The one on her jaw was almost as green as her eyes now, though it was fading. Her knuckles were raw, scabbing and deep purple. They had to hurt. And she was upset. He was upset, too.

She'd said he made her want things.

Well, she made Vincent want things, too, things he hadn't wanted since forever. Since before Madeline. It was folly. He liked to think his ex-wife had flushed those ambitions from his system, but here he sat on a bed in a hotel room, feeling emotions that had long been dormant. Emotions he didn't even want to name.

"Hey," he said. "It's late morning, day three of our search for the Coppola files. You're overdue to produce another excuse for why you're not handing them over." He glanced at his watch, and then nodded. "Yup. Overdue." He threw her an expectant smile, and then waited for her response.

She blushed and looked away. "We need to run an errand first, then you'll get your files."

And bam. An excuse, with barely any hesitation. She was getting good at this. *An errand.* Benton wasn't going to be happy. He could picture him now in his hotel room, pacing, wondering why Vincent wasn't texting him the location. In Vincent's estimation, that Benton wasn't calling for an update made him fucking Superman, because even Vincent's impatience was off the charts. "And will you be sharing the details of this "errand" we'll be running?"

She adjusted herself on the bed's edge, and quickly cleaned her plate, making him wonder if her appetite had returned, or if she was keeping her mouth full to have the excuse of delaying an answer. After she'd swallowed, patted her mouth with the cloth napkin, she took a sip of coffee. Only then did she looked at him.

"When we're in the car," she said, "I'll program the GPS. You will *not* share our destination with Benton, or I'll bail. Got that?" She widened her eyes, and her intensity told him it was a deal breaker. "I mean it, Vincent."

He sighed, thinking he was willing to lose this battle if it meant he'd win the war. "I want Coppola implicated and in jail. If this errand gives me that, I'm okay with it." She couldn't hide her relief. "When do we go?"

"One-thirty. The man I need to see won't be available until then."

Vincent grimaced. That meant hanging around the hotel room for two and a half hours. Two and a half hours of him not seducing her and wanting to. Two and a half hours of wondering if she'd kiss him back if he reached for her. Two and a half hours of hell.

"Fine," he said.

"Thank you." She nudged a wet lock behind her ear, sipping coffee, looking like just another woman who might be enjoying a vacation at a posh hotel. For her sake, he wished it was true, but it wasn't. She was burning her candle at both ends, and he was concerned. Shouldn't she be freebasing ibuprofen, taking ice baths, and pampering herself? Instead, she acted as if it was just another day in the life. It bothered him, making him fear Coppola conditioned her to take pain for granted.

"Did Coppola beat you?" Just the idea of someone putting violent hands on her filled him with rage.

Avery startled, paused, and then shook her head. "Not his style." Vincent felt a wave of relief run through him, and it was only then that he realized how badly he'd needed to hear her denial. "Dante isn't a hands-on kind of guy. He has others do his dirty work."

Shit. "And did they?"

"None of your business." She narrowed her eyes, as if offended he'd asked, yet there was no outrage in her tone. It sounded to him like she simply didn't want to talk about it, but he knew he wouldn't rest easy until he got that answer. He was having a hard time matching up the Avery he'd come to know, and the one in her files, who was raised in a crime family, who chose to marry the man responsible for her family's massacre. Physical abuse would explain it; Stockholm Syndrome. Otherwise, Avery didn't make sense. Deming would know. That's what her voodoo was all about; taking people apart and predicting their behavior.

"Why'd you leave your husband?" His ex, Madeline, left for money and social status, or at least that's what he'd told himself. Avery lost both of those things when she'd left Coppola, but she'd left him anyway.

She sipped her coffee, agitated. "That's personal, and you're a Fed. When this is over, I don't want my secrets used to fatten that thin file you showed me back at the sheriff's office."

"I wouldn't do that." Probably.

Avery must have seen his internal waffling, because she cracked a smile. "You're horrible, but I shouldn't be surprised. Your life is your job. Have you ever had a successful relationship? I mean, other than with a gun?"

Hmm. She made him wonder if she had access to that same voodoo Deming used, because she'd zeroed in on his flaws without noticeable effort. Deming called her a quick study. As much as he was having a hard time understanding her decisions, Avery didn't seem to have difficulty filling in all his blanks. He blamed his inability to understand women; not their priorities, their mercurial moods. Lots of guys didn't understand women, but he seemed to have a bigger deficit than most.

"My ex-wife said she loved me," he said, "and then cheated on me because she'd missed me so much." He narrowed his eyes, curious if Avery would sympathize with his ex-wife or him. With women, it was always a coin toss. "She couldn't handle me being away from her while I did my tours in Afghanistan, but then married an officer two weeks after our divorce was final, who then went to Afghanistan. She had the loyalty of a flea." Avery compressed her lips and batted her eyelashes, the image of sympathy.

"She was a fool," she said.

He sipped his coffee, feeling embarrassment scratch at his pride. "I've bared my soul. Your turn."

"That was your soul?" She snorted, making him smile. "Your ex wasn't worthy of you. Better luck next time."

"There will be no next time." He shook his head. "I'm not looking for love."

"Men rarely are."

"And you?" he said, more curious than sensible.

She avoided his gaze. "I have other priorities." Setting her cup aside, she stood, and gathered up her newly-purchased clothes.

"When this operation is over, you'll be free. Have you thought of what you'll do?" He braced himself to hear that she'd want to settle down, maybe marry, have kids. It made him uncomfortable thinking of her with another man.

She shook her head, upset for some reason. "What are you doing, Vincent?" When he had no ready answer, she glared at him. "Just stop it. Okay?" She turned and disappeared into the bathroom with her clothes.

What *was* he doing? He feared the real question was *what had he done?* He'd become personally invested in Avery and wanted her happy. No, he'd done much worse. He wanted to be in her life. When had he become such a dumb ass?

Fifteen minutes later, she came out of the bathroom, fully dressed, acting as if their previous conversation had never happened. When she flopped on the second double bed, as far from him as the hotel room allowed, she turned on the television full blast, aiming the clicker like a weapon. And that's how she remained for the next two hours while Vincent worried his problem, pacing and climbing the walls.

When he finally had reached his patience's limit, and putting his fist through the television seemed like his only recourse, Avery turned the set off. "One-thirty." She looked at her new gold watch. "Time to go."

"Where?" He wasn't in the mood to coddle her, and his tone and expression must have tipped her off, because she refused to meet his gaze.

"I know a guy," she said.

"Enough, Avery. At least tell me *what* we're doing."

She adjusted her leather jacket, making sure it hid her gun and knife sheaths. "I need something to gain access to the files. We're getting it now."

"What?" His belligerence had his arms folded, and him glaring.

"A…key."

"You sure? You don't sound sure."

"A key. I'm sure. Okay?" Clearly agitated, she nonetheless took his aggression, without pushing back. "Listen, we have to go *now,* otherwise we might miss him."

"Him. So, a "him" has a key. Fine. That's more intel than I had before. We're making progress." He dropped a fifty on the bed's side table for housekeeping, and then headed for the door. "I like your shiny stuff."

Avery looked at him over her shoulder, confused. He flicked a wrist bangle. "The gold seems more your style than those clunky silver rings." Avery curled her fingers, but that was the only indication that she'd heard him, or cared what he thought as they stepped into the hotel's hall.

With his tone deafness with women, he supposed her reaction meant he'd probably made a faux pas somehow. Avery saw him as the enemy. Why would she care what he thought about her bracelet? She probably hated him. It did beg a question, however.

Why did he care so damn much what she thought of him?

Chapter 14

She gave Vincent directions to the restaurant, and as they drove through Jersey City, it left her feeling a terrible nostalgia. It weighed her down as familiar streets, stores, sights, and sounds of the neighborhood triggered memories, good and bad. This place had been her world, where her childhood and married life had been spent. When she'd left three years ago, she'd promised herself she'd never return, because coming back meant embracing uncertainty. It would mean accepting Dante, becoming like her father before her, so she'd run, and put her life and Millie's on the line to do it. Now, three years later, only the threat to her sister's life could get her back here, and all this felt like her fault…but it wasn't. None of it was her fault. It was Dante's, and somehow, she'd make him pay.

The GPS directed Vincent to pull off the busy city street, onto a side road, then into a nearby Italian restaurant's parking lot. "Pull into that space," she said, "back into it." It gave her full view of the street, and the restaurant's parking lot.

"Quick getaway?" Vincent arched a brow, smiling. He wasn't taking this seriously, and, why should he? She'd kept him in the dark, so he didn't know better, because she wanted him safe, but feared his interference. This was her fault.

"Listen." She didn't open the door, just sat in the parked car, peering down the street, scanning passersby's faces. She was grateful not to see anyone she knew. "Maybe you should stay in the car." The moment he was seen with her, he'd have a target on his back. "Walking in there exposes you to certain dangers that you can't understand." Vincent saw her through the lens of law enforcement, but couldn't fully understand how the syndicate worked. Not internally. He saw her as *the daughter of,* or *the wife of,* when what she really was would curl his hair. There were people in that restaurant that knew who she really was, suspected what she'd done, and more would flood the restaurant once they knew she was there.

"I'm not leaving your side," he said.

"I won't run."

"I never thought you would." When she grimaced, he shrugged. "I meant from here. The restaurant. I can see you're nervous. Just know that I'll protect you in there, Avery." He tilted her chin up with a finger, and forced her to meet his gaze. *"With my life."*

"Because you're a Fed." His job.

"Because you're you." Then he pressed a gentle kiss to her lips, and she felt it to her toes. When he lifted his head, she felt raw and exposed, and Vincent wasn't helping, because he seemed equally unnerved by the effect of their kiss. "Are we about to do something stupid, Avery?" She nodded. "But it's necessary?" She nodded again.

"I'm sorry," she said. And she was. "I'm sorry you're messed up in this, and I'm sorry things are so complicated, but… Vincent, I'm doing the best I can."

He nodded. "Okay. Then let's get this done." He kicked up a cheek and winked. "I'll follow your lead."

He really was very sweet. "Thanks." She dropped her forehead to his chest, unable to hold his gaze, because other than Millie, no one had ever given her this level of trust before. He was literally putting his life in her hands, trusting that the risk she took was worth the payout. It was, but maybe not to him. And for that, she *was* sorry. "I don't want to see you get hurt." She pushed off his chest, needing to make him see reason. "I really wish you'd stay in the car. People around me get hurt, Vincent. Yeah, you're the toughest sonavabitch I've ever met, and if ever I wanted someone with me in a tight jam, you'd be it, but…." He was watching her with amused curiosity, as if she was teasing, rather than spilling her heart out to him. Suddenly, she wanted to smack him upside the head, and she was yelling. "Once we step into the restaurant, people will connect you with me. *Forever.* Somewhere, in some file, there will always be a photo of you, of us, walking into this restaurant. When they can't find *me*, they'll come looking for you, thinking I'm with you. *Forever, Vincent.*" She searched his gaze, hoping he could comprehend the enormity of that danger.

"Is this how people from Jersey propose?" Vincent's brows lifted, as he pretended to be surprised. "We step into the restaurant, and we're together forever?"

He shocked a laugh out of her, or maybe it was a sob. "What am I going to do with you?"

He dropped a kiss on her lips. "Let's talk about that later, when you don't have to worry your ex-husband is trying to kill you."

Was he saying he wanted a future with her? That was impossible. If she survived negotiations with her ex, odds were, she'd still have to run. "Okay." It was nice to pretend.

His face blossomed into a full-blown smile, and all Avery could think was...damn. She liked him. More than liked him. She pulled him into a kiss, and he took control, dragging her over the console to cradle her in his arms, squeezing and kissing her like he would never let her go. When he broke for air, he pressed his face to her neck, tasting her skin, nipping at her jaw, and her whole body trembled in his arms.

"I am a bad, bad, *bad* person," she sighed. If she were good, she'd confess all and trust him to help her, but she'd been burned too badly, and trust was a luxury neither she nor Millie could afford.

He chuckled, his hand cupping her ass. "I like you just the way you are."

Guilt had her pushing out of his arms, and hurrying from the car. If they were going to do this, they needed to get it over with. The suspense was killing her. Vincent must have been feeling impatient, too, because he beat her to the restaurant's entryway, grabbing its ornate door knob. He paused to give the equally ornate, carved door the appreciative glance it deserved.

"Pete's dad carved it back when he lived in Italy," she said.

"It's amazing craftsmanship." Vincent opened the door, indicating with a nod she should enter first, but they walked into the dimly lit, hostess area, nearly attached at the hip. A sparkly, crystal chandelier sent fractals of light across the red carpet, and dark wood wainscoting. All familiar, though the hostess was nowhere to be found. Avery couldn't remember a time where the hostess' desk was empty, and it felt a bit shocking. After all, the desk hid a loaded weapon large enough to fell an elephant.

"When they moved their business to the states, Pete's dad took it off their restaurant there, and brought the door with them," she said.

Vincent's hand was on her waist as they waited for the hostess. Soon, a blond, young, woman wearing a tight skirt and feminine, flouncy blouse, waved from the back of the restaurant, and smiled. Avery smiled back, while noting that tables were still lined up in familiar diagonal rows, still draped in white linen, and topped with cloth napkins, stemware, and silverware. Nothing had changed here. Still thirty tables, mostly filled with middle-aged adults. The restaurant wasn't very large, but it was still bustling. Always had been.

"Who's Pete?" Vincent whispered, watching the hostess's slow, hips-swaying approach that Avery ascribed to inordinately high heels.

"Pete's the owner." Avery attempted to reacclimate to this place, to breathe through her nerves. She'd never thought she'd come back here, so the smells of sauce and pasta on to boil hit her with a powerful wave of nostalgia. Memories returned of tables brimming with good food, surrounded by family and friends, and sounds of loud, raucous laughter. So many happy moments had happened here. It made her miss her parents, her cousins, her aunts and uncles. So many gone, murdered.

Being back in this restaurant was breaking her heart.

She was risking her life being here, but she needed to speak with Pete. And his cook, Vito? His Shrimp Scampi was to die for.

The hostess finally arrived, out of breath and smiling brightly, and then stepped behind the waist-height, wooden desk. Avery hadn't see anyone she knew in the dining area, so she felt it safe enough to direct her attention to the hostess. A new girl. Up close, Avery saw the blond came from a bottle, and her skirt showed more leg than allowed at St. Bernadette's Parochial School down the street. *Totally* Pete's type.

Avery reached behind the desk, and wrapped her hand around the familiar weight of a 500 Smith & Wesson revolver. Some things never changed, she thought, hiding the weapon under her leather jacket. The hostess startled, and opened her mouth repeatedly, like a guppy.

"Sweetheart," Avery said to the blond, "don't ever use this gun. It will knock you on your ass and the recoil will smash your pretty face. Everyone will get a good laugh, but you'll be looking through shiners for a month. We'll seat ourselves. And don't worry. I'll return the revolver before we leave." Avery walked deeper into the restaurant, glad that Vincent stayed close. Things were about to get hairy.

"What are you doing?" he said, sounding more casual than he had to be feeling. A 500 Smith & Wesson had a way of making anyone nervous.

"I announced my arrival," Avery said, "and stopped anyone from using this to shoot us. It won't be long now." Other than a slight elevation of his brows, he seemed calm as she chose a corner booth. It allowed both she and Vincent to sit with their backs to the wall, facing the restaurant's entrance. Once she was positioned, she put the revolver on her lap for easy access.

"We're here for a key, right?" he said.

"Yeah." A dark-haired waitress arrived at the table, her curls in a high ponytail. She was young and unsure, and approached reluctantly. Avery smiled. "Two Shrimp Scampi's and a pot of coffee." The girl nodded and then rushed into the kitchen. "You're going to love the Scampi. Family recipe."

He smiled, but it didn't seem authentic. "*Family*, huh?" She supposed he was referring to the restaurant's syndicate connection. Well, it wasn't as if she could deny it, so she let the remark hang in the air between them. "I love Scampi. Will we survive long enough to enjoy it?"

She avoided his gaze. "Too soon to tell."

"If these people are so dangerous, why would you trust their food? They might poison you."

"I can think of worse ways to die than by Mama Patron's recipe for Shrimp Scampi," she said. "But they'd assume if I had the nerve to come here, it would be sanctioned by Dante. Don't worry. If we die here, it won't be by poison." Her mouth watered thinking about the Scampi. It would be her last chance to taste it. After this meeting, she'd be ostracized, never welcomed again. Or dead.

His cheek kicked up. "Is it strange that I find your assurances comforting?"

Avery lifted the large revolver to the table's top, and covered it with her napkin, her finger on the trigger just in case bad luck came sooner than even she feared. Some of Dante's men were in the kitchen. "Be ready. You'll either taste the best Scampi of your life, or contract killers are about to spill from the kitchen, and we're about to have a gunfight with people who have never lost."

Vincent followed her example, slipping his gun from his holster, setting it on the table, and covering it with his cloth napkin. "I vote Scampi."

Her upper lip broke out into a sweat, and her heart raced as she stared at the kitchen's swinging doors. "Ah, Vincent? I wanted to thank you."

He also kept his gaze on the kitchen doors. "Yeah? For what?"

Lips compressed, she knew she should tell him now. They might not have a later. "Last three days. You being there for me. I'm not used to that, and it means a lot."

He nodded, but kept his eyes fixed on the doors. "Avery?"

"Yeah?"

"I'm making love to you before I die, so we're not dying. Not today, anyway."

She smiled and felt her body flush with joy.

Then the kitchen doors opened and she shut that shit down. The key to getting Millie back just walked in the room.

* * * *

People were staring, and normally, Vincent wouldn't have a problem with that, but he and Avery were hiding guns under napkins on the table. It was awkward. He didn't know whether to expect sirens, or bullets, and if that wasn't bad enough, the tiny twitch on Avery's right eyelid was going batshit crazy.

When their waitress and an older man, about five nine, balding, mid-sixties, wearing a tan suit, burst through the kitchen doors, Vincent heard Avery pull back the hammer on the Smith & Wesson. When more wait staff came through and served them coffee, two plates of Scampi, bread, salad, and dipping sauce, the man held back, watching them watch him. Avery lifted her fork just as he pivoted to the hostess desk, and picked up a phone.

Her moan of pleasure, caught Vincent's full attention. "How can you eat?" he said.

She licked her lips, and swirled her fork in the pasta using her left hand, the one not clutching a revolver under a napkin. "You'll never taste a better Scampi."

He surveilled the room, didn't see any movement beyond the everyday, so he also ate, using his left hand, like Avery was, which wasn't easy. But no way was he taking his finger off the trigger. Avery kept her eye on the guy, who now had his back to them.

"Oh, wow." It was Vincent's turn to moan. "This has ruined me for other Scampi."

"Right? I told you. It's the gravy." She nodded solemnly, lifting the pasta to her mouth. "Better than sex." He coughed as food went down the wrong way. "You okay?" she said. Her concern, however, didn't interrupt her food orgy.

"You've been doing it wrong," he croaked, doing his best to breathe again.

"Hmm?"

"If you think this Scampi is better than sex." He speared another shrimp. "You've been doing it wrong." He popped it into his mouth, saw the guy hang up the phone, and heard Avery put her fork down. They both had eyes on the guy as he made his way to the table.

After a quick, if self-conscious glance over his shoulder, the man sat across from Avery. "Don't forget to return my revolver when you leave," he said. "It has sentimental value." He placed a smartphone on the table.

"I know who gave it to you." She waved her fork between Vincent and the man in the tan suit. "Pete, Vincent, Vincent, Pete." She speared a shrimp. "You won't mind if I keep eating. It's been a while."

"Three years." He indicated Vincent with a tilt of his head, not looking at him. "Vincent, huh?"

"I'm her bodyguard," he said.

Pete laughed, as if Vincent had made a joke. "Is he for real?"

Avery grabbed Pete's phone with her left hand, and had her own laugh when she got the passcode on the first try. "You really need to change your passcode, Pete. Your birth date is too obvious." Pete slowly lowered his hands to his lap.

Vincent adjusted the napkin to show the muzzle of his gun, aimed at Pete. "Keep your hands where I can see them." Pete splayed his hands on the tablecloth, revealing a pinky ring like Avery's.

"Control your bodyguard, Avery."

"Now where would the fun in that be?" She kept her gaze on his phone. Her thumb worked fast, typing something. "Now pay attention. I'm inputting my number into your contact list. Get it to Dante. I need to speak with him." Then she tossed the phone back on the table and picked up her fork again. "This is delicious." She speared the pasta, and twisted her fork. "You should patent the recipe. You'd make millions. Maybe you could finally get that promised place in Boca for your mom. Get her out of that steaming kitchen." She lifted the pasta to her mouth, and the way she enjoyed it was one of the most sensuous things Vincent had ever seen. Food porn.

"Mom retired last year. Heart attack. She's in a home nearby." Pete shrugged. "I visit her every day. That seems to make her happy."

Vincent looked between Avery and Pete. From all of Avery's earlier warnings, and their precaution of pointing guns at this man, Vincent had expected more than conversation over Scampi. Where were the nest of contract killers? So far, there'd only been a blond and a rude guy. This meet was more family squabble, then gun fight. Though, as promised, the food was great. He took another bite.

"She wanted Boca, Pete. She earned it," she said. Yup, sure *sounded* like a family argument.

"What do you care? You left." Pete squirmed. "Look. I got things to do. I can't do what you want."

She narrowed her eyes. "What?"

Pete shook his head. "Things are different. Mr. Coppola's circle is smaller now."

Avery licked her lips, wiped her mouth with her napkin, purposefully revealing the 500 Smith & Wesson. No, her move wasn't subtle, but it was effective. Pete sat up straighter. "You'll give him my number."

Pete grimaced. "Why would Dante want anything to do with you? He has everything he wants. He has Millie. In a few years, that girl will be old enough to marry. She doesn't have your skills—"

"Shut up, Pete." Avery blanched.

"But you proved teachable." He snickered, wiggling his eyebrows in a crass manner, just in case his meaning wasn't crystal clear. "Millie will make Dante a good wife." Then he dropped his smile, and grabbed Vincent's steak knife, lunging for her. "Traitor!"

Avery buried her fork in Pete's wrist before the knife even got near her, and it flew, skittering toward a neighboring table. Pete didn't scream, but rather clutched his wrist, closed his eyes and inhaled sharply through his nose. Avery pushed her plate away, as if taking a moment to gather her composure.

Pete pulled the fork from his wrist, and placed it on Avery's plate.

"Give Dante my message," she said, her right eye twitching. "And you won't see me again. Don't make me come back, Pete. We clear?"

Vincent couldn't take his eyes off them, and his finger felt heavy on his gun's trigger. Pete said Dante had Millie, and Avery was anything but surprised.

"Why me?" Pete had grown pale; fear and pain having replaced his arrogance. "Why pick on me?"

Avery produced a smile both kind and sad. "Because, Pete, you have the best Scampi in town." She scooted from behind the table, gun pointed at Pete. "Put lunch on Dante's tab. I'm sure he's good for it."

Pete bled on the white tablecloth, and he was sweating. "I'll get the message to him." The smell of fear and Scampi would forever be linked in Vincent's mind.

Her gaze hardened. "And move your mom to Boca. She's earned it."

Vincent grabbed her elbow and hustled her to the exit. She paused at the hostess desk as Vincent opened the door, peering outside. Emptying the revolver's cylinder of bullets, she tossed them over her shoulder, then inexplicably replaced the gun back behind the desk.

"It was a present from his mom," she explained, hurrying outside. "We don't need it, and it does have a kick, which truthfully," she scanned the parking lot, "is probably why his mother gave it to him. Pete is a prick, if you hadn't noticed."

He was remembering the fork in his wrist. "I noticed a lot of things." He hurried her toward the car. "Turned me off Scampi for life."

Her face pinched, and he saw her defensiveness. "He suggested my ten-year-old sister *marry* Dante. Who do you think put that idea into his head?" She clenched her teeth, shaking her head. "Dante is playing mind games."

"Are you saying Pete lied? That he does have Coppola's ear?"

She scoffed, hurrying past cars, moving toward the edge of the lot where he'd parked. "Of course, Pete lied."

"And Dante has Millie." She didn't deny it. "What about the key? For the files?"

She glanced at him. "Pete *was* the key. And I already told you. There are no files."

"Dammit, Avery." All the missing pieces fell into place. All Avery's weird comments, odd choices, and *it doesn't matters* now made sense. This had always been about Millie. It was never about the files. "You should have said something. Why didn't you say something?" He pulled out his phone, needing to call Benton and tell him Millie had been kidnapped.

Avery held out her hand, avoiding his gaze as he paced next to her. "I have to sit down, or I'll fall down. Give me the keys," she said, swaying on her feet. She'd lost all the color in her cheeks, though sweat beaded on her forehead.

"I have to read Benton in." He handed her the car keys. Benton wouldn't take this news well, and Vincent wasn't sure how to control the narrative. There'd be consequences for Avery's deception.

She opened the car, and slid inside. "I know. Do it." She slammed the door behind her, leaving him to the chore.

"*Shit.*" He turned his back, attempting to hide his unease as he dialed. He still wasn't sure what to say to his team leader. When Benton's clipped greeting sounded in his ear, Vincent's stomach clenched as he hesitated to speak.

"Modena?"

The sedan's engine turned over. Vincent pivoted toward the car, and saw she'd slipped behind the wheel, and was now driving away. Vincent lunged for the door knob. It was locked. He slammed his palm against the side window. "Stop, Avery! Open the door now!"

Eyes forward, she peeled out, showering him with grit and dirt from the parking lot's gravel surface. Then she was on the road, driving off, him running after her. When he reached the main drag, he slowed his gait, feeling like a fool.

Benton was still on the line, yelling. Vincent pressed the phone to his ear. "She's gone. Avery played us from the beginning. We came to Jersey because this is where her sister is. Millie was kidnapped by Dante Coppola."

"Did she give you the files?" Benton said.

Vincent winced. "You're not hearing me. There are no files. Avery spent two days telling us she didn't have them, before she flipped her story. Now, she's saying they don't exist again. I'm thinking we need to believe her this time. The files are a false lead, Benton. I'm sorry." Benton swore up a blue streak, and there seemed no end to it, though the jist was he didn't want to believe Vincent's conclusion. "Listen, I'm stranded in Jersey City, and she has ten thousand dollars of FBI money in the trunk. She's not thinking clearly, and I don't know what she's going to do. We need to find her and stop her before she does something crazy."

There was silence on the other end. Then Vincent heard a sigh of disgust. "Go home, Modena. You're compromised."

"What? No way. Where are you?"

"Twenty minutes away," he said.

"Pick me up!" No fucking way this was ending now. Not this way.

"Go home."

"We get a warrant," Vincent said. "Who cares how we bring Coppola down, as long as we do it? Coppola kidnapped Millie Toner. Are you listening to me? Last I checked, that's a federal crime. Avery is waiting for him to contact her for an exchange. Let's use her phone to track her. Maybe your intel is right. Maybe she's leveraging the files to get Millie back. One way or the other, we get Coppola on kidnapping charges."

There was more silence on the line, and just as Vincent took a breath to continue arguing, Benton sighed. "Give me her number."

He did. "Call me when you get the trace."

Vincent disconnected the line, slipped his phone back into his pocket, and then started walking. He couldn't wait here. He had no idea what Pete would do, maybe call in his cavalry, but Vincent didn't want to wait around to find out.

Dante Coppola kidnapped Avery's sister. Damn. Looking back, he supposed she'd tried to tell him in so many ways; warning him that Millie had to come first, her erratic behavior after meeting "Fingers" Pinnella. He wished she'd trusted him enough to confide in him. He wished a lot of things, but mostly he wished he didn't feel so betrayed.

Chapter 15

Hours later, Avery entered the dilapidated hourly hotel rental she'd paid cash for until nine tonight, and slammed the door. The room was tiny, walls thin, the location inconvenient, but it wasn't associated with the syndicate. It was someplace to hide while she waited for Dante's call. She was freaking out, torturing herself about Vincent. She shouldn't have ditched him like that. The restaurant wasn't safe…and she missed him. Surprise, surprise, he'd become her security blanket. Her gorgeous, muscular, tactically proficient, killing machine sort of security blanket. Just being around him made her feel invincible, and as happy as she'd ever been. Now, she was alone, Millie's only hope, feeling inadequate to the task.

Millie. Avery told herself that her sister was a tough little girl. She'd had to be, so Avery made sure of it, but she was still a little girl.

"Shit, shit, shit." She covered her face, squeezing her eyes shut.

She was afraid—of Dante, of what he might do to Millie—but keeping Vincent would have been selfish, and foolish. Fucking Pete confirmed that. Her dragging Vincent into the syndicate's focus was reprehensible. She'd warned Vincent, but he didn't care. Well, she cared. He deserved better than to have to worry about looking over his shoulder for the rest of his life.

Avery paced the tiny room, not wanting to touch anything, thinking about those that had been there before her, renting hourly. And she worried. Her chest was tight with it as she paced and paced, until it was hard to think, and sobs hitched her breath.

It wasn't as if she'd had a choice in the restaurant's parking lot. She'd had to escape. Once Vincent reported she'd "bait and switched" the Feds, he'd be the hammer and Avery the nail. Not to mention, he'd be forced to choose between her and the Feds. No surprise where his loyalty would land.

So, she ran...and felt guilty as sin about it. Dante always said she didn't play well with others. Now it was Vincent's turn to learn that hard truth.

Flopping on the bed, sunlit dust motes kicked up around her. She clutched the money bag, thinking of her tomorrows. If she survived her encounter with Dante, this money would seed her and Millie's future, get them where they needed to go, and set them up until Avery could find a new school for Millie and a new job. Best case scenario. Worse? She wouldn't survive the day, because as much as Avery knew Dante inside and out, he knew Avery. He had set Millie up as an irresistible bait, and was springing his trap. Dante knew Avery would do anything to get her back. She'd be anything, sacrifice anything, to save her sister. All that was left to do was reel Avery in. She was helpless to resist.

Avery wiped a tear, hating her weakness.

Lifting both hands, she studied her six titanium rings. Dull with wear, she could still see their faint inscribed initials. Three years ago, after "graduating" from her "classes" with Dante's contract killers, her ex brought her into a room and told her who'd killed her family five years before.

The six men who'd trained her.

At the time, she couldn't believe it. Of course, now, she knew it was predictable Dante behavior, cruelty for cruelty's sake. He had Coppola men lead these six killers into the training room, where she'd spent the last five years learning how to fight, then those men left, leaving her, Dante, and the six killers behind. One by one, they'd confessed their roles in the Toner Family Massacre as Avery listened, mute with shock. Dante saw these confessions as a graduation present, of sorts, to finally tell Avery who'd killed her family. There were no guilty consciences in that room.

Then Dante gave her a choice: fight them, one on one to the death, and avenge her family, or give up her right for vengeance forever. He was basically telling her to shut up about her family's deaths, or face the consequences. That's when she'd realized two things: Dante had known who'd killed her family all along, and he was simply tired of keeping his secret. Most importantly, there wasn't one person in that room that thought she'd fight them.

It could have been the shock of finally discovering who'd killed her family, or it could have been the rage she'd felt to realize the men who'd beaten her for five years under the guise of "training" were the men who'd killed all that she'd held dear. Whatever had cranked her into action, Avery took Dante up on his offer. Shocked the shit out of everyone. Some were happy, others nervous.

They fought with her weapon of choice, a knife, while Dante's gun aimed at the men, keeping the fights one on one. She didn't kill them. She dominated them, her rage and skill used in the service of justice. And when they lay on the floor, helpless, she humiliated them by removing their rings and placing it on her fingers. Six rings. And when the sixth fight was won, the sixth ring donned, Dante execute them in his signature way, one shot to the skull.

She blamed trauma, exhaustion, her injuries for her lack of empathy, but when the last bullet pierced the last killer's skull, Avery didn't feel a thing. In hindsight, she supposed she should have predicted her ex-husband's savagery. These men were humiliated, so Dante had no use for them anymore, nor could he trust them again. He'd tasked his contract killers to train her, and they'd completed their mission. They created the monster that ended them.

And so began the legend of *The Stinger*. Someone had to take the blame for these deaths.

When Avery escaped Dante, unwilling to remain married to a monster, she became a loose end. The truth could cause him trouble within the syndicate, and yeah, he could call her a liar, but the rings… They were her proof that she'd been there, saw what happened, and he couldn't dispute them.

Dante had to die. It was him or her. Dante knew it. Avery knew it.

But Avery didn't *want* to kill Dante. She didn't want to kill anyone. Scooching down the headboard until she rested her head on the pillow, she covered her face, fighting tears. What was she going to do?

The hotel room's lock clicked.

Avery rolled off the bed, Glock in hand, just as the door flew opened. She greeted her unwelcome visitor on the floor, gun aimed at his center mass.

Vincent.

He held up a key card. Avery didn't move beyond blinking, and then she was breathing again. Gun still trained on him, she attempted to think, to reason why or how he was here. Vincent kept his expression blank, giving no indication of his thoughts, and then he stepped away from the door and allowed it to close behind him. The lock clicked into place, and the sound broke through her shock.

"Don't move," she said.

"I convinced the guy out front to give me your room key." He arched a brow. "Cost me a hundred-dollar bill. If I was you, I'd complain to management."

"He is management." She kept the gun aimed at him, not sure what he wanted from her, other than bringing her into custody, which she could not allow. Her choices were shoot him, tie him up, or hear what he had to say. No matter her choice, she was still lying on a gross floor. Rug burned and sore, she stood, doing her best to avoid touching the carpet more than necessary. "You're a pain in my ass, you know that?" Her dive had irritated the bruise on her knee.

"I knew you'd miss me." He wasn't smiling, or even smirking. He seemed cautious, still holding the key card in the air. His other hand hung at his side, near the gun she knew was tucked in his waistband.

"You alone?" she said, gun hand steady, her expression wiped clean.

"For now."

"When will they arrive?" She licked her lips, her hand tightening on the gun's grip.

"When I call them."

That had her frowning, because it made no sense. *When he called them?* As if Benton and the Feds gave Vincent leeway to negotiate with her. Benton was frothing at the mouth to destroy the Coppola syndicate. Why would he show restraint when he didn't need to? Something was going on, but if Vincent were telling the truth, and Benton was truly disinterested in her now, the Feds might be a problem she could back burner while she saved Millie. It was problematic that Vincent had tracked her down so quickly though. All her reasons for leaving him behind remained, and she feared he'd mess up Millie's rescue, maybe get himself killed.

"How did you find me?" It didn't really matter, she supposed. What mattered was getting rid of him again.

"I'm not just a pretty face. I had your cellphone traced. I'm FBI, remember?"

Crap. She pulled the offending iPhone from her pants pocket, hating that she still needed it because she was waiting on a call from Dante. Avery tossed it on the side table, and then tensed, using both hands to aim the gun when Vincent slipped his key card into his jacket pocket.

"Relax," he said. "I'm not going to shoot you, though you deserve it. What about you?"

She narrowed her eyes, a bit confused. "What about me?"

"You going to shoot me?"

She studied his stance; arms folded over his chest, a simmering rage just below his calm. Hmm. He was a dangerous man, and it was best that she remember that. "I'm thinking about it."

"We had a deal," he said. "A plan." She saw hurt on his face. *Damn.*

"Give me a break." She climbed on the bed, propped herself up against the headboard, while keeping the Glock aimed at his belly. "A deal implies I had a choice." She narrowed her eyes. "I should tie you up."

"Don't try to distract me with sexy talk. I want some answers."

She suppressed a smile. So, he wasn't as angry as he was making himself out to be. "I'm trying to do the right thing, Vincent. You're making it hard to be a good guy."

Her words had him shaking his head, staring at the ceiling, and then finally he rubbed his hands over his face. "Right back at you." He sounded exhausted.

And was making her feel bad. "I'm all she has, Vincent."

If he sympathized, he hid it well. "I don't understand why you think you have to do it alone."

Because Dante knew her secrets. He'd implicate her in his murders, or lie, and say she killed those men. She was *The Stinger*, after all. Her knife fights with them were brutal, bloody, so her DNA was on their bodies. Dante's accusations would hold up in court. "I know you don't understand. I'm sorry." But she couldn't trust him with her truth. Not when Millie needed her. Not when she wasn't the only person who'd suffer consequences.

He indicated the gun, appearing more irritated than afraid. "Have you decided yet? You going to shoot me?"

"I should." She was such a fraud. She couldn't shoot him anymore than she could shoot Millie, and that was a huge problem. She needed to be *The Stinger* again—brutal, heartless—or Millie might die. And Vincent was confusing her. "You should be very, very nervous right now. I'm not right in my head. I… I'm confused."

"Lady, I've been nervous since I laid eyes on you." He'd somehow made his words sound romantic. "And if you're confused, I can only think that's a start. It means you're willing to think things through. Put the gun down and talk to me."

She glared at him. "You can be such an idiot." Avery put the gun on the side table.

"Right back at you." Vincent sat on the bed next to her, propping his back against the headboard, and they both stared at the television's blank screen. "You don't want the Feds' help, so I'm assuming you have a plan that leaves them out of the loop."

"Them? You mean *you*. You're a Fed."

"You know what I mean."

She nodded. "There is only one plan that will work. I drive into the complex, say *here I am, give me Millie,* and then run away with my sister.

The rest is on Dante. He allows me and Millie to leave, or life becomes reacting to whatever he does to stop us."

"So, suicide?"

"If that's what it takes. You have a better plan?"

"We will." And by *we* she knew he meant the Feds. "They'll be here in a half an hour."

"So much for you saying they'll come when you call." She glanced at the door. "Honestly, I'd assumed they were outside the door."

"I hitched a ride and beat them here."

"Sorry about that." That he found her, that he was a target of the syndicate, that she'd ditched him at the restaurant, but she wasn't sorry he was here.

"This is what we do, Avery. Use us. Promise Benton whatever he wants. It will bring you a ton of goodwill and then you and Millie will be safe."

She shook her head. "Those files don't exist, or rather, if they do, I have no idea where they'd be. When "Fingers" gave me Dante's message, I didn't have any choices left and I didn't know what else to do, so I said I knew where they were."

"You should have—"

"Should have, could have, would have. You wanted two things from me. To meet with "Fingers" and you wanted the nonexistent files. One came up snake eyes, so that left the files. I had to lie. It's not like you'd have allowed me to come to Jersey otherwise."

"So, Pinnella told you Dante took Millie. And who's Jason Chadwick to you?"

"I hired him to keep Millie safe." She sighed. "He wasn't as good as I'd been led to believe, and now he's dead."

"You should have said something to me at the hospital. I could have helped."

"You mean you would have stopped me. I had to lie. It got me here, waiting on Dante's call."

He nodded. "Benton was the snitch you guessed existed in the syndicate. He was outed a day before we found you, but he left with the rumor you had files. He'd sacrificed a lot for that lead, so he's having a hard time giving it up. He doesn't want to believe you."

"Dante invented "incriminating files" to justify putting the hit out on me. Tell Benton he's lucky he left the syndicate with his life. Console himself with that. Most people aren't so lucky."

"You did. You left."

She shook her head. "Dante took everything from me and Millie. Took her childhood. Took…" She inhaled sharply, forcing down her emotions.

"This isn't living." The money bag had worked its way under her hip and was biting into a bruise. She pulled it out and set it on the side table.

"All because you left him?" Vincent was trying so hard to understand, she felt bad for him, because when it came to her and Dante, very little made sense. "He allowed you to divorce him. Why bother with the hit?"

She shrugged, not wanting to lie to him anymore, but having no choice. That was one secret she'd bring to her grave. "Scorned entitled man syndrome. Is that a thing? Your guess is as good as mine, but once he decided to do it, he needed a good enough excuse to warrant a contract on Ralph Toner's little girl. Family is everything in the syndicate. Dante knew what he had to do to justify calling out a hit on me." Vincent closed his eyes and rested his head against the headboard with a thump. "Do you believe me?" He met her gaze, grimacing.

She wanted him to believe her. Most of it was true.

"I believe you." He put his arm around her and tugged her to his side. She pressed her face to his chest and did her best to hide that she was smelling him. She loved his smell. "We'll figure this out. Problem is, Benton has nothing to support his warrant now. No files, no case. Coppola walks."

"That means you have no right to keep me in custody?"

"None."

It also meant Vincent had no official reason to stay and help her. The Feds would go back to wherever they came from and Avery and Dante would be left to hash it out in private. It's what she needed, so why did she feel so devastated?

"Maybe we can get Coppola on kidnapping." A volume of words pressed against her lips to shut him down. *There was no way to save Millie from Dante legally.* How could he not see that? The law took time to use, and men like Dante didn't follow rules. Vincent noticed she'd tensed in his arms. She couldn't help it. She was freaking. "What are you afraid of?" he said.

She punched his chest, and a spike of pain shot through her hand, forcing her to shake it out. "You tell me!" *A million things.*

"Those rings are brutal." Vincent rubbed his chest. "What did I say?"

"I'm *afraid*, Vincent, because Dante wants me dead, and he has Millie!"

"That's not what I meant. I'm talking about me. What are you afraid will happen if you allow me to help? If you trusted me?"

Her eyes welled up. "That you'll be someone else to save."

"What?" He laughed in her face, and then he scowled, tugging her onto his lap, cradling her in his arms. "You're a hundred pounds soaking wet. Why would I *expect* you to save me?"

She lowered her eyes, taking comfort in his words. "Pete will have told him about you. Remember? I said walking into the restaurant with me would put a target on your back. It did." She licked her lower lip, feeling nervous, but loving how it felt to be in his arms. "Dante will assume we're lovers. He won't let you die easily." She adjusted her position, easing her weight off her bruise.

His eyes narrowed. "Stop wiggling. You're turning me on." His words rendered her speechless, even as he continued to scowl. "What is it about you that makes me put up with your shit? You should be over my knee, or...or I should be bringing you in cuffed and shackled, but..." He tilted her chin up with his fingertip, bringing their lips close.

"You should go," she whispered. He nodded, but didn't move.

"I should. Then I catch sight of your ass, or the curve of your hip, or I drown in your mesmerizing green eyes." A shadow fell over his features, and she recognized pain. "And you make me feel..." He was out of control. Avery sympathized. So was she.

"Feel?" she said.

"Yes. You make me *feel*. I don't like it."

Her heart clutched. She couldn't handle this. "Vincent—"

"Ignore me." He rested his forehead on hers, sinking his fingers into her hair, holding her in place, closing his eyes. He was the most beautiful thing she'd ever seen. "When it comes to women I'm stupid," he whispered. Then he lifted his head, drew his thumb over her lower lip. She found herself parting her lips for him, wanting his kiss, but she was unable to ask, never having learned how. "But I know men," Vincent said. "And real men don't expect their women to save them." His smile seemed sad. "Though they appreciate the offer."

Her chin quivered, tears welled in her eyes. She was a mess.

He dropped a kiss on her forehead, and then peppered her cheeks with tiny, gentle kisses, smearing her tears. She clutched his shirt, felt his heart racing under her hand. "Stop running from me," he said. "Allow me to save you for a change."

Avery's head was spinning with *what-if's* and *buts*. How had she gotten here? A desirable lawman was making a commitment to save her, urging her to don the mantel of damsel in distress. He wanted her, or rather, he wanted the woman he thought she was, trusting that she'd be straight with him. How was she any better than his ex-wife? Omission was just as bad as lying, *so Avery wasn't any better.*

She turned her head, unable to meet his gaze, and accidentally brushed her lips against his. They tingled, so she licked them to make the sensation

Kris Rafferty

go away, but it left her wanting more. Vincent nudged her chin, so she'd look at him again. His breath was coming in shallow bursts, mirroring hers. Then he lowered his lips to hers, though didn't linger. It was a short, exploratory kiss. He was asking a question, and it was up to her to decide, but he wasn't making it easy to deny him. His fingertips moved from her jaw, down her neck, her collarbone, and just as she thought he'd cup her breast, he drew his palm down her arm, taking her hand and pressing it over his heart.

"I want you, Avery. You're all I can think about, and... I think you want me back."

She felt overwhelmingly shy. When he'd touched her at the cabin, she'd been off her game, barely awake, so by the time she was aware of what was going on, she was already fully aroused. And it had been *dark*. She didn't have to look at him looking at her.

"Vincent, I don't think you understand. Dante wants me back," she said. "To kill me or control me, I don't know. He sees me as a trophy. As his. I won't know what he has planned until I see him, but you must see how you and me is a bad idea. A death sentence."

Vincent's gaze hardened, and then he lay her down, and lay side by side with her. "Listen. You talk about your ex like he's all powerful. He's not. Do you know who is? Me. Because I'm on your side, and I have the full power of the FBI behind me, and I won't fucking let him have you." He covered her mouth with his, his hands clutching her to him, mashing their lips together. She held on, slammed with desire and hope. When he broke the kiss, he kept their faces close. "Do you hear me? He can't have you," Vincent growled. "I won't let him hurt you."

"But..." She shook her head weakly. "Why?" She didn't understand *why*.

Vincent closed his eyes, squeezing them tightly. His chest rose and fell, and she could see him restraining his emotions. The sight excited and impressed her, made her feel like she mattered to him. It brought on feelings of wonder, as if it were happening in a dream, and she didn't trust them one bit.

"Vincent?"

He opened his eyes, and she saw his confusion all mixed up with something else. That something else was what had her fingertips touching his cheekbone, exploring the hollow below, and gently raking her nails against his thick stubble. He was so beautiful. Wonderful. She ran her palm over his strong chest, his shoulder, loving how he felt, how he made her feel when she touched him.

He was touching her, too. His hand slipped under her shirt, reached behind her and unsnapped her bra; then they were pulling off their weapon sheaths, tossing them to the floor. And then he was kissing her again, sweetly, at first, and then deeper, drugging her with his focused passion, making her feel like the most desirable woman on the planet. He wanted her, as she wanted him, and that had never happened to her before. She'd never wanted a man back. Not like Vincent. He'd become important to her and precious...someone to protect. She broke the kiss, out of breath and feeling vulnerable.

"Somewhere along the way, Vincent, you forgot I was a means to an end. Cut your losses. Save yourself."

His hand was under her shirt, cupping her breast as he rubbed his lips against hers, mingling their breaths. "I don't want to be saved."

His words startled her, and then she realized this was the permission she'd been waiting for. He was telling her to take him. Just...take him.

Avery tugged his shirt up, and with trembling hands, bared his abs, pressing her mouth to his rippling muscles. She wanted to see him, touch his skin. Vincent allowed her to push him onto his back, watching her with dark, haunted eyes. Off came his shirt, and when she reached for his belt, she paused, losing courage. Until Vincent helped and unbuckled it for her. He unzipped his fly, and she watched him, breathless.

Then he reached for her, and she was triggered. She pulled her shirt over her head before throwing it and her bra aside, and then they were shucking their boots. Her Doc Martens took the longest time because they had to be untie, but breathless, their eyes bright with anticipation, they did it together. Pants gone, naked, they met on the bed, knee to knee, facing each other, looking their fill. She admired his beauty, as he explored the scars on her belly, hips, and legs, mementos of her final battle with the six contract killers. She had more knife scars on her forearms, too, but they'd faded against the paleness of her skin, and didn't pucker, because those cuts hadn't been as deep.

His gaze was intense, and grim, but his hands never stopped caressing her, his eyes never stopped admiring her curves. "Tell me you want this as much as I do," he said. "For the right reasons." They both knew what he was saying. He feared she was playing him. Again.

She swallowed hard. "Making love to you is the most selfish thing I'll ever do, and if you had even an ounce of self-preservation, you'd run from me, and count yourself lucky." She pressed her hand over his heart, felt it racing, and drew her other hand down his arm until she reached his hand, and pressed it over her heart, relishing the feel of his callused fingers against her skin. "Touch me."

He leaned, swept his tongue along her lower lip, tickling it open, and then plunged inside, sealing their mouth together. He kissed her with a gentleness and expertise she'd come to associate with Vincent. He had her near swooning within moments, and all the while, she trembled, loving how his muscles grew taut at her touch. His strength, the gloriousness of his physique, was all hers. All of him. Maybe just for now, but she'd take it.

"This is insane." She barely recognized her voice. "We'll pay for this. I know it. We'll pay." She lowered her mouth to his chest, tasting him.

"What *wouldn't* I pay?" His words sent tingles through her body as he caressed her back, her ass, squeezing her as he pulled her hips toward him, making her feel his arousal. The tips of her breasts mashed against him. She lifted her mouth, seeking his kiss, moaning when he drew her tongue into his mouth. Melting in his arms, she felt the tension build in her lower belly, making her swell with want, become wet with need. She wanted him inside her.

Vincent lowered her to the mattress, slipped a knee between her knees, and spread her wide as he positioned himself above her. With Dante, once he was inside her, it was soon over, and she'd always been left wanting. Avery couldn't survive if that happened now. Her body was on fire, desperate for release.

Then Vincent surprised her, growing still. Elbows supporting his weight, he held her gaze, and waited. For what, Avery had no idea. With fluttering hands, she ran them across his chest, lifting her chin, hoping to make him kiss her, touch her. Yet, he hesitated, poised to sheath himself inside her, studying her body.

"What? What should I do?" She knew how this worked. Dante had been a demanding lover. What was she doing wrong?

"Just...let me look at you." His gaze lingered on her hair, her eyes, her lips. "You're so damn sexy. So. Damn. Sexy." He moved lower on her body, tasting the tip of her breast, swirling his tongue around the nipple. Her thighs trembled as they squeezed together, pinning his waist, wanting him to touch her more intimately, to ease her growing need.

Arching upward, she felt his mouth suckle her. She threaded her fingers through his hair, holding him at her breast, overwhelmed by her wanting, but needing more. She whimpered when he lifted his head. But Vincent had moved on to her other breast, teasing this one now with a flick of his thumb. Soon, his caress moved down her stomach, over her scars, kissing them. Then he cupped her between her legs, and she was more than ready for him, wiggling against his hand, his questing finger. She gasped when he sheathed it inside her, bucking at his first stroke, even as his tongue thrust inside her mouth. Moaning, lightheaded, she edged toward climax. Then Vincent stopped and pulled back.

"Huh?" She lifted herself onto her elbows, having a hard time focusing. Vincent reached for his pants on the floor, and pull a wrapped condom from his pocket.

"Call me a cockeyed optimist." He tore it open with his teeth, handed it to her, and then lay on his back. "Put it on me."

Eyes wide, she eagerly complied, reveling in the hungry look on his face. He focused on her hands moving over his erection, and gasped when she gave him a tiny squeeze when she was done. Smiling, Avery pushed Vincent onto his back. He chuckled, helping her straddle him. Then she positioned him between her legs and sheathed herself with one downward movement.

Her eyes lost focus, and suddenly it felt as if she didn't need to breathe. Vincent inhaled sharply, dug his fingers into her hips, holding her in place. When she could focus, she saw his eyes had become heavy-lidded, and his mouth seemed poised to bite. Then he moved beneath her, guiding her hips, showing her what he wanted, creating their rhythm. Sweat broke out on her upper lip and cooled her back as pleasure made her weak, and soon it became a struggle to stay upright. Then he was moving faster inside her, adjusting her on him. She wanted to watch him, to enjoy his arousal, but she was too busy throwing her head back and moaning as stroke after stroke buffeted her with pleasure.

Vincent *blew...her...mind.*

Filled her completely. Had her arching toward him even as his hips surged inside her. She'd never felt the like as Vincent controlled her completely. He whispered her name, hot and breathy, as if against his will. Then he pulled her chest down to him, mashing her breasts against his hardness. He flipped them, until she was on her back and he was pinning her hips to the mattress, burying himself even deeper. She gasped, saw stars, and then his rhythm became fierce as he moved inside her, tipping her over an edge to orgasm, to...ecstasy.

"Vincent!" She turned her face, hiding it in the hollow of his neck. She felt him shudder, knew he'd found his release, even as he continued to move, longer strokes now, feeding her climax aftershocks.

The whole thing was heartrending, devastating, and... Avery couldn't wait to do it again. She laughed, floored by the enormity of it all. Vincent pressed his lips to her neck, his chest shaking, silently laughing. Happy. They were happy.

She rubbed his back, grabbed his ass and squeezed, and then locked her legs around his waist, not wanting to let him go. She wanted to thank him, to congratulate him for showing her what sex could be like, but feared it was a novice move, and would reveal her inexperience with orgasms.

He pressed a lingering kiss to her lips, and then pressed his face in the hollow of her neck, nuzzling. Time stood still and neither spoke as they caught their breath and calmed their racing hearts. It was wonderful. Avery felt amazing, and she wanted to memorize the feeling, memorize everything about this moment. His embrace, the tickling of his breath as it moved the tiny hairs on the nape of her neck. She wanted to remember every detail, so when he was gone, and when life got so bad she thought nothing could warrant the effort to survive, she'd have this memory: his protective embrace, his scratchy cheek on her neck, their sweat and heat mingling.

Because bad times were coming.

Soon, Vincent would know everything; who she was, what she'd done.

That was inevitable. He'd stick with her until he knew, because he was that kind of guy…the good kind. Only the truth about who she was would make him abandon her, but she had now, and this memory. It would have to be enough.

Her phone rang, and her heart skipped with fear. She unlocked her legs, and lay splayed on the bed, staring at the ceiling as he remained buried inside her. "I can't breathe."

Vincent rolled off her, sitting on the bed's edge as he picked up her ringing phone. "Do you think it's Coppola?"

"It has to be, unless it's the Feds." And why would they call Avery, instead of Vincent? They wouldn't. The phone continued to ring.

He glanced at the incoming phone number. "It's not Benton."

Pressing her palm to her forehead, she held her breath, struggling to compose herself. She waited as long as she dared before snatching the phone from Vincent's hand and hitting the accept button. She pressed it to her ear. "Yeah?" She held her breath, staring at the water-stained ceiling.

"Hello, baby. Miss me?" Dante's smooth, deep tone gave her a chill.

She caught Vincent's gaze and held it. He was all that was good in a man. All that Dante wasn't. Whatever he saw in her eyes had Vincent grabbing his Glock off the side table.

"You got my message." She bit her lip.

"Yes, I did," Dante said. "Poor Pete. He wanted you to know he was sending his mother to Boca to retire. You certainly made an impression, but then again, you always do."

"I want proof of life. Put Millie on."

"You shouldn't have betrayed me, Avery."

"I didn't betray you."

"You know what you did."

"I want to speak to Millie."

"She's fine, swimming in the pool. Don't worry about her. Beautiful things always have their value in my home."

Avery swallowed hard. So, Millie was at the mansion and Dante wanted her to know. "She's not yours to keep, Dante. You know that, right?" She wouldn't allow it.

"Who's the man you're with? Pete told me you had a bodyguard. Are you lovers?" He couldn't hide his jealousy, and knowing Dante, he probably felt as if he had a right to it.

She reached for Vincent, gripping his thigh, needing the assurance of his solidness, his strength. Vincent covered her hand, squeezing gently. "We're divorced, Dante. You have no right to ask about my personal life."

He chuckled. "In the eyes of the church we're married until one of us dies."

There was a knock on the door, loud and insistent. The Feds had arrived. She turned to Vincent, used her free hand to indicate her nakedness, and that he needed to buy them time for her to finish this call and get dressed. He nodded and stood, moving toward the door, showing her his fine ass. Even freaked by talking with her psychopathic ex, there was still a portion of her mind devoted to admiring the insane beauty of Special Agent Vincent Modena's naked glory.

"Goodbye, Avery. I'll miss you." The way he said it scared her.

"Let me talk to Millie!"

"That would upset her and she's only now calmed from that messiness in Boston." Jason Chadwick's murder. Millie's kidnapping. "She doesn't have your constitution, baby. A little blood and she fainted dead away." The knocking continued, but Avery ignored it. Vincent, gun in hand, peered through the peep hole. What he saw had him shaking his head impatiently, walking back to Avery and the bed.

"I'm coming, Dante." She squeezed the phone so hard it bit into her hand. "No need to kill anyone else."

"You should have left the rings."

"You want them? I'll give you anything, just let me speak to her," Avery said. The line disconnected.

A deafening boom coincided with a hole the size of a grapefruit being blown from the door's lock. Her mind registered the sound of a shotgun blast, even as a large woman appeared behind the now open door. Dark brown hair in a bun, wearing a housekeeping uniform, her brown eyes promised violence as she aimed her shotgun at Avery.

Angelina Modelli. One of Dante's preferred contract killers.

Avery rolled to the floor, and seconds later the mattress's edge disintegrated with a shotgun blast. Vincent got off three rounds, which bought him time to run into the bathroom. Avery low crawled to the bed's edge, peeking around. Lina had taken cover in the hall, but her shotgun's barrel was still in view, aimed toward the bathroom.

"Lina!" Avery bit off an expletive. The contract killer's presence here meant Dante had known Avery was at the hotel this whole time. "Don't do this! He's lying to you!"

"I don't care! I've wanted to kill you for years, Avery! Don't try to ruin my fun!" Lina cackled from the hall. On Avery's wedding day, she'd caught her French-kissing Dante in his office. "He requested your hands as proof of death." She laughed. "Just your hands. Wants to make sure you're good and dead." *The rings.* But Lina would recognize the six rings, too. Did that mean Lina was in Dante's confidence?

Vincent was giving minimal cover fire, making her think he was conserving rounds. Avery's gun was by her feet, so she grabbed it, chambered a round, and aimed toward the door. Lina shot the floor next to her, forcing Avery to scurrying back, seeking cover.

"Lina! I'm only back for Millie!"

"I don't care. I earned this kill. For the last three years, all I've heard is Avery this and Avery that." The distinct sound of a shotgun being reloaded had Avery on her feet, rushing the door. She grabbed the barrel just as Lina had it cocked and ready to go.

Avery pulled. Lina's grip was sure. A tug of war ensued, bringing them both into the room. The shotgun discharged, blowing a hole in the ceiling, just as Avery kicked Lina's knee out. It buckled, and Lina fell to one knee, swinging a handgun up with her other hand.

Vincent, still naked, rushed from the bathroom, gun extended. He pulled the trigger, his bullet grazing Lina's shoulder. "Drop it!" Lina recoiled as her shoulder was thrown back, but didn't lose her grip on the gun, so Avery kicked it from her hand. It hurting like hell, making her foot scream with pain, but it was a twofer, because Lina lost her balance, allowing Avery to grab the shotgun and toss it aside.

Vincent rushed them, pressing his gun to Lina's head. It should have ended there, but Lina risked it all, slapping his wrist. Vincent got off a shot, missed, but it was fired close enough to Avery to force an instinctive recoil, giving Lina an opening. She locked Avery's arm behind her back, and used her as a shield against Vincent. Avery stomped on Lina's foot, and found herself thrown into Vincent for her troubles. He caught her, and then dove with her to the floor as Lina retrieved her gun and fired. It clicked, empty.

Vincent jumped to his feet, and lunged at Lina, who lashed out. Vincent ducked and came up with a hook punch, which Lina parried before unsheathing a knife and slashing. Vincent evaded, but barely.

Avery howled, furious that Lina had come so close to killing him. She rushed Lina, chopped her wrist, and the knife fell to the floor as Vincent retrieved his gun. But in her rush to overpower Lina, Avery got hit with a sucker punch, and fell on her face.

Lina followed her to the floor, putting her in a rear choke. Dazed, unable to break Lina's hold, she saw Vincent above them, his gun aimed at Lina. He didn't have a clear shot, and Lina was using her as a shield. Avery palm-heeled Lina's elbow, turning her face toward Lina's chest, desperate to break the hold, to breathe, as they scrambled on the floor.

"Shoot her." Avery's words came out as a croak. Lina squeezed harder, continuing to position Avery between her and Vincent.

"Who's the guy, Avery?" Lina snickered in her ear. "You're not the type to work with a partner, and I obviously interrupted something." Avery was seeing stars. "Can't wait to tell Dante I killed you after you cheated on him. He'll love that." Avery gagged, pulling on Lina's wrist. "You stole files. You're a snitch. Dante *hates* you now."

"Let her go." Vincent looked as if he had a shot, but wasn't taking it. "She dies, you die. Shots have been fired. Cops will be here soon. I'd rather they not find two bodies."

"Oh, they'll find two bodies. The files, Avery. Where are they?"

Avery bucked her hips, and jammed her fingers between Lina's wrist and her throat, pulling hard enough to gain breath enough to shout, "Shoot her!"

Lina swore. "What the hell! Where'd you get those rings?" Lina squeezed harder, but Avery's fingers were protecting her neck, rendering the choke ineffective. "Answer me!"

Avery caught Vincent's eye, saw him staring at her, waiting *with Lina* for her answer. Shock, and then gutting betrayal slammed into her, forcing Avery to dig deep. She grabbed Lina's hair, bumped her with her hip, and switched their positions. Now Lina was under Avery, and though she still had her arms around Avery's neck, Avery's forearm was on Lina's throat, with all her weight behind it. Lina pushed at Avery, who grabbed her wrist. Flipping onto her back, Avery put Lina into an arm bar, draping her calves over Lina's face and torso to complete the pin.

"Where'd you get them?" Lina was screaming, enraged and unable to move.

With a brutal skyward thrust of Avery's hips, she yanked on Lina's wrist, breaking the bitch's elbow. Lina released a guttural scream. It was a horrible sound, and then Vincent was there, resting a knee on Lina's chest. He pressed his gun to Lina's forehead as Avery scrambled away. The contract killer was half unconscious, and didn't resist.

Vincent was furious. "Why was she so upset about your rings? You said they'd belonged to your family."

Avery's throat hurt, and she was sore. Every injury she'd acquired in the last few days were protesting, and Vincent... He was looking at her like she was the enemy.

"Leave me alone." Her words came out like a croak. She held her throat, flinching with every swallow.

Vincent was so busy glaring at Avery, he'd missed Lina reviving from her near faint. Lina swept his leg out from under him, and though Vincent's leg flew into the air, it came down hard, as an ax kick to Lina's head. She was unconscious by the time he hopped to his feet.

"No more lies, Avery."

She pushed off the floor and swayed when she stood upright. Life's pendulum had swung from heaven back to hell, and it was time to shoulder soul-crushing sadness again. She didn't welcome it, but it was familiar, so she knew what to do. Time to move on.

Chapter 16

Vincent grabbed Lina's arms and indicated that Avery help drag the woman across the room to the bathroom. "I deserve an explanation," he said, and then rifled through Lina's pockets, and found nothing.

"Yes, you do," she said, her voice a near whisper as she helped drag Lina. "But you're not getting one." Once inside the bathroom, she dropped the woman's legs, and pivoted back out into the bedroom.

Vincent followed, furious, slamming the door behind him. Then he propped a chair under the doorknob to prevent Lina's escape before his task force could round her up. "You and your damn secrets." They were going to get them killed.

He kicked aside shotgun shells and casings as he gathered his clothes and quickly dressed. Avery dressed, too, but with greater care. She moved as if in pain, which created the first crack in his rage, because he felt bad for her. When they were dressed, weapons in place, Avery grabbed the money bag and tucked it into her waistband.

"You wouldn't take the shot," she rasped, holding her throat. "I saw you had one, but you didn't take it. Why?"

So, she'd noticed, huh? He'd hoped she hadn't. "I wanted to question her. You were doing fine. You'd countered her choke."

Avery stopped walking to the door, turned on him and glared, her rage unleashed. "You didn't know that!" Half her words were barely understandable, but he understood the jist of it.

"You had it under control. If that had changed, *I would have shot her.* Okay? But I wanted her alive for questioning." He could tell she wasn't satisfied with his answer. "Listen, we need to get Benton in here before local police stumble on her, or they won't know what hit them."

Avery's eyes narrowed, and she folded her arms over her chest. "*Be honest*," she rasped. "You wanted her to interrogate me and it almost got me killed."

He shook his head, knowing there was nothing he could say to convince her otherwise. The woman couldn't trust him. No...she *wouldn't*.

When he didn't respond, she grabbed her boots, slipped them on, but didn't take the time to tie them before stepping over the destroyed door and disappearing into the hall. Vincent followed, wondering how he was supposed to explain this crime scene to Benton.

People had gathered in the hall, so he grabbed Avery's elbow, and hustled her around the corner, through a stairwell door. Avery pulled from his grip, hurrying down the stairs, leaning her weight on the railing. It made him think she'd reinjured her knee.

"You almost got me killed," she said.

"Bullshit." He easily kept up with her on the stairs, keeping an eye on their six and his gun at the ready. If Lina found them, odds were others had, too.

She stopped on the stairs, glaring at him over her shoulder. "Bullshit?"

"Yeah," he said. "Bullshit. No way I'd let her hurt you, never mind kill you." He stepped close enough for her not to have to look over her shoulder to meet his gaze. "I've fought you on the ground. You were like a wild animal, but with Lina? You were barely trying. Why is that? Why didn't you fight as hard as you'd fought with me?"

Her features twisted with pain. "Because I didn't want to kill her!"

He pulled her into his arms, and she surprised him when she sobbed against his chest. Her exhaustion was showing. He recognized the signs, had experienced them himself. "I wanted her alive for questioning, but Avery—"

She sniffed, clutching at him. "Yeah?"

"Next time, don't hesitate. Kill her." Avery drew back, confused. "When it's them against you, *you* walk away. *You* live. Got it?" She gave him a shaky nod, her chin quivering. "We can't stay here. When the cops find your friend upstairs—"

Avery winced, and gave herself a little shake. "She was never my friend."

"Well, they'll print the room and know we've been there. Unless I can get Benton in there first."

Avery scrubbed tears from her cheeks. "It doesn't matter. Lina was only the beginning." Her legs seemed to give out, and she sat on the stair. "Now we know what Dante wants."

Her dead. Vincent wasn't letting that happen. He texted Benton about Lina upstairs, and then put his phone away. "You need to start believing in me." He sat next to her, glancing up the stairwell. They were out in the open, but she didn't look as if she could move, and he wasn't sure she'd allow him to carry her. He felt exposed. "Have some faith."

"Millie's waiting," she said. "She has to be so afraid."

Millie. Avery loved her little sister more than herself. Vincent could only wonder what that must be like. To love like that. To *receive* love like that. In Afghanistan, he'd had his unit, risked his life for them more times than he could count. That was a type of love, all mixed up with duty, but the most he'd sacrificed was his time, effort…and his marriage. Just didn't seem on the same level as Avery's relationship with Millie.

Vincent put his arm around her and pressed a kiss to the top of her head. He expected her to push him away. He certainly didn't expect her to wrap her arms around him and hold on as if she were drowning. When she released him, he was weak enough to need to know why…why she hugged him.

"What was that for?" She shrugged, making him think, *even her hugs are shrouded with secrets.* "You need to start trusting me."

"Like you trust me?"

Touché. He wanted to tell her he trusted her, but he knew he only trusted her to a point.

When she started down the stairs again, he followed, easily keeping up with her pace. Making sure no one snuck up on their rear. All the while he worried. She still didn't trust him, and he was having a hard time being okay with that. He'd spent his life being trustworthy and was used to people automatically knowing it was a given. He was the one who didn't trust people. That was *his* thing. Sure, he understood her resistance when they were on different sides of an agenda, but her secrets had been outed. He was here to help her, so why? Why the resistance to trust him?

Vincent descended the stairwell just ahead of her when they reached the bottom, because he didn't want her rushing into the underground garage. She was upset and not thinking clearly. When he opened the door, he peeked into the darkened lot, looked left and right, and only saw parked cars. Avery barreled on through, breezing past him, as if getting away from him was her one goal.

A squeal of tires had her pivoting back to Vincent. He saw her panic, saw the advancing men in suits behind her and aimed his gun. He reached for her. More men bled from between parked cars. Coppola's men. It was a trap.

They distracted him, making him miss the man who rushed him from the side. He got off two bullets before his gun was stripped from his hand. A van squealed to a stop in front of them, two masked men jumped out, grabbed Avery, and forced a hood over her head. Vincent lunged after them, but he was hit hard, a shoulder connecting with his solar plexus, doubling him over.

He couldn't breathe. Then he was lifted—no easy feat—and thrown into the van with Avery, hitting the interior hard. He lashed out, stopping his punch mere inches from Special Agent Cynthia Deming's face. Deming dismissed him with a frown, and turned toward a still-hooded Avery, who was fighting for her life. Benton knelt on her chest, but she'd broken free, and was swinging. The van jolted forward, its tires screaming, and the sliding door slammed shut during acceleration.

"Stop!" Vincent pulled Avery's hood off, and was clocked in the jaw for his troubles. "Shit!" He glared at everyone, holding his palm up. "*Everybody stop!*"

Avery scurried to the van's back wall, more caged animal than woman. She saw the three agents hovering, and then released a shuddering breath. Benton scowled at Avery, giving Vincent a preview of the shit they had coming, and Gilroy was up front, doing his best to lose their tail. But Deming…Deming could have been having tea with the Queen. Sporting a sweet smile, dressed in her usual expensive pantsuit, perfectly coiffed, her patent leather heels were pristine, and he knew for a fact that her string of pearls was an heirloom. Deming couldn't have looked more out of place. She studied Avery in her academic way, doing her profiler voodoo thing, while everyone else sought to regain their breath and calm down. "It's just us, Avery. No worries," Deming said.

"Gilroy?" Benton called to the driver. "How are we doing? Anyone tailing us?"

"Not yet, and not if I have anything to say about it," the big guy said.

Vincent pushed down his anger and did his best to appear calm. "Why the *snatch and grab*?"

"We didn't want to get made," Deming said.

"*Made* by whom? Did you get a call about the shooting?" Vincent said.

"What shooting?" she said.

"I texted Benton." He scowled at his team leader, who pulled out his phone and seemed surprised to see his text. "*Made* by who?"

"Coppola's men were in the parking garage," Benton said. "We'd just arrived, saw them lying in wait, and had to make some decisions."

"I recognized a few," Deming said. "Most of them, actually. That was his full stable of contract killers in that garage." She arched a brow, studying Avery again. "Makes a person wonder."

Benton caught Vincent's attention. "Tell me about what happened upstairs."

"One of Coppola's killers. Room 339. Alive, unconscious when we left her, and scrappy. If local law stumbles upon her, there will be blood. She's dangerous."

"Name?" Deming said. Vincent glanced at Avery.

"Angelina Modelli," Avery said. "Lina."

"What's wrong with your throat, Avery?" Deming said. She reached behind her and pulled out a bottle of water from the cooler. The van filled with a horrible fish smell.

"Damn, Deming. Didn't you throw that fish out?" Vincent said.

"Yeah, but soap and water doesn't cut it and I haven't had time to buy bleach." She scowled at him, making her pert nose wrinkle. "I've been busy."

Benton was ignoring Deming and staring at Avery. "Coppola has your sister."

Deming handed Avery the water. "Let's go save your sister."

"Where are you taking me?" Avery said.

"That's up to you and how willing you are to be straight with us," Benton said. "So far, you've been anything but." He pulled out a file and laid photos in front of her. "These were taken from the coroner's records. Coppola's men. Take a close look at the hands."

Vincent picked up one of the photos, noticing how Avery refused to even look at them. He studied the hands, recognizing rings like the ones Avery wore.

"The rings, Modena." Deming sounded impatient.

So, the rings *were* important. His stomach tightened as he lifted another photo. Identical rings from the previous photo. All pinkie rings on dead shooters. Like Avery's rings. "What of them?"

"Those are custom made," Deming said. "They're made by a particular jewelry shop in Jersey City for Coppola's contract killers, apparently a tightknit crew."

"Each ring is titanium," Gilroy said from the front of the van, "worn on the pinkie, with their initials inscribed on them."

"I thought they were silver." Vincent looked closer at the photos, panic growing as he began to piece together what was being suggested. The profiler put more photos in his hands.

"These are *The Stinger's* victims," she said.

Vincent glanced at the photos. That's all it took to see what Deming wanted him to see. "No rings."

Deming nodded. "Six rings are missing. The shopkeeper was happy to talk about them. Protocol is that the men are buried with their rings. These rings were stolen. It's a sign of disrespect. Isn't that right, Avery?"

Leaning against the van's interior, Avery curled herself into a ball, resting her chin on her knees as she hid her hands between her thighs and her chest.

"Let me see the rings," Vincent said. Avery didn't resist. She held her hands out, showing the rings, revealing the initials inscribed on their tops. "Dammit, Avery." He didn't even have it in him to raise his voice.

"They're the ones." Deming gathered up the photos and tucked them into a manila folder. "Who gave those to you? Your ex-husband?" She glanced at Vincent. "This might be all we need to take Coppola down. If we can pin those murders on him, he's ours."

Benton grimaced, studying Avery. "Look at her. Do you see her testifying?"

"Avery," Vincent said. She wouldn't look at him. "Where did you get those rings?"

"It doesn't matter." She shook her head. "You wouldn't believe me if I told you, and I have no proof to make you believe."

"Modena, come on. We *know* where she got them," Deming said. "It has to be Coppola. We suspected he was behind their deaths, and these rings prove it. Avery can prove it!"

"She could have gotten them anywhere," Benton said. "Without her testimony, they're useless as evidence, and even then, it would be a he said, she said." He exchanged glances with Vincent. "She knows this. She won't testify. Remember, I lived with these people for a year. I was one of them. She won't testify."

Deming narrowed her eyes, pinning Avery with a stare. "She'll testify. Between the files and those rings, we'll take Coppola down. She'll never have to be afraid of him again. Isn't that right, Avery?"

Vincent realized Benton hadn't shared his intel on the "files" with the team. "Deming, the files don't exist." They'd believe him, if not Avery. "They're a rumor Coppola created to justify his hit on Avery."

"Of course," Deming said. "Of course, they don't exist. Everything else about this case has cratered. Why wouldn't that, too?" She sighed, lowering her head.

Benton leaned into the front of the van. "Gilroy, get us to the safehouse." Then he turned back around, exchanging glances with the rest of them. "We'll verify Coppola has her sister, get the necessary warrants, and see what happens."

"No. We need to get to Saddle River," Avery said. Benton shook his head.

"Avery, we don't know if that's where she is," Vincent said.

"She's there." Avery sounded positive.

"I'm not bringing his ex-wife to Dante Coppola," Benton said. "Look at her. She has the dead men's rings on her hands. She's involved and probably complicit. The last thing we should do is *anything* she wants us to do."

"Millie is ten," Vincent said. "She'll need her sister when we grab her. I just don't think we know she's there."

"She is there," Avery said. "I know it. He'd want her close, and... And he said she was in the pool." She swallowed hard. "Take me to Saddle River and I'll do whatever you want. I'll tell you everything. Even the stuff I know you won't believe."

Gilroy cleared his throat, interrupting Benton's deliberations. "There's a safehouse close to Saddle River. Close enough to Coppola's complex to be acceptable. And we should keep the asset close by in case things go south."

"You mean, *Avery.*" Vincent instantly regretted his snappishness, but Gilroy shouldn't have called her the *asset*. It was dehumanizing and intolerable.

Gilroy nodded. "Exactly. Right. I mean, Avery. We don't know what Coppola will do. The safe bet is to keep the asset close during negotiations." Vincent told himself to shut up. Just shut up.

Benton nodded. "Fine."

Deming pulled an ice pack from the cooler, and again, a wave of fish smell. "You're injured. Press this to the bruise."

He saw Avery wave it away, and was about to protest, maybe demand she take a Tylenol, but then Deming pressed the ice pack to his swelling cheek. Avery saw her mistake immediately and cringed, clearly embarrassed. That small misunderstanding startled him. *When had everything become about Avery to him?*

Vincent took the ice pack from Deming. "Thank you." Then he crawled across the van's interior and sat next to Avery. Tugging her onto his lap, he made her hold the ice pack to her neck, and pressed her swelling hand to it, to keep the ice pack in place. "Deming, you got any pain meds?"

Deming nodded, and reached into a first aid kit affixed to the van's interior wall. She tossed a packet of ibuprofen to him. Adjusting Avery on his lap, he felt her face turn into his neck as she slumped into his arms. She was exhausted.

"No, come on. Take them." He tore open the small paper container, and held out the two pills, then opened the water bottle for her. When she'd swallowed it, she leaned on him again, limp as a dish rag. He was worried about her. She needed to regain her strength, because things were about to get harder, not easier.

What with the quiet inside the van, and the white noise of them driving on the interstate, Avery drifted off to sleep, her hand pressed to his chest, her breathing synced with his. It gave him plenty of time to study those damn rings, worry about who gave them to her, and how he'd feel once her latest secret was revealed. He was falling hard for her, and felt stupid about it. He suspected Deming and Benton had already guessed. They weren't staring at Avery. They were studying the tableau of Avery sleeping in his arms.

Vincent allowed himself a sigh, and pretended not to notice their worries, because…well, *whatever*. His feelings were what they were, and right or wrong, they were his. *So, what* if he was being stupid. It wouldn't be the first time.

Chapter 17

Cradled in Vincent's arms, Avery woke to find it nighttime. He felt warm, and she was cold, so she pressed against him, her face against his neck. She felt safe and cozy, surrounded by his scent. Then she heard Benton speaking to the team in quiet tones, and remembered just how far up the creek she was without a paddle.

The van's side sliding door rumbled as it opened. "Vincent, get her inside," Benton said. "Gilroy, Deming, scout the perimeter while I log us into the safehouse."

Safehouse. Those words nudged Avery more fully awake, though sleep pulled at her as Vincent lifted her from the van and into the cool night. Cicadas chirped about them as she struggled to open her eyes. She saw a well-lit white Colonial ahead, surrounded by an expanse of lawn and then dense woods beyond that. The gravel driveway crunched beneath Vincent's boots, until they arrived on a cobblestone walkway that lead to the front landing.

They'd arrived at Saddle River, and that meant Millie was about twenty minutes away, hopefully sleeping and unaware of the showdown between good and evil that was ratcheting up to its conclusion. Avery's heart beat faster as her anxiety curdled her belly. *Soon, Millie, soon.*

Avery was coming.

Vincent carried her up the granite stairs to an intricately carved wood overhang. The large front door opened as soon as they reached it, revealing a sparsely furnished foyer. There was nothing on the walls, and the wallpaper looked at least thirty years old. Immediately ahead, about ten feet into the house, were stairs leading to the second floor. The house's hardwood flooring, banisters, and trim had probably been something to see in the house's heyday, but now, everything was worn; the furnishings were mismatched and yard-sale quality. There was a mustiness to the place that had her wrinkling her nose. She pressed her face to Vincent's neck again. He smelled better.

Avery could have, probably should have, forced herself to wake up completely and wriggle from Vincent's arms. She knew this, but she ached, and her knee was bothering her again despite the ibuprofen she'd taken earlier. And her throat was killing her. It would probably take a week to fully heal, but she didn't have a week. If she had anything to say about it, this rescue was happening soon, so she shamelessly took this respite, allowing Vincent to hold her as she took her time waking up.

"What time is it?" She sounded like she had a bad case of laryngitis.

"Paley?" Vincent was ignoring her, talking with a safehouse agent, a thin, dark-haired man, wiry, maybe mid-thirties. His red polo shirt and khakis made him look as if he worked for the Geek Squad at Best Buy rather than the FBI. His clipboard and pocket protector fueled the impression. The man's brown eyes focused on her first, before moving on to Vincent.

"Yeah, I'm Paley. You're Modena, right?" He inclined his head toward the stairs. "We prepared a room for the asset. Top of the stairs, first room on the right." Vincent gave no indication that they were going anywhere, top of the stairs or otherwise. He just kept her in his arms, holding her, his attention focused on Paley and Benton, who'd just entered the house.

Benton exchanged glances with Vincent, and then took the clipboard Paley offered him. "I'm Benton." He nodded to Paley.

"I had Modelli's interview transcribed for you," Paley said. "The video, and its transcription are on this." He handed Benton a flash drive. "She suffered a hairline fracture to the skull and a compound fracture to her elbow. So, the interview was done while she had meds in her." He glanced at Avery. "I only mention that because we believe it explains some of her...odd comments."

"Anything about incriminating files?" Benton said.

"Nothing beyond what you've said," Paley said.

Avery grimaced. Benton was still sniffing after the "files." Ahab, fishing for his white whale. On some level, she admired his drive. It kind of reassured her, too, that maybe these people knew what they were doing, and they'd leave no stone unturned. Benton and his team, gathering their slivers of evidence like squirrels gathering nuts, would chip away at the unknown until Dante was stopped.

But not today. Today they weren't even close, and no surprise. In Avery's experience, Dante was someone you survived, not punished, and at the rate she was going, her odds of surviving him were becoming more and more slim by the hour.

Vincent took the stairs. "You okay?"

She kept her head on his shoulder. "How do I look?"

He crested the top of the stairs and stepped to a bedroom door. "Death warmed over. Can you reach the knob?" Avery's bruised knuckles protested as she squeezed and turned the knob, and then Vincent's shoulder nudged the door open, and they were inside. The room was dark, but outdoor perimeter lights streamed in from the windows. He put her down. Avery found a wall switch, and flip it on.

"What time is it?" she said.

There were no clocks in this flowery bedroom of muted tones, flouncy drapes and a cabbage flower upholstered chair to the left of the bed. Avery lay on the queen-sized bed in the center of the room. It had *looked* cozy, with its crocheted coverlet, but Avery found the mattress too lumpy and hard to be comfortable, so sat up. Vincent stood in front of her, resting his hands on his hips.

"It's nine," he said. "We've got a judge willing to give us the necessary warrants to search Coppola's mansion for Millie. We'll stay here while we wait for them to be signed. Then we'll show up at his door and deliver the warrant. This is over by tomorrow morning. Promise."

"He won't get caught with Millie at the mansion. He'll get tipped off. He'll do something. He's smart, Vincent. You have to talk to Benton, tell him it won't work." Dante would kill Millie first before he'd allow her to be taken from him. Or maybe, hopefully, he'd hide her somewhere out of Avery's reach.

Vincent seemed unconvinced, if sympathetic, and she blamed it on his conviction that law and order was the only way to solve a problem. There was no fighting that kind of bias. It meant Avery had to move on her own before the Feds got their warrants and ruined her one chance to rescue Millie.

"Right now," Vincent said, "the warrants are our only play. If she's not at the mansion, we'll think of something else, but you need to wrap your brain around the consequences of a fail here. If she's not there, Millie is a missing persons case. I could expedite it—"

"No." If it got to that point, Millie would be long gone or dead.

"Listen, we're rushing in there with a warrant on your say so. That's happening. I promise. But if she's not there, your credibility is shot, and the bureau will shut this case down. The task force will be reassigned. Do you understand?"

"Yes." She'd have one less problem to deal with, but it would also mean her Dante problem had grown exponentially.

"The only reason it's gotten this far is because Benton was convinced you have information that will take down your ex-husband, and"—he shook his head, grimacing—"now that we believe you don't, it's hemmed us in on what we can do to take down your ex."

Avery nodded, falling back on the bed, ignoring its lumpiness. She covered her face, too tired, too *upset* to hide her emotions. The bed dipped, and Vincent sat next to her. When he pulled her hands down, she saw his sympathy, and then his gaze drop to her hands. "We need the rings for evidence."

Her knuckles were swollen, deep blue, and cut to shit. "You'll have to snip them off or wait until the swelling goes down."

He nodded. "I'll leave that decision to Benton." She didn't want to give up her rings. Their cost had been too high. "It's almost over," he said.

And the worst had just begun. Everything else had led up to this, and every move they made from here on out would tip the balance toward saving Millie or losing her forever.

He kissed her, sweetly, and she kissed him back because she couldn't help herself. She was weak and needed the comfort he was offering. She didn't care that they had no future. She needed him now.

"Talk to me, Avery." His arms wrapped around her as tears spilled past her lashes.

"There's nothing more to say." His sympathy was dangerous. It made her cry, made her weak when she needed to be strong. Vincent made her want to lean on him, but it was a dangerous trap, that could only lead to failure.

"They want to question you downstairs," he said. "I'll be there. I'll help you, but Avery, you have to answer their questions. Okay?"

She nodded. "Okay, but…give me a second to compose myself."

Avery turned her back on him, and curled into a ball on the mattress, hugging the pillow to her chest. She'd thought to get rid of him, that her turning might indicate she wanted to be alone, but Vincent surprised her by spooning her, tugging her close to his body. Avery didn't fight it, because it felt too good. He was so big, and she loved how it felt to be in his arms, surrounded by his strength. She rested her head on his bicep and allowed herself a moment to pretend they were a couple, with normal problems, looking forward to a normal life.

They lay there for a while, Avery lingering in her malaise as he caressed her side, kissed her hair, basically made her feel cherished…and guilty. Vincent saw her as the person he wanted her to be, maybe even needed her to be, much like she'd done with Dante. At seventeen, her family dead, she'd needed Dante to be her hero. Traumatized, she'd made a deal that she'd marry him, allow him to use her to solidify his position in the syndicate, if he'd arrange to have her trained to fight. It seemed the only way for her and Millie to survive, and now she knew she'd been a fool. Once she became *The Stinger*, there was no turning back. It set in motion a series of events that were culminating now…and putting it off was killing her. Time to go.

"Go tell them I'll be down in a minute," Avery said.

Vincent dropped a kiss on her temple, and then rolled off the bed. "Try not to worry. It will all work out, Avery."

She nodded, hoping to placate him, allowing herself the luxury of looking at him one last time, from the tips of his black boots, up his strong legs, hips to die for, flat abs, and broad chest. She settled her gaze on his lips, making her silent farewells to what he represented—a different life, lover, future, because her sister needed her, because it was the right thing to do. And if she were perfectly honest, because Vincent deserved more than what she could give him. Hell, so did Avery.

When he continued to hover over the bed, staring down at her, she lifted her brows, forcing a small smile. "I'm okay. I'll use the bathroom and then be right down." He nodded, but they both knew when he walked away, he was leaving things unsaid.

The moment the door closed behind him, Avery shot off the bed and turned off the overhead light. She hurried to the window and pushed aside the dusty drape. Deming came into view on the driveway below. She was walking the house's perimeter, gun in hand, while Gilroy walked down the gravel driveway toward the road. He had a purpose to his step that made her think he was expecting company.

She needed a car.

The van's keys were probably in Gilroy's pocket, but she remembered seeing a two-car detached garage on the left side of the property. If she could sneak there, maybe she could boost a ride. She was due some luck, if not a miracle.

As quietly as she could, Avery opened her room's door, and took a moment to quickly peek into the second-floor rooms. She was alone up here, the windows were alarmed, but some dweeb—who she would be forever in their debt—had left a window cracked in a bedroom that faced the backyard. The smell of cigarette smoke made her think it was the designated smoking room. She lifted the screen and peered down, having flashbacks from the sheriff's office, and her fall with only an extension cord to save her. This time, there was a ledge. It led to a first-floor porch rooftop. The climb down was touch and go, but by using the gutter, she soon had her feet on the grass and her back pressed to the siding.

She spied two men near the driveway, both smoking, leaning against a tree while they chatted. One wore a red polo shirt. Paley, the safehouse administrator. The other man, a suit, seemed familiar, but she couldn't quite make out his face, and she didn't feel secure enough in her position by the house to wait and find out, so Avery crouched, poised to make a run for the garage. Then the man moved so the security lighting lit his face.

She gasped and then covered her mouth, afraid she'd be heard. Heart racing, she looked again, hoping she'd made a mistake, but no, it was Bernard Ponte, Dante's lawyer. If Bernard was *here*, this place was under Dante's control. Which meant Paley was a snitch! Images of the sheriff's office, all shot up, flooded her mind.

She didn't know what to do and felt helpless, until her eyes dropped to her hands. She clenched them and stared at the rings, the initials inscribed on them, and remembered what she was capable of. She was not a victim. She was someone Bernard Ponte needed to fear, because he didn't have the leverage over her that Dante did, and she wasn't about to allow him to hurt Vincent.

Avery took a steadying breath, and wondered when she'd forgotten who she was…Ralph Toner's daughter. Dante Coppola's ex-wife. She certainly wasn't Patty, the waitress, though Patty had kicked some serious ass in that diner before that identity was retired. No, she was *The Stinger,* and she'd take care of Bernard Ponte herself, and that snitch, Paley, too.

Avery ran toward the garage like her pants were on fire, and didn't stop until she was leaning against its siding, wild-eyed and out of breath. Gilroy stepped out of the shadows, mere feet from where she'd been standing before, and checked the perimeter. It was a reminder that she had no time to waste, so she hurried to the garage's side door, and ducked inside, seeing two cars, outlined by security lighting from outside. None of the cars were old enough models to allow hot wiring, so she'd have to return to the house to lift someone's keys.

A male hand covered her mouth, then his other clamped around her wrist as she reached for his groin. She stopped her rear scoop kick just in time, because his scent triggered recognition. Vincent. Her shoulders sagged, as she peeled his hand from her mouth, turning in his arms. He scowled.

She whispered. "Bernard Ponte is out there talking with Paley."

"And you're in the garage, because—" He was also whispering, but didn't sound as if he was taking her concern seriously. His arms wrapped around her waist loosely, as if this were a social occasion and he was multitasking.

"Vincent, focus."

"I am. What are you doing here?"

"I'm going to steal a car and run them over. I've been distracted lately, so it didn't occur to me that I'd need keys until I stepped inside the garage. You stopped me as I was about to return to the house to steal them."

Vincent nodded, giving the impression that he was humoring her. "We're waiting for you in the kitchen. Benton has questions that you've agreed to answer."

She pushed out of his arms, and then folded hers over her chest. "Vincent." She made her tone biting, hoping to wake him up to reality. "It's Ponte. Dante's lawyer. I'm telling you the truth."

He sighed and then nodded. "You stay here. *Don't move.*" He pointed at her face. "I mean it, Avery."

She nodded and watched him until he was out of sight, leaving her standing at the garage's side doorway. Instinct told her to follow him, to make sure he was safe, but…Millie or Vincent? Fact was, it was a no-brainer. Vincent, who'd grown larger than life in her estimation, would be better off if she fell off the face of the planet. She'd been nothing but trouble to him since he'd met her in the diner. Dante's lawyer had to be here to out her as *The Stinger* and pin the murders on her. It wasn't a big stretch to assume the man knew her secrets, and Benton was rabid enough to take the bait. He'd jump at the chance to have *The Stinger* in custody.

So, this might be Avery's last chance to escape and save Millie. She had to take it.

Wiping a tear from her cheek, she checked the two cars and searched for keys. She found nothing, until she slid behind the wheel of the beige sedan and flipped down the visor. Keys plopped onto her lap.

The universe was telling her to run.

Vincent was warned about Ponte. She'd done her part to keep him safe.

Slipping the key into the sedan's ignition, Avery forced herself not to second-guess this decision, and hit the garage door opener on the visor, putting the car into gear. Soon, she was pulling out onto the gravel driveway. Headlights off, she idled there as she scanned the grounds for Paley and Ponte, who had moved since she'd seen them last. They were chatting at the end of the driveway, secluded from the other agents, as if they had secrets to share.

Avery knew what she had to do.

Chapter 18

Vincent saw Paley, the safehouse staffer, speaking with an unfamiliar man in front of the property, on the driveway. He'd only seen pictures of Bernard Ponte, and they'd been blurry, but yeah, it looked like Coppola's number two guy. What the hell was Ponte doing here? Vincent caught sight of Gilroy in the backyard, so he hustled over to him for a consult, not wanting to bust in uninvited into what looked like a heated conversation between the two men.

He nodded to Gilroy as he approached. "Avery's in the garage. I looked out the kitchen window and saw her running across the backyard. She saw Ponte and had a meltdown. What's he doing here?"

Gilroy lifted his brows and grimaced. "Negotiations. Benton has been on the phone since we got here."

"Secure Avery, please." Vincent glanced at the garage door. "She's not thinking straight. Make sure she goes nowhere, okay?" He hustled into the house via the back porch, and found Benton in the front hall, pacing, on the phone. A glance at Deming told him she was worried.

"Looks like this thing is going to end sooner rather than later," she said. "Coppola got wind of the warrants and is working back channels."

"Yeah?" That sounded bad, so why did Benton look happy?

A screech of tires sent a jolt of adrenaline through him, and then all of them ran to the front door to find Gilroy running full tilt after a sedan leaving the driveway...*toward Ponte and Paley*. Deming gave chase, but Vincent froze, looking on in horror as Paley jumped out of the way. Bernard Ponte didn't, and Avery clipped him. Ponte flew in the air, fell hard, and lay unmoving when he hit the ground.

Avery kept her foot on the gas, and was soon gone. Gilroy and Deming ran after the sedan, but stopped at the end of the driveway.

"Gilroy!" Vincent roared, throwing his hands in the air as he hurried to the agent's side. No less than five minutes ago, he'd told him to watch her, that Avery wasn't thinking straight. "I gave you one job!" Out of breath, Gilroy met up with Vincent, his finger pressing his wireless earwig radio receiver deeper into his ear.

"I'm getting reports," Gilroy said, "that she sliced a tire on every vehicle on the property. We're dead in the water." Vincent shook his head, speechless. Gilroy avoided his gaze.

"One job!" Vincent paced the driveway, gravel crunching underfoot. His mind couldn't shake his rage, and it was making it hard to think through this fuck up. Paley was hovering over Ponte, but the lawyer still hadn't moved. Vincent didn't want to even think about the repercussions to Avery if the man died.

"You're one to talk." Deming was pissed, too. She was huffing and puffing after running after the sedan. "What's the use of romancing an asset if you can't control her?"

"Screw you, Deming." It was nothing like that. He wouldn't let it be like that. Paley was hovering over Ponte, fists on his hips, looking worried.

Deming holstered her weapon, pulling out her phone. "I'm calling an ambulance."

Benton ran out of the house toward Vincent, though his eyes were on Paley and Ponte. His iPhone, however, was still pressed to his ear. "What the fuck?"

Gilroy sighed, catching Vincent's gaze. "Do you think the NSA is hiring?" Then the agent sent Benton a worried glance, before jogging to Ponte's side.

Vincent's kingdom for a car with working tires.

He held up a hand, stopping Benton's tirade before it started. "Avery hit him. I think it's safe to assume she's going to the Coppola mansion."

"Look, I'll call you back," Benton said into the phone, his voice tense, his eyes near panic. Deming shot Vincent a glance that seemed chockful of sympathy, but she didn't say anything, just turned her back, and continued her conversation with the ambulance company.

Benton slipped his phone into his suit jacket pocket and approached Vincent's side, standing shoulder to shoulder, frowning at the crowd around the lawyer. "This isn't happening. Do you hear me?"

"I'm sorry," Vincent said, and he was. He should have known better than to think he could control Avery.

Benton folded his arms over his chest, looking a hairsbreadth away from losing his cool. "I just got off the phone with the bureau. They sealed a deal with Coppola, who is now on the FBI's payroll as of five minutes ago. Full immunity. No one touches Coppola." He pressed his lips together, glaring at Vincent, as if that would settle the matter, but they both knew better. Avery was out there, a wild card, and she was looking for blood. "You listen to me, Modena, I did not sacrifice a year of my life for your girlfriend to ruin my endgame! Do you hear me?"

Girlfriend. Deal. Full immunity. Vincent heard probably more than Benton realized. More than he'd wanted to hear. Avery saw this coming days ago. Predicted it. She'd told him from the start the Feds would never take Dante Coppola down, and she was right. Coppola cutting a deal with the Feds left Avery in the wind.

"Deming?" Vincent said. She hung up the phone and pocketed it.

"Ambulance is on the way," she said.

"Please tell Gilroy to meet me in the garage," Vincent said. "We have tires to change."

"What are you planning?" Benton walked with him, their feet kicking up gravel. "This is the endgame. You know what I've gone through to get here. Coppola is selling his syndicate out. We could take down the competing east coast syndicates, too. It's huge. Don't mess with this deal, Modena."

"I'm not planning anything," Vincent said. He still couldn't believe the Feds had sold Avery out, after promising her the moon. After *he'd* promised her the moon. "Except changing a few tires."

"He's alive." Deming shouted from across the yard. She and Paley stared down at Ponte, who flopped a bit on the ground, but neither agent touched him.

Gilroy jogged Vincent's way, still looking chastised as an ambulance siren sounded off in the distance. He slowed his gait when he reached Vincent, and they walked into the garage together.

Vincent wasn't looking forward to repairing the damage Avery wrought, but he was happy to have something to distract him. She was out there, alone, looking to get herself killed.

This delay gave him time to figure out what he wanted to do about it, or if he should even try.

Chapter 19

It was early morning before the task force was informed that their request for court orders to search the Coppola mansion for Millie Toner were denied. The bureau accepted Coppola's deal when Benton was forced to admit there was no "incriminating files," and his superiors didn't want to hear anything about Millie being kidnapped, potentially in the mansion, because the team had no evidence. Though Millie had been declared missing three years ago, a rumor that she was at the mansion wasn't enough to kill the bureau's hard-won deal. Coppola promised names, dates, and evidence galore if they gave him immunity, so the court orders were denied and Federal Marshalls were flying out now to collect Coppola.

And, not incidentally, the task force was to be reassigned.

Oddly enough, it was the Feds' deal with Coppola that made Vincent suspect Millie was, indeed, at the mansion. Why else would Coppola make a deal? Nothing had changed. They had no evidence to charge him. If he did have a snitch in the FBI, Coppola knew they had nothing to pin on him, so why make a deal? Coppola had to be afraid the Feds would find Millie at the mansion, and then he'd be charged with kidnapping. Forgoing another explanation, it was a motive Vincent was willing to run with.

At the mansion or not, Avery thought Millie was there, so that's where she'd go. Instead of booking a flight, Vincent decided to stay and save her ass. Once the task force discovered what he was doing, they canceled their flights and told him they were sticking around long enough to make sure he didn't destroy his career…or maybe die. Vincent was grateful, but anxious, because their involvement now meant it wasn't just his career he was risking. It was all their careers.

By ten a.m., they were in the van, on the road leading to the Coppola mansion's complex, parked beyond the stone walls, just outside of the mansion's many security cameras' range. The team was irritable and hungry as they waited for Avery to make her move. Vincent's plan was simple. Stop Avery. His team's plan was just as simple. They wanted to stop *him* from doing something stupid. He feared that was too late, that he'd fallen in love with Avery. If she died... He wouldn't be able to handle it.

"Are you getting this, Benton? Do you have the PDF?" Sitting inside the van on one of the two stools next to the computer shelving, Deming frowned at her phone, slowly scrolling.

"Yeah." Benton sat before her, on the van's floor, his legs hanging out its open side door. He, too, was focused on his phone, frowning. He swiped left.

Gilroy sat in the van's driver's seat, peering into the rearview mirror. "Head's up, folks. I think I see her driving toward us."

Vincent looked out the van's tinted back window and recognized the stolen sedan heading their way. His heart clutched as he hurried out of the van, pushing past Deming and Benton, who didn't move an inch.

"This is it," Vincent said. "We can't allow her to pass. Once she drives onto the property, we'll be breaking the law to retrieve her."

"Shit," Benton whispered, still reading. "You need to see this, Modena."

Vincent refused to be distracted by whatever was consuming them. He had this one shot to stop Avery, and he couldn't screw it up. She was convinced Millie was at the mansion, but after a long night of thinking things over, he wasn't. He didn't know why Coppola decided to make a deal with the Feds, but it wasn't because he feared being charged with kidnapping. It was a felony, and if caught, it would kill Coppola's deal. The court order to search the mansion was denied by a random judge, and no one knew which way the ruling would land. To keep his immunity, Coppola had to have assumed the worst; that Feds were coming, and they'd find Millie at the mansion. He moved her.

Millie wasn't at the mansion.

Vincent stared down the road, watching Avery's car fast approach. Benton lifted a hand, eyes still on his screen. "Wait. Things are moving fast, Modena." He held up his phone.

Vincent stepped into the center of the road. "I have to stop her. Coppola wants her dead." She was driving straight at him, and the car's speed seemed to increase rather than slow.

Deming remained in the van, her attention torn between what she was seeing on her phone and Avery's speedy progress. "Once she's past us, she'll be within range of the mansion's security cameras. Coppola's been searching for her for years. Finding her outside his property's walls will be an early Christmas."

"She isn't driving past me," Vincent said. "I won't allow it. She'll stop."

He lifted his hands over his head and waved his arms. Soon, he could make out her features. Their gazes locked, but he saw no recognition there...nothing. Stone cold. And her car wasn't slowing. Only then did it occur to him that she was playing fucking chicken with him, assuming he'd step out of her way. It infuriated him.

He inhaled the crisp, morning air, as blood pounded in his head, sharpening his senses, and wondered what the hell he was doing. She wasn't stopping. He knew she wouldn't stop. What he didn't know was... would she hit him?

"Ah, Vincent?" Gilroy said. "Last time she did this, she nearly killed Bernard Ponte. Why don't you—"

"Avery! She is not in there!" Fists clenched, he held his ground, unwilling to allow her to hurt herself this way. "Millie's not in there!" The car was almost upon him, and he saw her eyes widen with panic. They'd both waited too long. There wasn't enough time for her to avoid hitting Vincent, and just as he was about to jump out of the way, Gilroy plowed into him, lifting him off his feet, and hurtling them toward the embankment. Avery's car zoomed past as they landed with a thud.

Spitting dirt and brush, Vincent pushed away from Gilroy, furious and afraid. "She tried to kill you," Gilroy said, climbing to his feet, dusting himself off.

Vincent shook his head, standing. "She's sacrificing herself to save her sister."

After seeing Bernard Ponte speaking with Paley last night, she'd deduced the Feds were in Coppola's pocket, and, in a way, she wasn't wrong. The Feds chose to value what Coppola could give them instead of seeking justice for Coppola's victims.

"She's on her own now." Gilroy turned, watching Avery pause the sedan at the security gate about a hundred yards away. His tackle had tweaked Vincent's bum shoulder, forcing him to crack his neck and roll his shoulders a bit before he could walk to the van.

"Gilroy?" Vincent groaned. "Last time I was hit that hard, it was by a rocket launcher's concussion."

Gilroy surveilled the road as they walked back to the van, wiping dirt off his close cropped blond hair. "You're welcome."

Angry and frustrated, Vincent turned his glare toward his other teammates, curious to see what Deming and Benton found so fucking interesting that they couldn't help stop Avery.

Deming waved him over, her eyes still reading. When he stepped to her side, she peeked to the left, watching Avery's sedan at the security gate. "She doesn't even know if her sister is in there, yet she's going in anyway. That's love."

Benton was still reading his download and didn't even look up as he spoke. "We can't go in after her. If Millie is in there, maybe Avery's right."

"What are you reading?" Vincent peered over Benton's shoulder to see.

Benton sighed. "Maybe Avery inside that mansion isn't a bad thing." He glanced up at Vincent, lifted his brows, and then returned to reading. "Especially if Millie is in there."

"Spill it," Vincent snapped.

Deming glanced at Benton, and then turned to Vincent. "I think Coppola is playing us all, pretending to deal with the Feds to get his hands around his ex-wife's throat. He's crazy." She shook her head, making her disheveled blond hair fall over her cheeks.

Gilroy lifted his brows, pressing his lips together. "He killed her family and then married her. We already knew he was crazy."

"No, Gilroy," Vincent said. "I know that's what the file says, but Avery explained. There was a coup by Toner's contract killers." Vincent saw their skepticism. "They put Coppola into power after killing the Toner family. Something about Avery's father wanting to go legit and disbanding the contract killers. Coppola found out after the fact, but let it go, because they'd done him a favor by setting him up as boss."

Deming frowned. "Did Avery tell you this? It would explain why she still married him."

"And it's not true," Benton said, lifting his phone, indicating what he was reading. "Coppola ordered the hit on the Toner family. Avery was either lied to, or she lied to you." When Vincent opened his mouth to argue, Benton shook his head, stopping him. "Coppola's guy, Joseph Pinnella—"

"Avery calls him "Fingers"," Vincent said.

"—he spilled his guts after a Coppola-affiliated lawyer tried to kill him," Benton said. "It was a failed hit. I'm reading Pinnella's transcripts now. He says Coppola was behind the syndicate coup that killed Avery's family."

Deming shrugged. "Which makes the deal the Feds made even more strange. Why deal with Coppola, if we have Pinnella?"

"Good question. Pinnella's intel is the jackpot, folks." Benton continued to read, bent over his phone.

Vincent wasn't convinced. "I saw Pinnella try to shoot Avery point blank. She'd be dead if his gun hadn't tapped out. The man can't be trusted."

"No one trusts Pinnella," Gilroy said.

Benton nodded. "But he says he has proof," he said. "A flash drive found in the belongings of one of *The Stinger's* victims. The transcripts are here, but I haven't gotten to them yet. Have you, Deming?"

"No." She was peering at her phone, swiping left.

Benton nodded. "The six contract killer deaths were apparently recorded. The whole thing. The flash drive is being vetted even as we speak, and it's supposedly some rough stuff. Probably proves who *The Stinger* is, and that Coppola ordered the executions. I know Pinnella's decision to snitch is what convinced Coppola to cut a deal, but I don't know if he knows about the audio."

Vincent's stomach was in knots. The mansion's gate was almost completely open, and Avery's idling sedan would soon be out of his reach. He had to decide, roll up shop, and see how things worked themselves out between Coppola, the Feds, and Pinnella, or run like he'd never run in his life and catch up with that infuriating woman and convince her she was being stupid.

He ran.

And ignored his team's shouts to come back as his phone vibrated in his pocket. He ran like his life depended on it, because it felt that way. When he reached the gate, adrenaline pumping, he forced himself not to yell, to catch her attention, because he wanted to stay under the radar for as long as possible. Once detected, security would descend, and then he would no longer be her ace in the hole, he'd be screwed alongside her.

He managed to slip through the gate before it closed, but even at a full run, he wasn't fast enough to catch up with her car. Then Avery floored the gas pedal, and sped off, making the distance between them grow even more. Still his phone vibrated. He ignored it, because his team believed Coppola's deal with the Feds should be preserved, it would save lives, and Pinnella's evidence would close their case. They were right, and he had no excuses for what he did now. But he had to save her.

He kept low, bobbing and weaving between shrubs and statuary when the cameras aimed in his direction over the manicured grounds. When there was no more cover, and Avery's car had pulled up to the mansion, a guard spotted Vincent, so he stopped hiding and ran straight for her car. All hell broke loose. Security spilled from behind trees, out of the mansion, all running toward him, guns drawn, shouting.

Still running, he found himself waiting for the sound of a gun's discharge, for the pain of a bullet ripping through his flesh. Yet, his goal remained clear. Save Avery, because at some point over the last four days, he couldn't imagine life without her.

Chapter 20

Avery was exhausted, in pain from spending the night in the cramped sedan, and scared to death as she parked in front of the mansion. Built to impress, the stately granite façade towered over her, but Avery only saw a gorgeous prison. She dialed Vincent's phone number *again*, knowing Gilroy had tackled him in time to save his life, but wanted to yell at him for not having more sense than a cow going to slaughter.

Who stood in the middle of the road as a car raced toward them? Vincent did. Had he expected her to stop? *For what?* Cuffs and confessions? No closer to Millie? It was impossible, because Avery was tortured by *what ifs*, knowing how brutal Dante could be, and those *what ifs* forced her foot to stay on the gas pedal. Biting her lip, listening to his line ring, Avery promised herself that if she survived her meeting with Dante, she'd send Gilroy a bouquet of flowers as a thank-you. *Dammit!* Why didn't Vincent pick up his phone?

She disconnected the line, foregoing a message, because really… What could she say? *Just checking in.* She threw the phone on the passenger seat. Did he see it was her number, so he was ignoring it? She wanted to say *I'm sorry.* He probably thought she'd tried to run him over. It would have been nice to set the record straight, but—leaning forward, peering up at the mansion through the windshield—she'd run out of time.

Hands gripping the steering wheel, shaking, she wasn't sure if her legs would support her when she stepped out of the car. Last time she saw her ex, he'd just executed six men, while she stood bleeding, clutching a bloody knife. In her nightmares, Dante was huge, and frightening. He'd terrorized her for too long to walk inside the mansion now anything but afraid. She should have killed him when she'd had a chance. Now she had no power. Not while he had Millie. He could do whatever he wanted with her. With both of them.

She got out of the car, surprising herself when her knees didn't buckle.

"Avery!" She turned, saw Vincent running up the driveway.

"No!" *The idiot.* She raced around the car and waved him off. "Get out! Vincent, go!" It was too late. A security guard caught up with him and cudgeled his head with the grip of his gun. Vincent went down, face-planting on the gravel. Avery hurried to his side, then kicked the security guard in the groin. He fell back, clutching himself. "Back off!" she shouted. Another guard stepped up and sought to back hand her, but she parried it and punched him in the throat. That guard fell to his knees, bent at the waist. She disarmed him and aimed the gun at him, then at the four guards that swarmed around her and Vincent. "I said, *back off*!"

Hands in the air, they retreated, looking beyond her toward the mansion. Vincent groaned, and then stood, clutching the back of his head. "Well, that sucked," he said.

The guards exchanged glances, as if coordinating an attack. She aimed the gun at one after the other, wondering who would rush her first.

"Are you insane, Vincent?" What the hell was he doing here? Where were his people? A glance back at the gate showed nothing but a great expanse of lawn and woods. No task force. He was on his own. "*Shit.*"

"Well, hello there, Avery." Dante's voice sent a chill through her. "Give that guard his weapon, please." He stood on the stair's landing, smiling, watching her, as trim and fit as always. She'd forgotten how tall her ex-husband was. His black hair, graying at the temples, was neat, slicked back, emphasizing his strong features, his hollowed cheeks. His brown eyes—so dark they seemed black—stared directly at her, promising familiar pain.

Everything felt familiar; being helpless, feeling hopeless and afraid.

Eyes front, Avery obeyed without hesitation, flipping the gun, holding the barrel and offering the guard the gun's grip. She had no other choice… And Vincent had made his. He chose to save her. *The idiot.* Meddling in a deal between Dante and the Feds. The man would be crushed between them. The thought had her near panic, on the verge of crying.

Shut it down, Avery. Shut your thoughts, your feelings down. She'd done it before, and would do it again. She'd become what she had to be, still had to be. Hard. Cold. *The Stinger.*

The security guard, still holding his throat, took the gun back. She caught Vincent's gaze, and allowed herself one word. "Why?" she said.

Vincent winked. "Can't let you have all the fun."

"Avery, come." Dante turned, showcasing the perfect lines of his expensive black suit as he walked into the mansion.

She struggled not to think, or care. "Vincent—" She wanted to tell him she admired him, was grateful for him. He deserved that. "—you're such an idiot."

Vincent glanced past her to Dante, not hiding his worry. "Right back at you."

She pivoted away, hurrying after her ex-husband. He waited for her inside the palatial white marble foyer. "Where is Millie?" she said.

"Upstairs in your room, waiting for you." Dante slid his hand into his suit jacket and pulled out a pack of cigarette. "Go. See for yourself."

Glancing up the wide, palatial stairwell, she felt torn, not wanting to leave Vincent. The security guards were already treating him rough, dragging him into the foyer behind her. She noticed they'd bound his hands at his front with a zip tie.

"Coppola," Vincent said, "I'm sure your deal with the Feds doesn't cover killing an FBI Special Agent."

"You'd think, right?" Eyes wide, Dante smiled, like it was all a big joke. He tapped a cigarette out of his pack, and then tucked the remainder in his suit jacket pocket. "Stick him in the dining room while she dresses for brunch." Then he put the cigarette between his lips, lighting its tip as he climbed the stairs. "Come, Avery. Let's get you out of those clothes. I want you to shower before we eat." Still not looking at her, he continued climbing the stairs, exhaling a stream of smoke. "He's touched you, and you smell of him."

Ignoring Dante's taunt, she leveled a hard glare on the guards manhandling Vincent. "Stop hurting him. Not even a bruise. Got it? Or I'll come for you." The private security guards looked mean, and were intimidating. There were five of them in the foyer, big, brawny, young, and they scoffed at her, as if she'd made a joke. She didn't know how to make them obey her, because she had no power here. She was helpless.

"I've been remiss," Dante said. His cultured tones echoed in the large foyer, and instantly caught the attention of everyone present. "I'm sorry, Avery. It's been three years since you've lived here, and these men are relatively new hires." He paused on the stairs, brows lifted, and tapped his cigarette ash over the railing. "Please allow me to introduce you." He took another drag, and then released a stream of smoke. "Men, this is my wife. *The Stinger.*"

As one, the guards looked at Avery's hands and blanched. These men didn't need to be convinced, because the rings indicted her. Everyone in the syndicate knew *The Stinger* stole them after killing the six men. Her heart skipped a beat, and she looked at Vincent, saw his disbelief quickly turn to shock. It didn't last long, and was soon replaced with something else.

Chapter 21

The Stinger. Avery Toner Coppola was *The Stinger*? Vincent couldn't believe it, and yet she didn't deny it. She just stood there, staring at him, looking as if her dog just died. Coppola, meanwhile, was preening it up, treating Avery as if she were the finest grade of weaponry, another threat to hold over the guards' heads. And *still*, Vincent couldn't process the truth. Shaking with rage, trussed up with zip ties, he felt...betrayed.

"Isn't she wonderful? My creation." Coppola descended the stairwell, moving swiftly toward his ex-wife, kissing her cheek, and then turned to their audience as he took a deep drag off his cigarette. It was hard to believe he was the same man that ordered Avery's family murdered, gave his wife to killers to play with, and then divorced her, and put a hit out on her. Vincent began to wonder if he'd been fed a bunch of lies.

And Avery... Where was the victim, the older sister doing her best to be strong and courageous? The one who'd made him love her. He didn't recognize *The Stinger.*

How was she not Coppola's accomplice? Familiar feelings of betrayal roiled in his belly as he reinterpreted the last week through the lens of her being *The Stinger*; all her deflections, her determination to leave him behind, escape the task force's protections. Like a blurry kaleidoscope coalescing into clarity, facts jumped out at him. She was trained by contract killers, and then killed her teachers, solidifying Coppola's leadership in the syndicate. During her interrogation, Avery insisted Dante had saved her when she'd needed him. The team had assumed Avery lied, that she feared Coppola, but now he knew she'd just moved on, used her ex and then discarded him. Like Madeline, Vincent's ex-wife. That made Avery smart, but didn't absolve her of one damn sin.

He loved her. And it broke his heart. Shaking, teeth bared, he lunged at her, his zip tied wrists extended, fingers clawed, reaching. A guard kicked his leg out from the side, and down he fell to the foyer's marble floor, a gun pressed to his head. His rage was such he didn't feel the pain. It protected him, filled his lungs, his head, and had him teetering on the edge of risking a bullet to punish her, no matter the cost. To break her as she'd broken him.

Avery's eyes flashed, and then he saw her reach behind her. "I said not even a bruise."

She moved so fast, he didn't know what happened until he heard the scream. The guard who'd kicked his knee out was pinned to the floor by a knife embedded in his boot. Then Avery turned her back, and walked up the stairs like she was the grand mistress of the mansion. This angle revealed her back, her leather jacket tucked up, and her now empty knife sheath.

How had Benton lived in this world for a year, and missed that Avery and Coppola were a modern-day Bonnie and Clyde? Obviously, they had some sick thing going on, or why this show of unity?

Coppola flicked his cigarette toward the dining room, signaling with a tilt of his head that two guards should drag Vincent there. They did, and then propped him against a pristine wall covered with silver threaded paper. A guard stayed with him, holding him at gunpoint as a chair was brought, and then sat him down, and tied his ankles to the legs. They left his wrists zip tied as they were, so his upper body remained relatively free, and that's where he sat for a half hour, stewing, scheming, thinking up ways to ruin Avery and Coppola's day.

It didn't take him long to decide Coppola wouldn't kill him. No upside. And if Coppola could have gotten away with it, Vincent would already be dead. So, him being tied to the chair was probably theatrics. He knew Benton and the team were working some plan outside, doing what they could to get him out. That meant Vincent needed to do his part by biding his time, not making any waves. He'd come here to save someone that didn't need saving, so he'd settle for leaving and then count himself lucky. Let the Coppola Syndicate feed on itself without Vincent's help. He was done.

Servants brought in tray after tray of brunch offerings. Muffins of all sorts, croissants, platters of scrambled eggs, poached eggs, fried eggs, omelets, toast of all varieties, pastries, bacon, sausage, and three different empty glass goblets next to fine china and flatware. When they'd finished, there was enough food on the table to feed an army, and Vincent's damn stomach was growling.

He'd spent the last half hour demanding his release to servants who'd acted as if he were invisible, and his head throbbed from the pistol whipping. He'd moved in time to deflect most of the impact, but he had a headache, and was pissed, not enjoying this Saddle River "living" at all; a little brutality, a little brunch.

Fifteen minutes later, the staff stationed themselves against the wall, looking all starched and pressed, eyes front, expressions clear. Vincent got the impression something was about to happen. Soon, Avery, and a young blond, who had to be Millie, walked down the grand, white marble stairwell, their hair intricately pinned atop their heads. He got a good look at them as they passed, seeking their places at the expensively adorned, food-ladened dining table.

He'd never seen Avery like this. Not even in pictures. Pale, controlled, makeup expertly applied, she was stunningly beautiful in a pale blue dress that was cowled in the back to her ass, and hung from her shoulders with thin straps. Little more than a slip of silk, the dress glided over her skin, cut sharply at the décolletage, and under her arm, to revealed ample side breast as well as cleavage. It hung on her, revealing her legs to her hip as the skirt's slit widened and narrowed with every step. If she wore her signature knives, he had no idea where she'd hidden them.

Did Coppola have a hand in choosing this dress? Seeking to disarm her?

Her boots were replaced with strappy heels, delicate and high, and she wore large diamond bracelets, earrings and rings that sparkled under the chandelier's soft glow, completing the impression of Avery as ornament; a Stepford wife. Even her bruised jaw and knee had been cosmetically painted over. She wasn't *Patty, the waitress,* or *Avery, the victim.* Vincent only saw *The Stinger,* and that her beautiful perfection was a disguise to hide that she was a killer.

He hated that she took his breath away.

How had he not seen the killer inside her? The evidence had been staring at him the whole time. Avery ran away with Millie three years ago. *The Stinger* disappeared three years ago. Avery wore the rings of the men who'd killed her family, their fucking initials were inscribed on them. That alone was a circumstantial evidence bonanza. A good detective would have pushed off from there. He'd been blinded, couldn't see past her gorgeous eyes, her vulnerability, her love for her sister. But now he saw the killer. Now, after she'd descended the stairwell like an ice queen, and entered the dining room as if she were parting the Red Sea, he *saw* her... and hated that he still desired her, that she was now forever out of his reach.

He told himself she wasn't his to mourn, but it didn't hurt less to have lost her, and dammit—that dress, her perfection—he was aroused. If she'd straddled him now, he'd go along for the ride, hating her all the way, and enjoying the hell out of his agony. She had to know this. If she'd looked at him, she'd know, but she didn't. To Avery, he might as well have been furniture, a cog in her wheel of deceit.

Coppola stood next to Avery behind the table, pulling her chair out for her, and then Millie, before taking his own seat to Avery's right. Vincent wondered if Coppola realized how diminished he appeared next to Avery. A mere mortal.

Millie saw it, and unabashedly wore her adoration of her sister like a crown, clutching Avery's hand, happy, if a bit nervous. Vincent was tied to a chair, so her nervousness was understandable, but he did wonder if that was all Millie feared, if Avery's dire warnings of her sister in trouble had been lies. What was going on here? Was it simply just…Sunday brunch?

If Avery lifted her eyes, she'd see Vincent seated across the room, facing her, but she didn't. She kept her eyes on the fluted champagne glasses the staff filled for her and Millie. When Millie reached for it, Avery stopped her with a gentle hand on her wrist—a hand devoid of the incriminating rings, and instead adorned with diamonds. A wedding ring. Millie didn't complain or negotiate with Avery's decision, but rather kept her eyes on her lap and waited. For what? Vincent was dying to know.

"Give Detective Modena champagne," Coppola said. "I know it's early, but we're celebrating."

Vincent took the glass, his wrists still bound with the zip tie, and pretended to sip. "Tasty. Nothing like Moet in the morning."

Coppola arched a brow. "You're mighty cocky for a man tied to a chair."

"About that. Might as well release me." He pretended to sip again, trying to figure out what was going on in the crime lord's head. "When my people bust in, it'll be one more thing on the list of shit that will put you away."

"I don't think so. You trespassed on my property," Coppola said, "assaulted my security guards. My lawyers are drawing up the lawsuit as we speak. I'll call the police when I'm done with you, and they can release you. You've already stabbed one of my guards in the foot." His cheek kicked up when Vincent couldn't hide his annoyance at the false charge. "I can't risk any more violence."

Vincent tilted his head to the side, studying the man he'd only known through his files. "What do you want from me?"

"A pound of flesh." Coppola's eyes flashed with fury, but his mouth smiled. "You slept with my wife."

Vincent frowned. "Excuse me?" Only three people knew he and Avery had made love. Him, Avery, and a contract killer with a fractured skull in custody. "Who told you that?" Avery wouldn't look at him.

"Why"—Coppola glanced at Avery—"my wife did, and now that I know, I can't allow that to go unpunished." Great. It occurred to Vincent that whatever this champagne might be drugged with, it was preferable to what Coppola might do to him, so he downed the alcohol in two gulps.

"Go to hell, Coppola." He threw the fluted glass at the man, only to have Avery catch it just inches from her ex-husband's smirking face. She held Vincent's gaze as she placed it on the table. Millie's eyes widened, and Vincent saw her fear. *Of him.* He slumped in his chair. *Now I'm the scary one.* Terrific.

"No doubt, Special Agent Modena." Dante smiled, glancing at his serving staff who put food-ladened plates before him, Avery and Millie. "Until that day, let's clear a few things up. Shall we? Avery, tell him what really happened today."

Avery licked her lips, her gaze downcast. "Dante and I have decided to work out the problems in our marriage," she whispered. "Millie and I have moved back into the mansion."

Coppola took a bite of bacon and chewed. After he swallowed, he directed a smile at Vincent. "Nothing to see here. Just one big, happy family."

"Why should I care?" Vincent said.

"I don't care if *you* care, though I suspect you do. Am I right?" He chuckled. "But you're going to tell the FBI, verbatim, what she's said. I know your team is in their spiffy white van outside the perimeter of my property. If you and your people aren't gone within the next ten minutes, I'll have my lawyers—the ones you didn't hit with a car—contact your boss's boss." His smile turned reptilian. "Then your illusions won't be the only thing you've lost today."

"I can't lose something I never had," Vincent said.

That didn't mean he wasn't hurting. Avery's eyes were welled with tears, and one had spilled over and run down her cheek. It killed him that he still cared. She met his gaze, saluted him with her champagne flute, and drank it down without pausing for a breath. When it was gone, she inhaled sharply, and then slammed the glass down.

"You're such an idiot, Vincent. Just...*go*," she said.

Her tone, or the familiar complaint, triggered a memory, and he felt as if she were trying to tell him something. But Vincent had been wrong about her from the beginning and didn't trust his instincts. Coppola's eyes narrowed on his ex-wife, making Vincent think he wasn't the only one who felt the vibrations of uncertainty in the air. Something was up. And for the first time since he'd learned of Avery's identify, he felt a niggling of hope.

"Control yourself, Avery." Coppola pushed his full plate away and lit a cigarette.

"Dante, please get rid of him. We have things to discuss," Avery said. "And looking at the Fed is ruining my appetite." She turned to Millie. "Do me a favor, sweetie. I've become chilled. Will you find me the shawl that matches my dress?"

Without a word, Millie stood and walked toward the atrium and the stairwell beyond. A guard stopped her at the dining room's boundary, his gaze leveled on Coppola, waiting for a yeah or nay. Coppola kept his gaze on Avery, eyes narrowed, even when he waved his hand at the guard, allowing Millie's exit. The girl hurried up the stairs.

"You seem quite intent on clearing the room, my sweet," Coppola said. He drew his finger down Avery's arm until he held her hand. He lifted it to his lips and kissed her bruised knuckles. It mirrored the many times Vincent had kissed that hand, and he didn't like seeing Coppola touch her; it hurt, so he decided to share the pain.

"Coppola ordered the massacre of your family," Vincent said.

"Shut up," Avery said.

"'Fingers' Pinnella lifted a flash drive off one of the contract killers you murdered. There's audio of their executions. You're done, Avery. Coppola has immunity, but you don't. The FBI has all the evidence we could want to indict you." Vincent smiled at the crime lord. "Coppola, if you hadn't sent someone to kill Pinnella in the hospital, he never would have flipped. This is on you. Now he's testifying that you ordered the massacre of Avery's family. Says he has proof."

"Shut up." Avery's eyelid twitched, but other than that, she seemed unmoved.

That wasn't enough. Vincent wanted her as mad as he was, as hurt as he was, as devastated as he was. "He married you, slept with you, fed you to his contract killers, and you took the abuse, because you wanted vengeance."

"Did you say Pinnella has proof?" Avery's expression remained blank, but her tone grew faint, as if she were waking from a dream.

Coppola suddenly looked nervous. "Avery—"

"Yes!" Vincent said.

She slowly turned her head until she was glaring at her ex-husband; the ice queen gone, replaced with fire. Though she didn't move, her gaze seemed wild, her posture poised to spring. Vincent spilled a few facts, hoping to uncork this bottled-up rage.

"Think about it, Avery. Pinnella snitching is why Coppola made a deal with the Feds. He had no choice. Once the proof got out that he'd ordered your family massacred, had you clean up the loose ends by killing those responsible, he knew he'd have a target on his back, too. The Feds are his safety net. It's why he lured you here." If he could piece together the connection, Avery would, too, but would she see it in time? "He's pointing the finger at *The Stinger*, feeding you to the Feds and the syndicate. His part forgiven by immunity, as the Feds tuck him away somewhere safe, leaving you to take the fall."

Coppola glanced at Vincent, revealing a crack of fear in his composure. Avery remained still, glaring at her ex, as the room fell silent. The staff no longer seemed neutral witnesses, and the guards were watching, waiting to hear what Avery said in her defense. Everyone waited, including Vincent, because everything rested on Avery's response; her and Millie's future, Coppola's future, the Feds' case.

Coppola waved the nearest security guard forward, and the man stepped behind Avery, hand resting on his gun. The guard couldn't hide his nervousness, as Avery, *The Stinger*, radiated fury. And Coppola seemed unaware that his hand trembled as he sipped from his champagne flute.

"You really should be thanking me, Avery. You're alive, aren't you? I ordered the Toner family dead, yes, but when it was discovered you and Millie had survived, I chose not to kill you both. You were so young, so beautiful and alone." His smile faltered. "So, I kept you. Millie, well, she was my guarantee you'd behave. She still is." Coppola met Avery's gaze, his veiled threat unmistakable. From the look on Avery's face, she heard his threat, too, yet still did nothing. Vincent wondered if he was missing something.

A knife planted almost to its hilt between Vincent's thighs, and twanged as he pushed off the floor, his chair skittering back a foot. It took a heartbeat to understand where it had come from, and by then, he was slicing his zip tie bindings.

Avery lunged at Coppola. Gasps and shouts filled the dining room, staff ran out of the room as Vincent bent at the waist, and cut his binds. A hand grabbed his shoulder, pulling him back until he landed on the floor, resting on the chair's back, staring at the ceiling. A guard loomed, aiming a gun at his belly, but Avery split the guard's attention, so Vincent snuck in a kick to the gun, the groin, disabling the guard. He rolled to the left, now armed with a knife and a gun.

He ran toward Avery, and saw Coppola scurrying out from under the dining room table. Shots rang out, and tile fragments flew as bullets tore up the floor around Vincent. He dove to the side, not knowing where the shots came from, but knowing he couldn't stay there.

When he landed, he saw Avery, wielding a table knife, claw her way over the tabletop. Dishes of food, glasses and linens fell to the floor as she slashed at guards within range. Yet, no guard seemed willing to fight her. They avoided her, looking between her and Coppola, as they backed out of the room.

Crouched, Vincent surveilled the guards as they left, and saw one aim at Avery. Vincent lay down suppressing fire, giving her time to hide. Instead, she dove from the table, and landed on Coppola, embedding her knife to the hilt behind his knee.

Coppola screamed and fell, clawing at the tile.

Avery ripped the knife free, and then planted it behind his other one, provoking another scream. A guard ran toward Coppola, gun extended, shooting at Vincent, who tucked and rolled, returning fire. The guard fell before he reached the crime lord, and then two more guards, but another got past Vincent, and landed on Avery.

He punched her, and drew his fist back, sliced to the bone. He kicked, missed, and screamed when she stuck his calf and then left the knife in his hip. The guard fell, crawling away, leaving a trail of blood. All eyes were on Avery, but no one was moving. Vincent shot at their feet, hoping to trigger their survival instincts, because death waited for them in this room. This was their chance to run.

Guards ran, dragging their wounded with them. Then it was only him, Avery, and Coppola, who was writhing in pain on the tile. Covered in other's people's blood, she stood above him, legs shoulder width apart...an avenging angel. Vincent had never seen a more pitiless glare as she reached beneath her dress's hem and retrieved a small knife she'd hidden near her hip.

"Avery, enough!" Vincent shouted.

She crouched next to her ex-husband, and flipped him onto his back. Then she straddled his belly, like a lover, holding the small knife in her fist as she chambered a punch. "You, monster," she said.

"Avery?" Millie was standing in the doorway, scared, gripping a blue shawl.

"My parents!" She punched Coppola's face, making him bleed all over her sparkling diamond rings. "My family!" She punched him again, the stones tearing at his skin. "You ruined everything! You made me this!" She pressed her palm to her chest, trapping the knife between her palm and her heart, creating a bloody handprint, as she used her other hand to point at Millie. "You took her childhood!"

Vincent stood next to her, not wanting to touch her, fearing he might trigger more violence. "Stop, Avery." His words fell on deaf ears. She was beyond responding to anything but her rage unleashed, and Coppola seemed dazed, on the cusp of losing consciousness.

She bared her teeth. "You need to pay for what you did."

The Stinger's MO was cripple her victim, then one shot to the head. Vincent didn't know where she'd hidden her gun, but he was convinced she had it somewhere. He couldn't allow her to murder Coppola, no matter how much her ex deserved it.

"Stop, Avery." Vincent aimed his gun at her head. "I can't allow you to do it." It would make him complicit. "Stop." *Please.*

As he waited to see if she'd make a move, Vincent froze as he realized he was helpless, a fraud. He couldn't shoot her, because he loved Avery despite everything. He wanted to save her, but it had become clear she was a woman that didn't want to be saved.

Maybe *shouldn't* be saved.

Chapter 22

"Avery," her ex-husband begged, writhing in pain, showing his palms in surrender. She saw his panic, and wished she could enjoy this change in the all-powerful Dante Coppola. There was blood everywhere, his guards were gone, and now it was just him, and her...vengeance. "Please, Avery."

She covered her ex's mouth, digging her finger into his cheeks to shut him up. Had her mother begged for her life? What about her cousins? Her father?

Shaking, wild-eyed, Avery knew what she must look like; blood-soaked dress, her hands and legs smeared with it. Vincent must think her insane, and maybe she was. It was impossible to think beyond the certainty that Dante had to suffer.

Vincent knew she was *The Stinger*, and now Millie knew, too. They'd never see her the same. Even now, her little sister sobbed as she hovered just outside of the dining room, clutching the shawl she'd been tasked to find. Millie couldn't possibly understand this, and would only be harmed if she witnessed what Avery was about to do.

"Give me the knife, Avery." Vincent held out his hand, palm up.

Benton, Deming, and Gilroy rushed into the room, guns drawn, and for a second, she hoped they'd take the shot. Put her out of her misery. "Avery," Benton shouted, "put the knife down. Now!"

Knees pressed to the cold, blood-slick marble, she straddled Dante, her shoes long gone. Avery kept her ex pinned to the floor, knife to his throat. Hand shaking, she could visualize him dead. They'd shoot her, of course. She wasn't sure which agent would pull the trigger—Deming, Benton, or Gilroy—but they would. She suspected Vincent would try to stop them, but it would be too late. Avery thought killing Dante would be worth the price. Vengeance would be served and maybe end her pain. First, she needed them to understand. She needed Millie and Vincent to know.

"He's evil," she said, her voice warbling. A sob caught in her throat. "He...He destroyed *everything*, everyone I've ever loved. He made me this!" She grabbed Dante's slicked back hair, smelled the cigarettes on him and flinched, even as she pressed the flat of her knife harder against his throat. "You," she glared at Benton, "don't think beyond what he can give you." She lowered her gaze to Dante, saw him swallow hard, unable to hide his fear and pain. "But he lies." Dante spit in her face. Avery's resolve hardened. "Deming?" she said. "Take my sister from the room, please." Millie shouldn't see this, or witness her sister's death.

Vincent crouched mere feet from her. "No, Deming. Millie stays." He tucked his gun into the back of his waistband, inching forward, his eyes on Avery's face. "If you kill him, you do it in front of your sister. I'm not about to make this easy on you."

She shuddered, but her grip on the knife never faltered. "*Millie*, do what I say. Leave the room." A glance told her Millie was tearful, but shaking her head, unwilling to move.

"*Please, Millie.*" She couldn't do it with her sister looking on.

Avery's tears spilled down her cheeks, mixing with the blood spatter. Vincent inched closer, into Dante's blood. The agents remained silent, guns at the ready, while Millie looked on, quietly sobbing. "Give me the knife, Avery," Vincent said.

Trembling, her body swayed as her strength faded, as Vincent's beautiful, busted up face grew nearer. She wanted him to hold her, because...she couldn't make herself do it. She wanted to, but couldn't force her hand to end Dante's life. She wasn't strong enough, was failing her family. Panicked sobs escaped her throat.

No one would avenge her family.

And that was her fault, because *The Stinger* never existed. If *The Stinger* had, Avery would have killed Dante long ago. Instead, she ran when Dante killed those six men, because she'd never been more than the victim Dante created.

"You don't *know* what he did to me." Avery shook her head, blinking past tears, hating her weakness. She sounded like a little girl. Yet, her knife remained at Dante's throat, because she saw no way forward. Her *next* move didn't exist. "What he *took*. I'm..." She sniffed, blinking. "I'm not even *human*."

Vincent reached for her, but hate for Dante had shifted to self-loathing, and the pity in Vincent's eyes undid her. The fear in her sister's made her decision for her. It was a tipping point, and Avery snapped. She lifted the knife to her throat, and the sting felt like freedom.

She heard a shout, saw stars, and then there was nothing.

Chapter 23

"Dammit, Benton, did you have to hit her so hard?" Vincent caught Avery as she slumped, knocked out by Benton's right cross to her poor, bruised jaw. Coppola was complaining as Gilroy and Deming dragged the man away in cuffs, leaving a smear of blood in his wake.

Benton ran his fingers through his hair, looking more upset than he'd had ever seen him, and Vincent could have hugged him. "I didn't think," Benton said. "I just..." He glanced at Avery. "I hit her. Sorry, but she was about to off herself."

Vincent never would have allowed it. "I had her by the wrist. She wasn't offing anyone." He cradled her in his arms, worried that she was covered in blood, and not knowing how much was hers.

Millie stood over them, sobbing. "Avery. Avery, don't leave me." Vincent reached for her, thinking to pull the girl close, only to have Millie drape herself over Avery.

"She'll be fine." Vincent patted Millie's back, unsure of how to soothe a ten-year-old. Sirens grew louder outside. He glanced at the door. "Who's rounding up the guards?"

Deming stepped to his side, wiping blood off her hands with a linen handkerchief. "They're in the wind." She grimaced at her handkerchief, crumbled it, and stuffed it into her pocket. "We had to choose. Save your ass, or arrest them."

He nodded, turning back to Avery, worrying. "For shit's sake, Benton. You split her lip."

Deming crouched next to them, rubbing Millie's back. "She going to be okay?"

Vincent glanced at her, thinking she was referring to Avery, but Deming was looking at Millie. "Avery's *The Stinger*," he said. *She* was the one they needed to be worried about.

Deming nodded. "I listened to the recordings. She didn't kill those men, Vincent. Coppola forced her to fight them, she won each battle, but didn't kill anyone. He executed them afterward."

Vincent closed his eyes, overwhelmed with relief. Avery wasn't a killer. "Where the hell is the ambulance?"

"I hit her too hard," Benton said, guilt personified.

Deming pursed her lips. "You shouldn't have hit her at all."

EMTs wheeled a gurney in the room, and Vincent lay Avery on it, and then watched as the personnel strapped her on it. He followed, close by, as they wheeled her out of the house. The first ambulance had already driven off, presumably with Coppola and other injured syndicate men. When Vincent made moves to enter the ambulance with Avery, needing to ride with her to the hospital, Benton pressed his palm to Vincent's chest, stopping him.

"If you want a career after today, walk away." Benton's expression revealed more empathy than he'd expected, but he was adamant. "You disobeyed a direct order from Special Agent in Charge. I can fix it, but it means walking away now." Benton's phone rang, and after retrieving it from his pocket, soon narrowed his eyes, seeming unnerved by the caller's identity. "I have to take this." He turned his back on them.

Millie stepped into the ambulance after the gurney was secured. Avery, still unconscious, would wake upset. He wanted to be there. "What's going to happen to them?"

Deming rested a hand on his shoulder. "Leave, Modena. She's in good hands. I promise. It's not forever, it's just until Benton can smooth things over. Please. Go." She nudged him toward a cruiser. "One of the uniformed officers will drive you to the airport. We'll meet you there. Me and Gilroy have a few loose ends to tie up first." The ambulance drove away, and Vincent's opportunity to trash his career by stepping inside was gone. He regretted it immediately.

Local law enforcement had arrived a while ago, but more were still streaming onto the property, rounding up security guards, and leading them into cruisers. It was too much. He didn't care. He just wanted to follow Avery to the hospital, but no one here could take him and still keep their jobs, so he walked away, thinking to hitch a ride there on his own. To Avery.

He walked out the front gate, past the security booth and down the private road, thinking about the lies she'd told him. He thought about how they'd made love, how he'd thought it was special, life altering even. She'd made him want a future with her. Vincent wondered if she'd played him, and if that even mattered. He loved her. Yeah, his head was messed up, and he didn't know what to believe anymore. All he knew was how he felt, and how it didn't match up with the facts.

Avery Toner Coppola aka Patty Whitman was *The Stinger*. She'd lied as easily as she took a breath, and he didn't know how this would shake out, but this operation had left its mark on him, and it went deep, like a knife to his heart.

He loved *The Stinger*.

After a while, having already walked miles down the road, the task force van drove toward him. It was the first vehicle he'd seen since he began walking, so he stepped out of their way, hoping they'd pass because he still wanted to hitch a ride to the hospital. But the van pulled over, and its side door slid opened. First thing he saw was Deming's worried expression. Gilroy was driving, and Benton was seated in the passenger side, rolling down his window.

"Get in," Benton said. "We don't have time for this." Deming held out her hand, but Vincent shook his head.

"Don't be stupid," she whispered. Vincent grimaced, feeling hemmed in. With a sigh, he climbed inside. Moments later, Gilroy had the van moving again.

"They're expecting us in Boston," Deming said, sitting on the cooler, her forearms resting on her knees. She glanced at the team leader up front. "We've been reassigned. It happened quickly. I guess they have a serial killer, and Benton pulled some serious strings to acquire the case." She bit her lip. "I'm thinking it's personal."

Another case? Vincent felt as if he couldn't string two words together, and he was supposed to jump into a whole new case? He leaned back against the van's interior, his palms pressed to the floor to secure himself against the van's swerves.

It was all so depressing. His new normal. Other than his job, what did he have? Nothing. "Boston is as good a place as any."

"For what?" Deming studied his face, adjusting herself on the cooler as Gilroy took a turn fast.

"To hear Avery's killed herself. It's happening. We both know that." They'd stopped her at the mansion, but he'd seen her eyes. She'd wanted to die, and he feared next time she'd succeed.

Deming shook her head. "She has Millie. She'll be okay."

"Avery will never be okay." And neither would he. She'd gutted him, and he couldn't see a way back to normal.

Deming compressed her lips. "She's indestructible. She had a weak moment. It will pass."

Vincent didn't have it in him to argue. Instead, he brooded the whole drive to the airport, shutting everyone out. When the van parked, Vincent jumped out, and left them there without a word. Then he rented a car, and drove back to Saddle River, intent on seeing Avery in the hospital, because he couldn't stop himself. He needed to be with her, but the Federal Marshalls had arrived and blocked him. From Benton's many voice mails, Vincent knew the team was on a plane, headed to Boston, so he left a voice mail of his own. He'd meet them there. He didn't trust where his head was at. Hell, he didn't trust himself. He needed to be around his team.

Chapter 24

The next morning, just after sunrise in a downtown Boston diner, the team worked the problem of their new case. Gilroy took up a whole side of the booth, forcing Vincent to sit on the end in a chair, while Deming and Benton were squeezed into the other side. Vincent felt like the winner in the seating arrangement. Sipping his ice water, he saw Deming nudge a piece of paper in front of him. It was an obituary form for the *New York Times*. He glanced at it, and then her.

"Who's dead?" Vincent peered closer. *Avery Toner Coppola*. There was an attached photograph. She was seventeen, in her wedding gown. Even then Avery had a look about her that said she'd suffered too much.

"The Federal Marshalls are pulling strings," Benton said, "asking that they put it in this weekend's paper. They want the news to spread near and far that she's dead."

Deming compressed her lips, glancing between him and the form. "She's changed her name, but refused WITSEC."

"She made a deal with the Bureau," Gilroy said, rubbing his head, squinting, avoiding Vincent's gaze. Everyone was treating him with kid gloves, and it was getting annoying.

Benton shifted on the bench, almost jostling Deming to the floor. "The Bureau took into consideration her history with Coppola, the audio of her fighting the contract killers, Coppola clearly telling her they'd killed her family, his ultimatum. The audio absolves her."

"That's the FBI's official position?" Vincent arched a brow, finding that hard to believe. Like Coppola, they tended to want their pound of flesh. Benton nodded, so he figured it had to be true.

"So," Deming said. "Between her PTSD, and the evidence we have against Coppola, and the kidnapping of Millie, Avery's actions are being ruled self-defense."

Gilroy shrugged, leaning his elbows on the table. "No law against divorcing a psychopathic murderer."

Or marrying one, Vincent thought. Out of the corner of his eye he saw a waitress approach. He turned, and froze. It was Avery. His heart raced as he studied her, worried about the bruises, her obvious exhaustion. If her eyelid hadn't twitched, he would have thought she didn't recognize him. How could she pretend that way? It was a skill, that's for sure, and it irritated the hell out of him.

"Can I take your order?" she said. His mind went blank. Why hadn't he been warned? He glanced at his team, but no one was looking at him, except Deming. She sported a grin.

Shifting in his seat, he faced Avery, and saw sunlight reflect off her auburn hair. It was pulled back into a ponytail, making her look like Patty again, especially since this brown uniform was stained, too, and she was back to wearing those funky, functional white shoes. Her pencil hovered over her order pad as she waited for a response, her eye still twitching. He felt stupid.

Say something, he thought. But he didn't. His mind was on how much damage she could do with that pencil's sharpened end. She was a trained killer, masquerading as a waitress.

"Do you know what you want?" Avery swallowed hard, and now her bruised, abraded chin was quivering. Her eyes widened, and bled with vulnerability. Vincent got the impression that she was poised to run as she waited for his answer. Did he know what he wanted?

Damn, yeah. He did.

"*Charlotte*," Deming said, making a big deal about saying her name. "What's good on the menu?"

Avery's name tag, pinned above her heart, read *Charlotte*. So, Avery had moved to Boston, his hometown.

He exchanged glances with his team, and thought, hot damn, they'd *all* known she'd be here and kept it from him. Why? Then it hit him. He'd kept his feelings to himself. He hadn't come out and confirmed that he loved her, not even to Avery. Why would anyone have any idea what he felt or wanted? He'd just assumed they knew.

* * * *

Deming said something, but Avery didn't hear. It was like someone put a conch shell to her ear, and all she heard was ocean waves. This must be what it feels like to die, she thought.

He was looking at her, giving nothing away, and she supposed that made sense. He'd probably written her off already. Last time he saw her she was crazed, a blood-covered fiend wielding a knife, why wouldn't he feel well rid of her? It was nice to see him again, though. She hadn't thought that would ever happen.

Vincent turned to the others, looking them in the eye. "You should have told me she was here."

This was a mistake. She didn't even notice she was walking away until Deming ran to her side and pulled her back to the table. "Vincent," Deming said, scowling at him, "we want to introduce you to Charlotte. Charlotte? This is our stubborn, judgmental, scared of love friend, Special Agent Vincent Modena. Say hi to the woman, Vincent." Deming made a big show of pinching his arm, before sitting back down. Vincent acted as if he didn't feel it.

"Charlotte, huh?" Vincent grimaced.

Avery nodded so many times her ponytail wobbled loose. "I've applied to U/Mass. I want to major in mechanical engineering."

Vincent glanced at his coworkers. "What are you looking at? Stop staring."

"Vincent!" Deming snapped.

He narrowed his eyes at the profiler. "Are you waiting for us to exchange our sun signs?" He swung back to Avery, his smile forced and over bright. "Hi, Charlotte. I'm a Libra."

"I thought you were Taurus, *the bull*." Deming drummed her nails on the table.

Gilroy slipped out of the booth. "This is too intense. I'll meet you guys back at the precinct house." Benton looked longingly after the Fed, but Deming was sitting on the outside of the booth, and she wasn't moving, so Benton wasn't escaping anytime soon. Everyone was uncomfortable, Avery included, so she decided to make this quick. There was something Vincent deserved to hear, and from the looks of him, this would be her last chance to say it.

"I'm sorry," she said. "Vincent…I'm sorry…about everything."

Deming looked between her and Vincent, as if she were attending a high stakes tennis match. Vincent, however, seemed angrier upon hearing Avery's apology. So, she gave up. She dropped her pad and pencil on the table, untied her apron, and caught the other waitress's eye.

"Ethel, I'm sorry. I have to go." The middle-aged women nodded, walking her rounds, filling up coffee cups. Avery wiped a tear as soon as she stepped outside and struggled not to sob.

The air was warmer in the city, even this early in the morning. The traffic was loud, and her view outside the diner was of aging brownstones and beat-up cars. Not knowing where to go, she took a left and started walking, no destination in mind. It was hard to think when she was feeling so much, so she shut down, and told herself things could only get better. She'd hit bottom, so the sky was the limit.

Then Vincent was walking beside her. She didn't have the courage to stop or turn her head to see his expression. She continued walking, wiping tears, trying not to humiliate herself more than she already had. She'd spent an hour getting ready this morning, trying to make her hair look presentable in the ponytail. With all her tears, her eye makeup had to be smeared on her cheeks, and odds were she'd nervously bitten her lipstick off. He continued to walk next to her in silence, keeping pace, his hands in his pockets, making Avery wonder how this would end. She hadn't a clue.

When they got to a corner and were forced to stop for the light, she turned to him, ready to say the words again. He deserved to hear *I'm sorry* a million times, but the look on his face stopped her. She didn't see accusation, or horror, as she'd seen in her dreams last night. He was looking at her like she was *Charlotte, who wanted to go to U/Mass Boston.* Like she was a clean slate.

He took her right hand, studied every angry bruise and cut, and then pressed his lips to her knuckles. When the light changed, he kept hold of her hand as the crowd carried them across the street. Avery was so dazed by Vincent's behavior she could barely see, never mind think. They continued to walk until they reached Charles River, and once again, she wished she was wearing a heel, maybe a red pump, and maybe something other than her waitress uniform. Vincent's smile made her think he didn't care.

"I like the name Charlotte," he said. "What's your sister's name?"

"Brittany. She'd always wanted to be a Brittany, but I feared a name change would confuse a two-year-old." Avery licked her lips.

He nodded, and walked them to a bench overlooking the water. When they sat, it was in silence, still holding hands. She wondered if he noticed that her fingers were bare for the first time in his presence. No pinkie rings from murdered killers, no dazzling jewels from her psychopath ex.

Vincent opened her hand and lifted it to his mouth, pressing a kiss to her palm, his eyes closed, his head bowed. She could feel him trembling, and it humbled her. When he brought her hand to his lap, cupped it with both of his, he looked out over the water.

"I killed forty-three people when I was a sniper." He glanced at her. "I killed four more during my career as a FBI Special Agent. I did that. Not you. Of the two of us, only one has taken life."

She knew what he was doing, and she appreciated the sentiment, but it didn't change anything. "I made it possible for Dante to kill those men, Vincent. I carry some of the blame."

"I heard the audio. You survived that." He turned, holding her gaze. "Not many could."

Her eyes welled with tears, and she wasn't sure if she could speak without crying, but she felt like she should try. "I'm sorry I lied."

He kissed her knuckles again, holding them against his lips. "Can you forgive *me*?" His lips moved against her bruised skin.

Did he say *forgive*? "For what?"

He pulled her close, touching his forehead to hers. It created a precious intimacy, sectioning them off from the rest of the world. "For not trusting you more," he whispered. "For not telling you...." Vincent's forehead was warm against hers, and he suddenly seemed nervous. "So, ah, I love you."

Getting what you want shouldn't make a girl cry, but Avery found herself sobbing with happiness. Vincent laughed, and pulled her to him, lifting her onto his lap. "I... I love you," she sobbed. "I love you, too."

"Good." He wiped her tears. "That's good." He hugged her tightly. "So, yeah. You love me. Good. Even though I'm an idiot?"

She laughed, feeling crazed. "Yeah. I do! And if you're an idiot, I am, too!"

He laughed. "Okay. Good. We'll be idiots together."

"Okay." She nodded, pressing her face to his chest, not even hiding that she was smelling him. She'd missed his scent...missed everything about him.

"When does your shift end?" His eyes twinkled with happiness, and Avery got all tingly inside, because she remembered when she'd wanted to be *just a girl*, being picked up by *just a guy*, who wanted to be with her at the end of her shift. Had that only been a week ago? "Four o'clock. I pick Millie up from summer camp at six. I mean, Brittany."

He nodded, keeping his gaze on the river. "I'll pick you up at four. You and me, we're going on a date." He took a deep breath and released it slowly, as if he were trying to calm down. "And tomorrow, and the next day. It's you and me." He caught her gaze, his eyes intense. "Got it?"

She nodded, seeing the possibilities of a future with Vincent. *Yeah, she got it.* And couldn't wait. Everything was clear now. After she'd lost her family, she'd feared love, feared losing one more person she held dear, but now she knew better. Love was a risk, sure, but it was also what mattered the most. Maybe it was the only thing that mattered. True or not, it's what they'd got, and they were happy.

Epilogue

Special Agent Jack Benton stood and paid the diner's check. Breakfast was over and it was time to head to Boston Police Department's downtown precinct, homicide unit. He was nervous, and Deming was picking up on it.

"Now that I'm in town, I have some people I'd like to check in with," she said, "if you wouldn't mind, that is. I haven't been back in Boston for a while." She shrugged, looking uncomfortable. "Gilroy is already on his way over to the precinct, but I'm thinking Modena will be a while. He and Charlotte have a lot to discuss. I'll meet up with the team early afternoon, if that's okay. I'll take a cab."

Jack nodded. "Sure." He reached into his pocket and pulled out his keys. "There are a few things I need to iron out when I get there anyway. Probably best if you give me time to do that before the team jumps into the new case."

"You've been keeping details close to the vest on this one," she said. "Should I be worried?"

"Serial killer. We should all be worried."

Deming nodded, shoulders sagged. "I hate serial killers."

He walked with her out of the diner. "This one is…complicated, Deming, so get back as soon as you can, all right?"

"I promise." Then she was off, hailing a cab.

Jack looked left and right, a stranger in a strange land. No one was looking for him in this town, because one year ago, it had been *his* picture in the obituaries. With no living family, coming "back to life" seemed moot. The only people that did know he lived were his team members. His task force. And, of course, his supervisor, the Special Agent in Charge. They were all that mattered, or so he'd thought as of yesterday, when he'd gotten the call.

His ex-partner, Special Agent Hannah Cambridge, thought he was dead.

Jack was still reeling from that bombshell. When he'd taken the Coppola Syndicate undercover assignment, it was a promotion, and gave him team leader status over a task force. The promotion required him to "die" and take on a new identify. Who wouldn't jump at that opportunity? He did. Things had happened fast, so he'd asked his Special Agent in Charge to tell Hannah the news. Only he didn't, unaware that his partner, Hannah, was more than just a partner.

She was his lover. They'd kept it quiet, not wanting to cause gossip.

So, Hannah spent the last year believing him dead. Murdered. She went to his wake, for heaven's sake.

Sure, their relationship had always been rocky, and this year he'd suspected Hannah had been glad to see the back side of him, but this news changed everything. Jack never intended for Hannah to believe he'd died, but now that he'd arrive in Boston, Lazarus arisen from the grave, what was he supposed to tell her?

She had a temper, and a serial killer wanted her dead, so… He sighed. He'd save her, but first he had to convince her not to kill him.

Meet the Author

Kris Rafferty was born in Cambridge, Massachusetts. After earning a Bachelor in Arts from the University of Massachusetts Boston, she married her college sweetheart, traveled the country, and wrote books. Three children and a Pomeranian Shih Tzu mutt later, she spends her days devoting her life to her family and her craft.

Printed in the United States
by Baker & Taylor Publisher Services